C000007596

The Last Salmon

by the same author

fiction
WHALE
THE LONGEST FLIGHT
FUR
THE FAROES VENTURE

non-fiction
FLY-FISHER

The Last Salmon

JEREMY LUCAS

JONATHAN CAPE
LONDON

First published 1990
Copyright © Jeremy Lucas 1990
Jonathan Cape Ltd
20 Vauxhall Bridge Road
London SW1V 2SA

Jeremy Lucas has asserted his right
to be identified as the author of this work

A CIP catalogue record for this book is available
from the British Library

ISBN 0 224 02354 3

Photypeset by Computape (Pickering) Ltd, North Yorkshire
Printed and bound in Great Britain by
Mackays of Chatham PLC, Chatham, Kent

For my son, Peter Simon, in the hope that the Wealden landscape which charmed his father might survive for him and that he too will see wild salmon running into Loch Maree.

PART ONE

Riders of the rain

I

There was a place where mountains, sea and sky met and where migrant birds and migrant fish moved with the seasons, a coastscape in change, in hourly, daily and monthly change. There was a time when this place possessed a fierce abundance of life, when eagles soared across the mountain slopes, spying the land's wealth, and ospreys dived upon the elusive creatures of sea and loch. It was hardly man's place, though people made their homes in scattered, sheltered areas away from the wild, black mountains and the high moors. A Gaelic tongue was heard in the straths which cut into the land from the sea. The place remains, the time is gone and Gaelic is drowned by harder sounds.

Now there is mostly just memory and forgotten tales, legends and myths. There are those who say it happened because men forgot the ancient Gaelic way of taking from the land and sea and giving back in equal measure. And yet it was the men of the glens, pushing their herds of sheep farther north and west who both loved and began to destroy this wilderness.

Then there is the more recent memory of people who saw the last events. For there were changes like the seasons, like night and day, wild storm and quiet skies, and there were changes which brought catastrophe, as devastating as the ice sheets which once piled up across this place, and made it the way it is. No memory could reach back to that time or even to the time when the ice thawed, depositing its titanic load, laying bare the scars it had carved through the mountains, all the way to the wild, wild sea which it had sucked dry and stilled in a frozen, blue grasp. Memory began long after the land and coast had become an hospitable place, where life soared in the sky, roamed and burrowed the forests and the slopes, the straths and the moors,

3

and was powered on great fins in rivers, burns and deep, cold lochs.

The north-west coast of Scotland is remote in the British Isles, remoter still to Europe, the last of the land before the wildest of seas, the North Atlantic. A torn, entrenched coast where the rocks are changed infinitesimally by sucking currents, and irrevocably by gigantic, crushing tides and storms. Here the salmon swam, master of great seas, journeyer across thousands of miles, a homebound, silver fish, tasting, feeling and sensing the enormity of water around him, yet knowing which direction was home, knowing the place and the time. He knew, also, where the waters became little again, in rivers far into the hills, almost frozen beneath winter skies, as in that first great thaw, where life can be reclaimed from ancient, tired and journey-worn bodies.

Through the sea's prism light the Atlantic salmon swam, tumbling into the powerful turbulence thrown up by the Outer Isles. He slipped against the tide, not fighting it, beating his great tail at the swirling waters. For two months, and fifteen hundred miles, he had barely paused. Guided by currents and weather, by the ever-changing light at the surface, by tastes and vibrations in the mêlée of the open ocean, he had maintained his overall direction, south-east. Now, close to the islands, the tastes and vibrations were increasingly familiar as he searched for the ancient passage through to the Inner System and the Western Approaches.

Even after such a journey he was very powerful, master of twelve home runs, easily strong enough to shrug off the succession of rollers that spilled across the rapidly shelving sands. Lithe and muscular he knifed himself away from the vastness of ocean that he had crossed. It was July and the water was warm on the shoaling reefs, hissing and rich in oxygen. Explosions of bubbles glittered and spun in the forever moving element of the Hebridean coast. White water necklaced every stack and rock that jutted tentatively into the cool air. Spray was torn from the sea, hooked over the waves and thrown with a roar that was nothing against the ceaseless thunder of the pressing sea.

The salmon had returned yet again, his indomitable instincts far greater than the perpetual fears of the many dangers he faced during his home-bound voyage. He sculled quickly through the pattern of sunlight from the racing banks of water above him. In a moment he was dazzled, tired by the endless pounding of many-fisted currents. Then, a ferocious sweep of his tail and he had blasted his way through a sand-storm and out into the suction of a rip-tide.

Again the water deepened and the big fish hovered in a blue void, strangely silent now. His gill plates worked rapidly and his fins spread and quivered, his tail a giant, dangerous fork, his dorsal erect, his pectoral fins catching the light in a whisper of motion as they stabilised him. He was stationary, thirty feet below the surface. He waited.

Behind him, still on the shallows, two hen salmon slid with the cascading sea. One was large, almost as heavy as the cock fish, though shorter and fatter. The other was only half her size, younger by eight breeding runs, and swam quietly in the older hen's slipstream. Together they skirted the rim of an undersea sand dune, met momentarily with the tide's resistance, then with an identical, curving motion, as if there was a strange and instantaneous communication between them, sprung free, kicking down towards the cock fish.

The three paused, resting, while they tasted the changing flavours of the coast. They hung very close together, almost without motion. Here they were, alone where there should have been a great gathering, where a thousand salmon should have been spilling across the shallows, and another thousand on every tide, until the gathering was a silvered, swirling wall of salmon. But now there were only three, waiting in the blue vastness, alone on the home run. They orientated themselves towards the north-east and the hazardous channel-ways of deeps and sounds that led to the Inner Hebrides and beyond.

Fins flush to their bodies, with a harmonised pulse of energy, they were gone; shimmering, silent shapes merging with the nebulous grey-blue of hostile sea.

During the night the salmon navigated their way through the Sound of Harris, the main route for migrating fish from the open Atlantic into the more sheltered waters of the Minch. Three fish in darkness and sea-noise sped unseen through an emptiness which threatened to disorientate them. The cock fish swept ahead, thrumming his tail rhythmically, cruising at high speed.

There seemed to be no danger, but that was the greatest danger of all. It lent his fins a terrible urgency.

There was darkness, with so few companions and so many unknown dangers in home waters, a place he no longer mastered – where acceleration and speed and purpose, a salmon's lifeblood, were not enough to ensure survival; a time in which he seemed lost, an anachronism. But it had not always been like that.

Seven hundred miles away, south-east, a man stood in the peace of the Kentish Weald. It was hot and John Howard could see the horizon in a haze, just where the peach-girthed sun ate into the distant silhouette of hills. Even the landscape moved, the trees shimmering in the near distance, worn and drunk by the long months of summer heat.

How strange it was, thought John, that everything changed so much; now wilted and withered by the heavy summer, then awash with cool rains, vibrant and bursting with life, then again ensnared by cold, forced to sleep. It happened so quickly, the seasons pursuing one another, storms juggling cold fronts and humid southern breezes. Yet even the great and terrible changes occurred so quickly; catastrophic events undreamt of yesterday were actual and terrible components of existence today. He had been a witness to something traumatic and sudden. And the fury he felt would never leave him.

He heard the telephone ring and then his wife Anna calling from the back door.

'It's Iain in Kinlochewe. He wants to talk to you. He sounds a bit worked up.'

Even as John walked into the house something stirred in his mind, lifting the tempo of his thoughts. Iain calling him from Scotland; he hardly ever called nowadays. There was no reason.

'They're back, Johnny,' said the deep, Highlander voice. 'They've been seen; the salmon are back in the loch!'

Loch Maree, to John the most beautiful place on earth, a place out of a dream, where the salmon and sea-trout ran – where they used to run. The great mountains, Slioch and Beinn Eighe, towered above the loch's southern straights, near the Kinlochewe river. Were salmon, even at that moment, questing those waters where the Kinlochewe pushed its peaty load into the loch?

He looked up at the stars above Kent. It would barely be dark over Maree. At that time of year there would be but two or three hours of real darkness up there. The salmon would be exposed to light and near-light most of the time. They could lie deep when it was lightest, but they would have to move up to the surface eventually, into the waves, where the oxygen concentration was greatest, to exercise their thick muscle, to wash their bodies with that oxygen, to leap into the light and cool air. Who would see them? What dangers lay in the light?

Struggle, as life always is in wild places.

2

He remembered. It was a winter's night. That was it; he was a little boy sitting in front of a comforting log fire. His eyes seemed less tired than they should have been at that hour, for they sparkled in the glowing lights of the fire and a Christmas tree. Presents were scattered beneath the tree, secrets which were not yet ready to be revealed.

'Right, Johnny. Bed now, it's gone ten.' The voice of his mother interrupted his thoughts of the next day; of diving into those presents, of running outside, kicking at the snow, of throwing snowballs at his sister Charlotte, of Christmas lunch with Auntie Viv, toys all around him in the warm sitting room of the cottage ... 'Bed, now! Or Father Christmas won't be coming!' She tried to sound stern, but her voice was as warm as ever, like the lovely Christmas feeling which filled their home in the snowbound Kentish Weald.

'Go to bed little brother!' muttered Charlotte, smiling her stupid smile at him which said, 'I can stay up, 'cos I'm older. So there.'

'Shut up, Charlotte,' he reacted immediately, unable to think of a cleverer reply.

'That's enough. *Both* of you!' Their mother exploded. 'You're both going to bed now or neither of you will be getting any presents.'

'Oh Mum,' whined Charlotte, 'I can stay up a bit longer, can't I? I'm nine now and ... '

'She can't, she can't.' Johnny wanted to hit her.

'Bed!' screamed Mum. And the children made for the stairs, Charlotte frowning at her younger brother as she pushed past him. Johnny didn't care, so long as they were both having to go to bed, so long as Christmas was tomorrow and there would be a stocking left by Santa and there would be more snow falling as he slept and Auntie Viv would come in the morning, her old Morris stuffed with more presents.

As the children's dressing-gowned figures climbed the staircase Diana Howard sighed with relief. She shook her head as she heard them arguing on the landing. This would be the first Christmas without Jack, the sixth month since he was snatched from them by the drunk's car and the senseless accident, the sixth month without him. Now they all lived with the unthinkable: Christmas without him. They were good children, anyway. They would manage. They would *all* manage. Charlotte had her good looks and quick mind, while Johnny had his obsession with nature, just like his dad. But it was Christmas and she was determined that they would be happy.

Later, lying in his little attic bedroom, the cottage quiet and safe around him, Johnny thought over and over again about the presents around the Christmas tree, the intriguing shapes and sizes of them. There was a big rectangular one, a heavy wooden box. That could possibly be a train set. Then there was a long thin one which Mummy would not let him feel because she said he would be able to guess what it was if he felt it, but he was sure it was light in weight by the way Mum had so easily slipped it behind the tree, against the wall and out of his reach. Could that be it? It was the right shape and length.

And all the others – a small boring box from Uncle Robert, probably some medal he had won in the war or, at best, a model Spitfire or Corgi tank. Then there was some hopelessly wrapped thing from his sister which was bound to be utterly useless, something she had cooked or a hankie or something like the pair of gloves she had knitted, with lots of help from Mum, last year. But it was all so exciting and he could not sleep.

He thought of the snow outside. He climbed out of bed and went over to the little eaves window. He shivered even though the room was warm from the heat of the chimney breast which ran up through it. Outside, a nearly full moon lit the snowscape and he could see far beyond the farmer's field and the hedgerow, all layered in snow now, and the little road – would Auntie Viv's Morris get through that in the morning? – and the deep, still woodland where squirrels and badgers slept in warm, cosy places.

Flowing along the edge of that wood was a stream, the River Bewl it was called, a tributary of the Teise which, in turn, ran into the big Medway, Kent's mighty river. The Bewl was mostly frozen over now, but Johnny remembered how he had spent countless hours there last summer holidays with net and jam jar. And by his side or behind him, holding his hand, talking to him, pointing, revealing hidden things about the world that was the streamside, always there guiding him through the magic of the green Weald, was his father.

They had waded, sometimes right up to their knees, bare feet on the gravel, or on drowned branches or mud, the gorgeous thick stuff oozing between their toes. Usually they went upstream because then the mud and detritus they stirred up wafted off downstream and did not colour the water upstream. Johnny held his net in the water, using it to dislodge stones and bits of wood and weed. He caught sticklebacks and minnows, and once a roach a full four inches long. From the sandy bed on one stretch he often caught things that looked like little twigs, but, as his father showed him, proved to be the homes of caddis grubs, constructed by the little insect larvae themselves from the minuscule matter of the stream bed. Each day by the river he caught or found something new and put it in his jam jar to show Mummy and Charlotte later.

Johnny knew there must have been many days that he and Dad had been to the Bewl, because his head was still so full of the memory of it all. Yet it could not be like that anymore. Winter had come and Dad was gone. Next time, when the Bewl flowed sparkling and glittery yellow through the green fields again, he would have to carry on his explorations alone. That seemed strange, almost ridiculous. How would he do it alone, without the man who knew everything?

Clouds wafted swiftly across the sky and Johnny could see the moon only in glimpses and as a silver gash on the edge of the clouds. It was snowing again, yet his thoughts continued to race back to last spring and early summer on the Bewl.

He had a memory of Mr Billings, the farmer who owned the land through which this three-quarter mile length of the river flowed, popping his head above the nettles and tangled alder of the bankside.

'What y' caught today then?' he would invariably say, with a knowing wink towards Johnny's father, his ruddy face beaming at the sight of his young friend.

'Hello, Mr Billings,' Johnny would call, before clambering excitedly out of the stream to show Billings his latest triumph. Like when he had caught his first bullhead, a squat, blunt little fish, beautifully camouflaged against the multi-coloured stream bed.

There was that afternoon, while Daddy was asleep on the flattened, dry grass, when Johnny had sat down on a tree stump in the warm summer sun, his feet still in the stream. There was a heavy, summer quiet, at least in his memory; even the crickets seemed distant and the stream's flow muted, sidling through ranunculus beds. He had placed his net half in and half out of the water, its handle sticking out away to his right. A blue flash against the foliage of the other bank had signalled the arrival of a kingfisher. Keeping perfectly still Johnny watched, thrilled, as the dazzlingly coloured bird alighted on the handle of his net. There was so much orange on the bird's chest and chin, that it surprised Johnny who had always seen kingfishers only as a blue blur as they shot across the river. Why did you never see that hot orange when the birds flew? For what had seemed an age the bird had stood there, poised, its head quickly turning from side to side as it spied the water. He wondered if there could possibly be a more incredibly beautiful creature in the whole world, its feathers a blaze of startling iridescence. Then it looked up at him, ever so briefly, before darting off in a whirring blue flash downstream.

'It didn't!' exclaimed Mr Billings when Johnny told him about it later.

'It did. Honestly – for a whole minute.' And there was something in his raw excitement that told Mr Billings that it was true.

But there was horror, too, in Johnny's paradise of the Bewl. One hot early August day he had been watching the water intently, prodding at the base of a lily bed to see if some roach fry would dart out and into his net, when, suddenly, on the periphery of his vision, a greeny-brown movement was slithering down towards him. It was a female grass snake, very large, twisting sedately down the stream, her head held mere inches above the surface, the rest of her body almost hidden, but infinitely sinister, like her small, deadly eyes.

In a moment, Johnny had turned from the serpent and fled the water, clambering up the steep bank, ignoring his father's calls and the many stings inflicted upon him by the nettle bed, abandoning his jar and net, even his plimsoles left a hundred yards down the river; anything to escape the terrible snake.

From that day on Johnny never went into the water without wearing his wellingtons, even though he often went in so deep that the water filled them up. He just felt safer with them on, and preferred long trousers.

But on that Christmas Eve, any grass snake or adder would be deep underground, well away from the frost and snow. Every animal in the Weald, it seemed to Johnny, would be hidden in some warm burrow, the fish in the bottom of the deepest pools of the Bewl, the kingfisher in his tree, nestling up against his mate.

He went back to bed, still thinking about the river and then about the snow, and Christmas and presents. And soon, in the cottage in the snow-silenced Wealden landscape, Johnny was asleep.

Far to the north, in wild country, twenty-five miles from the sea by way of river and loch, the leapers swam. In a rushing burn ordinarily not a foot deep was a gravel-bedded pool, the only significant pool in the little burn which drained the bleak northern slopes of Sgurr Dubh, the Black Peak. The burn was an ancient breeding redd of salmon. It was a remote place where the big autumn-run salmon, as red and bronzed as the bracken and heather on the hills, headed to spawn.

The largest salmon and sea-trout in the system ran here although there were many redds which the fish would pass earlier in the journey, along the branch of the Kinlochewe called A' Ghairbhe. Then the homebound fish would meet Loch Clair where they would turn either west, into Loch Bharranch beneath Sgurr Dubh, or south-east into Loch Coulin and beyond to the waters draining into the Coulin pass. But the biggest fish of all ran into Bharranch to breed in the redd of Sgurr Dubh.

In this sheltered, hidden place the great thrashing and splash of the big fish as they dug their egg beds was unseen by all but the osprey, and the huge salmon on this redd were far too large to be worried by fish-hunting birds. Even otters questing up from Loch Clair did not swim this burn during the torrents of early winter. The flow of water was too fierce and the fish too large for otters' teeth. There was better hunting for brown trout and small sea-trout in Clair and Coulin.

There was nothing to bring men to the desolate slopes, though a few fishermen came for the brown trout in Loch Bharranch during the summer, when the salmon were not there.

But now it was not quiet, though safe, for it was mid-winter and the water from Sgurr Dubh, released from its northern heights, was seeping into the burn. The bed of the little pool lay two feet beneath the surface. It was clear, for the water oozing from sheer rock carried little peat stain. In its cold rush was a saturation of oxygen, gathered as it spilled from the slopes and over gravel higher up the burn.

Beneath the turbulence the gravel shifted slightly but was otherwise still. No eyes saw within the gravel bed, a mere twelve inches beneath the rounded pebbles, where a minute life was struggling against the enormity of natural forces. In near dark-ness and only a womb-like murmur of the stream above, the egg lay with a hundred others, all shielded by the loose gravel from the main force of the water. Over the past few days, its pinkness had flushed with orange. Through the translucent skin the black dots of eyes shone and there was the slightest movement, a con-torsion of the soft shell, a flicker of the eye-spots, a vague twist-ing of a skeletal shape and the furious beating of a tiny heart.

On the Sgurr Dubh redd were many thousands of such eggs, all laid there just weeks earlier by the massive salmon of the Ewe-Maree system. Great tails had worked the gravel then. Frost had shrunk the stream and the backs of the bronzed fish were above the water as they came in pairs from the black waters of Bharranch. Hollows had been gouged from the gravel while the flesh of the salmon had reddened with wounds and their scales had been ripped from where they rubbed on rock and their fins had split and worn.

A hen fish, swollen, small-headed, heavy in motion, yet gloriously powerful as she reached and found the purpose of her fantastic migration, had eased down into the redd she and the cock fish had dug. She arched and a hundred eggs gushed into the hollow. She arched again and another hundred joined the first, though many spilled off and away from the hollow, down into the merciless stream, the torrent, to be snapped up by hungry brown trout which had followed the salmon into the burn knowing that there would be good feeding or swept on down over the sill at the burn mouth and into the wastes of Bharranch.

Even as the eggs squirted down into the bowl of gravel, the great cock fish, leaner by far than the female, large-headed and with an enormous, curving kype of a lower jaw, the mark of a mature cock-salmon which had made several breeding runs, pressed down at her side, slightly upstream. He too arched, a marvellous poise as his body shook in the consummate reason for his terrible journey to the burn of the Sgurr Dubh. His milt swept over the eggs, those that remained in the hollow, those that would be the future of the giant salmon of the system.

Then the two fish together had swept a little upstream and again waved their tired, torn tails so that gravel wafted in the burn and showered down gently on to their eggs until they were covered and secret.

The long winter night had fallen and the two fish fell away downstream, together rolling across the sill and away from the redd, down into Bharranch. There lay the intrinsic decision, to fall further, deeper, to forget, to allow the northern cold to still their perpetual struggles in life now that they had fulfilled the purpose of salmon on a home run, or to gather what feeble strength remained in their battered bodies and turn back for the sea, down through Clair, the Kinlochewe, Maree, Ewe and the Minch? To travel round and through the mountain passes which led to the sea, where there was hope for their own future, or would they fall down into Bharranch and allow, instead, the eggs they had laid in the burn to be their future?

The moon-glinted slopes of the Sgurr Dubh stood above what was apparently a void of lifeless water, snow and rock. But in the loch, on that night of Christmas Eve, the waters shrunk around them by frost, and ice lying as an impenetrable screen between them and the air into which they yearned to leap, the appallingly tired and battered salmon rested their tails on the sandy loch bed. Since leaving the burn and the redd they had slipped down to the loch, out into its silence, to gather strength, whatever more of it there could possibly be in their bodies, for the next stage – the outbound run to the sea.

Above them, in the redd, was their hope, their future. It barely mattered what came next for them. If, by some fate of rushing water and kind currents their tired bodies could be guided back through Loch Maree, and out into coastal waters where, at last, they could begin again to feed, as had happened before on returning to the salt from other breeding runs, then ... Then there could be more, the great cyclical migration could begin again.

In the silvered water the two fish turned very slowly towards the exit river from Bharranch and they heard again the building threat of running water. But it would be running for them now. They could even hold it at their tails, if they had the strength at least to maintain their direction, and it could work for them.

The eggs on the redd of the Sgurr Dubh lay still but alive, the embryonic creatures within growing imperceptibly, their size, their silence, hiding the greatest of all secrets of migration.

It *was* a fishing rod; the long, light, mysterious present which Diana Howard had pushed beyond Johnny's reach behind the Christmas tree. And it had made all the other presents nothing, except for the reel which Charlotte had saved two month's pocket money to buy for him, or so she kept saying, and the miscellaneous bits and pieces of second-hand tackle in the big cardboard box which had been Auntie Viv's present.

'Oh Mum, a *fishing rod*!' he had gasped. 'A *fishing rod*. Look, Charlie.' He had taken it carefully from its partitioned cloth bag. There were three sections, coloured brown and made of hollow glass fibre, the rings whipped on with a very dark brown silk, like the colour of his hair, and heavily varnished. The handle was cork, cleanly sanded and with the lovely, dry smell of a fishing tackle shop.

Johnny had assembled the sections, gently pressing home the ferrules and aligning the rings. The rod, ten feet long, had reached dangerously across the sitting room. Mrs Howard began to tell him to be careful until she saw the extraordinary way he balanced it. With the cork handle resting under his forearm he looked slowly along its graceful length. Gently, he had moved his arm so that the tip dipped and there was a quiet swish in the room, and then another. His eyes had been wide with the joy and thrill of it, the beautiful fishing rod. Even Charlotte had been silent.

3

On the first day that the slight warmth of the spring sun really penetrated the redd on the Sgurr Dubh, the ovum hatched and the creature it had nurtured stretched its almost invisible fins against the flow of water. It was a male salmon, indistinguishable from all the others, known at this stage of development as alevins, that were struggling with the gravel around them and the current which it seemed would wash them all away in a moment.

But the tiny salmon clung to the pebbles of his redd, down in the crevices, the weight of the yolk sack he still carried, the heaviest and densest part of him, stabilising him and holding him down in the flow.

Some were swept away, caught in a sudden gush of cold water, ripped clear even as they took in the first gasping flood of oxygen through their barely formed gills, even as they stretched and faced the great waters, as a salmon bravely does; but the cruel flow caught some of them and tumbled them down, over the sill and into blackness of Bharranch and certain death at the jaws of waiting brown trout.

Now, with pebbles dwarfing his frail shape, with the burn's flow a torrent, though relatively slow since the thaw spates had finished, he learnt to keep his head to the stream and to press his figmentary pectoral fins outwards if the flow threatened to dig him out of the hollow. Even his tail was quiet, still, with no hint of the potential it contained for enormous power. The alevin barely moved as his first day faded on the redd and a dark, long night left him in a world which flowed and roared and was hostile.

*

In that early spring the Weald seemed bursting with life. Johnny spent every hour he could out of doors, always by the River Bewl. Instead of wandering quietly up the shallower stretches where his father had let him wade last spring he now sought out the deepest pools and dark, shaded runs, for this was where the biggest fish in the river hid and lived. As the memory of his father grew less distinct so it seemed that there was a benevolent, watchful haunting by the stream. It made Johnny turn his head sometimes to look behind him at a place where Jack Howard might have stood. Gnarled oaks kept sentinel and the branches of willows waved at him. Sometimes it was just the wind and rain and where he looked was, after all, empty space. He talked out loud, sharing the stream's intimate secrets which he uncovered. The spirit was strongest near the rushing water where it too spoke, though with a meaning which only Johnny could possibly understand.

He had favourite pools, like the one where the river had undercut a bank, right back to some oak and alder on a bend. Johnny set up his tackle on the inside of the bend, which was shallow and gently shelving, with gravel at the top and silt downstream. On the far bank the river ran darkly, smooth against the roots that had been exposed there. Right at the bottom of the pool the water eddied back upstream before falling away in mid-river.

It was on that pool that Johnny made some of his best discoveries. When at last it was the holidays, he managed to visit the pool almost every day. Diana Howard became plagued with a new and ghastly chore in her life. When out shopping she had to visit Corner Pets in Paddock Wood for a shilling's worth of maggots. She made Mr Holsworth, the pet-shop man, put the bait tin into a paper bag and then in the bottom of her basket.

'Johnny going fishing again, Mrs Howard?'

'What else? I wish he'd give the same attention to his books. Oh, he reads his fishing books, of course.'

'Ah, but it's good for the lad to be out in the air. So long as he's not up to mischief,' Mr Holsworth added as an afterthought.

'He wants another crow quill and a plummet. Whatever that is.' She read from the list which Johnny had dictated so that she would not get it wrong.

'Any particular colour?' asked Mr Holsworth as he rattled the container of quills, revealing the brilliant yellows, reds and oranges with which they had been painted at the top. To the boys who hung around Corner Pets, which doubled as the local fishing tackle shop, that big glass container was better even than a jar of gob-stoppers.

'A red one – he was particular about that. Says the red shows up best against the far bank.' She sighed. 'Oh, yes, it's got to be a medium one carrying, what's this, 3BBs?' She showed the list to Mr Holsworth so that he could decipher the fisherman's cryptic code.

'That's the shotting – the weight the floats carry, Mrs Howard.' He smiled but took the message very seriously as he sorted out a red-topped quill float which would take about three BB split shot to make it sit up nicely in the water.

That evening, the float did indeed sit perfectly in the stream, though with slightly more than three BBs. Johnny was at his pool in a small boy's heaven consisting of a shilling's worth of maggots, warm and squirming in the tin, and evening falling so slowly and the crushed water mint at his feet giving off its heady odour. First cast and the float landed within inches of the far bank, lay there a moment as the weights dragged down the line and baited hook, then stood vertically in the water with only a half inch of red top exposed.

Then the stream caught it and began trotting it down the pool, under the cut of the bank. Instinctively, Johnny reached down into the bait tin, never taking his eyes from the float's slow progress. His finger-tips told him that he had grasped a dozen maggots which he hurled across the river to drop into the head of the pool, two yards upstream of the float. Though he did not need to think about it, this 'groundbaiting' brought the fish on the feed and concentrated them in the area through which his hookbait would drift.

He barely felt the weight of the rod in his right arm. It had become like an animal extension of that limb, the most natural thing in the world. The rod tip followed the float round and downstream. With his left hand Johnny gently turned the reel drum to allow more line to run off so that the float did not drag.

Then, in that glorious moment that stirs the primitive hunter in a boy, the float dipped. Suddenly the red bob had gone and

Johnny swept the rod up in a thrilling split-second realisation that a fish had taken the bait and he had done everything right. There was the lovely thump of a hooked fish out there in the swirling pool.

The rod tip went over, right over this time, all the way to the rod's butt section and Johnny did not wind the reel but just held the tension to the invisible force out there, somewhere in the black-brown depths of the river. He could not wind this one straight in, like the five-inch roach or little perch which often plagued some of the pools. And his heart was thumping, his eyes wide, as he felt that mysterious power, twisting, driving upstream, then across, and, incredibly to Johnny, back out into the deep water with renewed strength.

Then, at last, he could wind in a little line, and more, and he saw a flash in the murk, then the silver form of a fish, and red fins and a faint olive hue. The fish was beaten, suddenly head up, no more fight left, and Johnny wound and applied side-ways strain with the rod until the fish slithered on to the gently shelving bank of gravel at his feet.

Quickly, he put down the rod and reached for the fish, wetting his hands in the river first so as not to damage the fish's protective mucus and scales. The *Fishing with Mr Crabtree* book, after-dark reading for Johnny with a torch under the bed clothes, had said: 'Always wet hands before touching a fish . . .' He held the little hook where it had dug into the fish's leathery mouth and twisted it out in a moment. He lifted the fish, firm and strong in his careful grasp, and placed it gently in the keep-net which he had already positioned in the river. It was over and yet it was still there, the dipping float, the strike, the fight, unhooking, touching the wet, cool flesh, putting it in the net . . . And now the fish, a big roach, its fins a fiery, translucent red, back olive, toning to brilliant silver on the flanks, swam in his net, trapped, for now, while he could admire its beauty from time to time between casts.

Later, as darkness fell and his mother would begin to worry if he stayed out any longer, he weighed his precious catch. He had returned the four other, smaller roach he had caught together with a little chub, and had saved the big fish to last. It pulled his spring balance down to one pound and two ounces. He had done it, beaten the magical barrier, a pounder roach, a *pounder*.

'Look,' he said to the spirit at his shoulder, 'look how beautiful it is.'

Wait till Mr Billings and Mr Holsworth heard about that. He had never heard of a pounder being caught from the Bewl. Never before had those waters yielded such a magnificent creature. It was a record for the river.

But who would believe him unless they saw the fish for themselves? His mother might, but not Charlie or the others. The fish lay on the wet gravel, its tail flapping as Johnny knelt over it, his hands ready to pick it up. He looked around for a heavy rock to bring down on its head, to kill it quickly so that he could take his prize home to show them all – his prize, his roach. He could see its gill plates working as it struggled for oxygen. Its cheeks and belly were iridescent in the fading light, as if brushed with mother of pearl. Who would believe him without the actual proof? Who could know that his big roach was so beautiful?

There was a stone in his hand and he could feel its lethal weight. He lifted it and he was the desperate, primitive hunter with his hard won catch. But then he could not take his gaze from the fish's eye, ruby and orange, alive, watching. He dropped the stone and in another moment grasped the roach, lifted it and eased it into the water. He held it there for a few seconds while it regained balance and its fins began to work, coral red as they spread again. Then it kicked, feebly, then more strongly as it recovered. He felt its strength, its need to live, and with one more kick it had opened his fingers and was heading out and away, into the freedom of the pool.

He had caught it, he *had*, and it gave him such a good feeling, such a strong emotion that it made him cry for a few seconds as he gathered his tackle together and turned for the field, heading for the lights that were on in the cottage.

There was no darkness beneath Sgurr Dubh and the burn's summer flow was feeble. The alevin had almost digested his yolk sack. It was merely an orange bump beneath him and he had doubled his length since hatching in March. Now he found it easy to maintain his position in the stream and could even dart up against the current for a few inches.

His siblings had, weeks earlier, carpeted the redd, but now there were fewer, for already the salmon's omnipresent enemies were taking the weak and the unlucky, those positioned on the most exposed gravel or those numbed by night-frost and allowing the flow to carry them down into dangers from which they had, at present, no means of protecting themselves.

For long hours a pair of herons worked the burn. Their camouflaged greyness stole above the shallows, perpetually poised and dangerous. On a grey day the alevin would see the herons as another cloud in the sky, until the explosive shift and stab, by which time it was over for another of their unsuspecting number. The lucky ones saw the slightest movement which lacked the fluidity of clouds and instinctively shrugged themselves into the gravel crevices.

On the days the herons visited the Sgurr Dubh redd, each bird took fifty of the little fish, although in May the hunting became more difficult. With fish so small, and with numbers falling off, during long hunting periods the herons turned to more profitable breeding burns in the Coulin pass.

By the end of May the alevin had completely digested the yolk and he had developed the streamlined shape of his kind. He had become a fry; as grey as a heron's secondary feather, as subtle a colour as the magnificent late-running cock fish that ran the Maree system in autumn floods, though he was still only an inch in length. Against the light he was translucent. Only slowly would his scales and flesh thicken to hide his skeleton and the livid red throat which was his quickly pumping heart.

Even as one threat disappeared, so another one presented itself. Again sinister, slow and methodical, sneaking across the burn, dark and sinuous as reed stems wafting in the current, stealing and skulking within beds of those very stems. Eels. As despised as parasitic, sucking lampreys, the eels had been the greatest threat when the salmon were still in the alevin state and relatively sluggish in motion. Worse, the sickly brown creatures had been marauders of the egg beds, searching throughout the redd for tell-tale signs of a salmon's spawning mark, then driving their snake-like heads between the pebbles as they sought the smell of eggs. If a weakness in the bed was found a single eel could devour every egg.

Now that the fry were more mobile, able to dash for cover at the slightest hint of danger, the eels were less successful. Even so, those fry which paused too long facing the slight current near the weeds, or at the tail of the pool, failed to notice the peat-brown sleekness slithering in from behind.

The threats of flood and frost, heron and eel, all diminished as the fry and his siblings grew larger, and fewer. Throughout the almost perpetual day of the northern summer he learnt the contours and nature of the burn. By June he had grown powerful enough to swim more than fifty yards upstream, in the weakest summer flow, from where he had hatched. The stream was shrunken up there and he explored tentatively, in the shadows, and with other salmon fry, never completely alone.

The burn was confined so far up from Bharranch, closed in by overhanging and undercut peat banks and heather stems, and the shadow of Sgurr Dubh was even more of a shroud than it was down on the spawning area. It drew the light from the southern sky and stilled the winds from that direction. The burn ran from the gathered waters at the mountain's base and always with the fresh water of melted snow or the frequent rain from the highest slopes, where cloud often hung. The young salmon fry was never to forget the taste of that water from the peak of the Sgurr Dubh.

4

'His spelling is appalling,' Miss Jackman, Johnny's teacher, told Diana Howard at a parents' evening. 'He just doesn't bother. I sometimes wonder if he isn't a little bit dyslexic.'

Miss Jackman was a gently spoken lady in middle age, a spinster who was devoted to her class. She liked Johnny even though she despaired of him.

'He's not a stupid boy, but he is simply not interested unless we're doing nature or geography, or some such.' She waved her arms as if to express the subjects in which Johnny was interested, subjects which she obviously felt would be of little use to the boy's future. Her thick glasses hung precariously between the tip and bridge of her nose. It was difficult to concentrate on what she was saying; Mrs Howard tensed herself in readiness to catch the spectacles when they fell. They bounced up and down as Miss Jackman talked.

'Surely he could catch up? What about homework?' suggested Diana Howard.

'Well, yes, but ... ' Miss Jackman shook her head and her spectacles rocked wildly on her nose. The 'but ... ' was meant to imply that she did not feel that Johnny would catch up unless some special measures were taken.

'You could try these.' Miss Jackman gathered together half a dozen books for young readers, all on subjects to do with animals. 'We just have to get him reading something, otherwise he will fall too far behind. He won't pass into Tonbridge unless there is an improvement soon.' Passing the eleven plus and thereby gaining a virtual passport for the local boys into Tonbridge public school was Miss Jackman's aim for all her boys. She saw it as her great purpose and responsibility in life.

She was measured, at least in her own opinion, by this achievement.

It was during that summer and autumn that John Howard grew to love the Wealden fields and the River Bewl with an intensity which overshadowed all else in his life. When the glorious summer holiday was over he found himself confronted by the awful prospect of a long school term. The routines of his days were punctuated by the enjoyable sights of the Weald; the walk and bus ride to Paddock Wood station and the train journey into Tonbridge, seeing the fields and hedgerows lush with a season's growth, the orchards ablaze with the colours of ripe apples and pears, the ranks and files of poles laden with gorgeous smelling hops. Johnny pressed against the train windows, pulling them down so that he could lean out and look into the depths of the meshwork of streams. He knew their names; the Beult and Teise, a section of his Bewl, tributaries of the mighty Medway.

On the walk to school he could see the Medway itself. Pulling himself up on to the bridge parapet he balanced on his elbows, the toes of his shoes scuffing against the stonework. From there he watched the flowing mystery beneath. On calm days, he could see the dimpling of roach and dace sucking down hatching flies from the surface. When the river was in flood it gushed in a thick brown mass and carried all manner of fascinating junk; paper bags, an old straw basket, a Tizer bottle ...

The final bit of the journey was the worst by far, three-quarters of a mile from the bridge, past the high street and on up the leafy roads at the top of the hill, each step taking him nearer to the place which was like a prison. He passed Tonbridge school where the boys wore strange hats and looked as if they belonged to quite another place and time. Don't they know they look silly? thought Johnny. Why didn't those boys run away to the fields and the river banks?

The dread mounted as he turned into the drive where his own school stood. There, for another day, yet another barely tolerable day, he would suffer the boredom and routines, the discipline and restraint.

On those days when rain clouds drifted over the Weald, Johnny could imagine himself taking shelter beneath the branches of oak and beech while the delicious, wet wind blew and the hedges dripped and there was no one around to disturb him in his adventures by the river; their adventures, his and Dad's. At school he would hear the brief rattle of an autumn cloud-burst against the window of Miss Jackman's classroom and then the satisfying sound of gusting wind and rain would be lost under the drone of her voice as she tried to teach arithmetic.

The salmon fry had explored throughout the burn, from its trickling summer source beneath the Sgurr to the dangerous glide above the sill. There the water opened and shallowed in a glare and tumble, disappearing over a gravel bar into the mysterious beyond, with a roar and a flash of bubbling light.

Above, slightly upstream, in the glide of smooth water, the fry fed, darting from side to side as he intercepted minute particles of detritus and phytoplankton. On calmer autumn days, when the air above the burn was humid and dank, the bodies of tiny midges drifted down on the stream. These enticed the little fry. He rose at them, at first whipping them with his tail to drown them, then approaching them head-on, rising over them with a splash and even with an open-mouthed, head-shaking slash at the surface, the tiny beasts smashed by his full-blooded attack.

Then he began to taste them, to crush them in his jaws and to swallow them. They would drift down to him, one after the other, in their tens and hundreds, and he would rise, an almost invisible plop as he sipped and drew them down, swallowing, and up for the next, and the next as he held his head to the current and slowly drifted downstream.

His siblings rose with him, crazed in the intensity of their feeding rise, oblivious to the dangers around and above them; predatory eels and brown trout, a heron's poise, and, now that the autumnal southward migration of birds had begun, the opportunistic terns and gulls, sheltering inland from storms at sea. The terns would hover on the updraft at the base of the Sgurr, hawking in the air, heads downpointed as they sighted the fry. Their wings half-closed while they dipped and stooped and their quick bills stabbed beneath them at the water's surface, whipping up a fry even as the birds gyred up into the sky, again to hover, again to sight a fry.

It was a tern which caused the young fish to swim, on his fleet fins, out into the unknown, beyond the burn that was his world. He had been rising at midge when a tern had spun in the sky above him. A white belly had streaked down towards him, and the shadow of angular wings had grown. There had been a dazzle of light and a splash which momentarily stunned him with its shock. Not two inches from his right flank another fry had been snatched up by the tern. He had seen the brilliant scarlet bill scything towards him, and he had spun away and upwards, leaping at the surface in some tiny mimicry of an adult salmon's great spectacle. A breeze had caught him and blown him two feet downstream.

He had found himself in the pool glide, with sucking water all around him and a roar and tremble at the sensitive lateral lines along his flanks. He was on the sill, driving himself at the quick current that bulged and spilled over the gravel, but he could make no progress against its force.

So he had turned, the tingle of oxygen in his muscle, the thrill of blasting water at his tail. He kicked and dived and he was swimming down into darkness. Only a murmur of the burn was behind him and then silence and a curious stillness. He had passed over the sill and had left the Sgurr Dubh burn. Now he lay on the lip of a great vastness, a salmon's joy in vastness, in open water, the dark Loch Bharranch.

For the first time in his life he was alone.

He swam three feet below the surface, deeper than he had ever been, and the peaty water around him shone in a bronze autumn light. Beyond, out into the loch, was a frightening darkness and he was not ready to go that way yet. Instead he turned back towards the orange, weed-strewn sands by the loch shore where there was light and motion in the waves breaking against stones.

There he met another enemy. As he approached the weeds a brown trout rose from the boulders of the loch bed where it had hidden, waiting for the fry which often were washed down in the current from the burn. But the trout had been too slow, having fed well on a hatch of silver sedge flies. It had risen with purpose but lacking the speed which hunger would have given it. Turning on the darting fry it snapped its jaws, expecting the soft crushing of flesh, but tasting only water and not feeling the twist and tremble of a little fish dying on its teeth. The salmon fry, for the second time in just a few minutes, bolted and flayed its minuscule fins at the surface, then turned and dived, zig-zagging downwards, and suddenly met with the safety of dense weeds.

Johnny had exhausted credibility with his excuses for not going to school. His mother did not believe anymore in the headaches and tummy upsets, and she would not yield to his screaming and ranting as she forced him to put on his uniform.

'You have to go to school,' she pleaded, 'or you won't learn anything and you won't be able to do what you want to when you grow up.'

'I don't want to do anything that they teach me in school,' he snivelled, 'it's boring. I just want to go fishing.'

'Well, you won't make a living out of fishing. Now, get those shoes on and go to school.'

Why not, why could he not make a living out of fishing? People did: fishermen. He had seen pictures of them in one of the books Miss Jackman had given him and it looked wonderful. They wore bright yellow oilskins and sou'westers and they fished from big wooden boats that pitched on the wild, wild sea. They caught cod and halibut, and great, bulging netfuls of silver herring. Sometimes, near northern shores, they went after salmon; the books called it the 'king of fish'. It was not fair. He was good at fishing, he enjoyed it. It was never boring like the six-times table and seeing how many syllables were in the word 'behaviour', let alone writing it out a hundred times after class.

The warm late summer weather had persisted well into October and it seemed to Johnny a terrible thing to be trapped in school while his river flowed rich with the colours of fallen leaves and the fish fed ravenously before winter set in. So, he planned the first great rebellion of his life.

It was a Wednesday, a clear morning when the sun came up over wet grass, glistening across the Wealden landscape. Johnny did not protest as he made ready for school and Mrs Howard gave him and Charlotte their porridge. In fact he was much quieter than usual and his mother caught herself glancing at him and she even felt his brow to see if he had a temperature.

When it was time to leave, Johnny picked up his satchel and rushed out after kissing his mother.

'Don't miss the train this afternoon,' she called after him. 'And have you got your two shillings?'

'Yes Mum, see you later.' And he was gone, down on to the little road, then on to the footpath which led through to the main road and the bus-stop.

When he had gone a few hundred yards along the footpath, he stopped, turned and walked slowly back. He waited near the end of the path, hidden from the road and the cottage, until he heard his mother start the Austin and drive off with Charlotte to Tunbridge Wells where she worked and his sister went to school. Then, quite suddenly, he realised he had done it. He was free. Miss Jackman would think he was ill again and that Mummy was keeping him home. So long as no one saw him, who would know?

Collecting his fishing rod which he had left strategically in the shed and swapping his school shoes for wellingtons, his fishing tackle and two Milky Ways already in his satchel, he climbed over the fence into Mr Billings's field and made for the river.

When he was older, Johnny could only remember two things with any clarity about his truancy. Firstly, there was his fathomless joy of having stolen some more time by his river, fishing, exploring the bankside, hiding from passers-by, walkers and farm workers. And secondly, there was the consternation he caused when his truancy was discovered.

His mother and the school found out, but not until he had got away with it for several days, when Mr Billings finally remarked one day to Diana Howard that he had seen Johnny's thatch of brown hair down by the river bank on a Friday and 'shouldn't the lad've been at school?'

'I were sure it were 'im, but when I looked 'e'd disappeared, the little blighter.' Mr Billings grinned toothlessly. And so it had been, as Mrs Howard later made Johnny tearfully admit.

'Oh Johnny . . . How many days have you been up to this?' she asked wearily. He could not remember exactly how many days. It had seemed a long time, all of it deliciously stolen, wonderfully fugitive, even though now he was going to have to pay.

Diana Howard had been obliged to go and see Johnny's headmaster and Miss Jackman on a Saturday morning in early November when, at last, the weather had changed and frosts and fogs had tightened their wintry hold upon the Weald.

'I really do not know what to do with him, Mrs Howard,' said

Miss Jackman, her spectacles bobbing about even more than usual. 'He is such a tearaway. A lovely boy, though, full of energy. I just cannot seem to direct that energy towards his work.'

Major William Skeetle-Smith (the boys called him SS Bill), Headmaster of Hilden Grange, sat with a stern expression, though he did not feel particularly stern. For he remembered, very vaguely, when he might have done the same as young John Howard. He felt like laughing at the thought of it: the little rascal running across the fields with his fishing rod. He wanted to laugh even more as he watched Miss Jackman's worried look and her ridiculous spectacles.

'Well,' he suggested at last, 'at least we know he's not dim. He has got away with it for rather a long time. Rather enterprising, really.' Then he saw that Mrs Howard might be about to lose her temper and Miss Jackman was staring at him open-mouthed. 'But I agree with you, ladies,' he hastily added. 'We really must do something to turn his attention to some good, solid work.' Miss Jackman closed her mouth.

The 'something' was a very tight rein on John Howard's life, so tight that he never played truant again while he was at his pre-paratory school. And it was also the cane. He became the only boy that year to receive 'six of the best'. It had not really physically hurt in the least. But it had bitten deeply into his pride, as his mother, Miss Jackman and poor Major Skeetle-Smith, who had to administer the punishment, had intended.

That cold November, as the river ran in brown flood, Johnny learnt that there was a wonderful essence in life, like being out in open country and by flowing water where fish swam and kingfishers dived. Also he discovered that you had to do certain things to earn the time to enjoy it all. You could steal time, yes, you could; but you had to give something back in the end. It was very confusing and he did not fully work it out for years, even though he instinctively understood it all the time. He knew that the headmaster's punishment, 'six of the best', and yet the man's understanding, was some small part of it. He had seen that understanding in his mother and Mr Billings and Mr Holsworth. Long, long ago, before a very sad time, he had seen it in the eyes of another man, his father, now shut away in dark, transient memory, to escape sometimes in tears in the night. He knew it was love. He knew the meaning, though he could not put a word to it.

The water temperature had held steady until the end of November and then had plummeted, bringing harsh winter to the Maree system. On Beinn Eighe, Slioch and the mountains of Torridon, including Sgurr Dubh, the screes whitened under snow, while ice built its rock-splitting hold on northern slopes. Wind keened across Bharranch and it seemed a desolate place, a freezing loch on a barren moor beneath black rock and icy crevice.

Yet, beneath the surface, the fry, two inches long now, watched a living loch. Torpor had silenced many of the hunters as lean winter slowed them and they conserved their energy, though the trout were gathering by the mouths of feeder streams where they would spawn. Heavy hen fish stole sedately from the loch's depths while cock fish, smaller and sinuous, sported the fierce reds and iridescent oranges of their spawning dress. They wielded the dangerous, hooked and toothy kypes of their lower jaws, slashing them at one another, or at other hapless creatures which ventured near.

In slightly deeper water the grey shapes of sea-trout gathered, also before a spawning run. They did not mix with the brown trout and would run slightly later, digging their redds in deeper water. They were the runners of the tide, fish of the rain, running up from the sea after big tides and flood waters in the rivers. They came and went mysteriously, large numbers one day, gone the next, on to another loch or burn in the system.

Then the salmon, huge and dark, driven on vast forked fins. These were the autumn runners, massive against the maiden fish, the silver grilse which had run earlier in the year. Above the fry, one December day when rain had lifted the Sgurr Dubh burn so that it hissed down into Bharranch, came the giant shadows of salmon. Like all the other fry he hid down among the boulders for fear of the great, silent fish. In that year he saw little of the spectacle of autumn salmon on a breeding run. It had no meaning, then, for the little creature which knew only fear and instinctive reaction in order that he might survive the terrible winter.

Just once, in the dull red of evening, as one of the huge salmon slid across the shallows, the fry felt a sudden excitement, a primitive call. It made him dart across the loch bed, beneath the fish's broad belly, kicking up sand as he sped along. Then again fear and pure instinct, diving into crevices, bolting into weeds, hiding from endless threats, the fry quivered unseen in the deep while salmon returned from the journey that all their surviving number and offspring would again have to make.

5

Diana Howard sat in her cottage garden in the mid-summer glow of late evening. The scents of jasmine, honeysuckle and stock wafted across to her and seemed as potent as the sherry to which she had treated herself, as she sometimes did after a long, hard day. She loved her garden and her home but making ends meet was not easy. There was always so little money now that Jack had gone. The store group for which she was a manageress was going to move her up to a London branch in the autumn. It would mean an awful train journey every day, but it would also mean more money.

She saw Johnny strolling across Billings' field from the river. He was ten now, wiry and sinuous, full of energy, and looking charmingly ridiculous in his wellingtons on that dry summer evening. He was so much smaller than Charlotte who was thirteen, a teenager, for goodness' sake; soon she would be a woman. It hardly bore thinking about. They still quarrelled relentlessly, little jealousies and absurdities between them, and sometimes they even came to blows. Oddly enough it was not Charlotte who always won, despite her age and strength. She would pull at Johnny's hair and bite him in a rage, but he was so fierce in reaction, so quick as he flayed his bony limbs. But their battles were quick, ending in tears for both.

They were so different, Charlotte like her, Johnny the image in miniature of his father. In him she saw the same humour in the blue eyes, the same mischievous charm, energy and enthusiasm for what he enjoyed, apathy for anything else. Charlotte was pretty, a winner, academically excellent, bound for university, medical school probably. That pleased Mrs Howard. She didn't worry about her daughter who would always come out on top in life. Johnny, however, could go either way. Depression could destroy him, but his energy was electric. He had something very strong which he revealed only in odd ways.

She watched him stop by the back gate and look up at something fluttering in the sky.

'Look, Mum,' he called across. 'We've bats roosting under the tiles.'

'What dear? Bats?' She had thought that the fluttering creatures above the cottage on those still evenings were the swifts and house martins she saw during the day.

'Pipistrelle bats. I can see where they're coming out from, under the attic window.'

There it was again. Now, how on earth did he know that? Strange facts that would never have occurred to her. He really did know so much about nature and animals. If only it was important. But, then, maybe it was. It was, after all, the whole world to Johnny.

The summer holidays arrived and Johnny found he had the freedom of the river again, even though his mother usually kept him in to do an hour's reading or holiday work. He fished, spending his days alone, and he was far less hurried than he had been in other summer holidays. He knew the river intimately and could pick out the right pool or run for whatever species he wanted to catch and also could match the bait to the fish and conditions. In a flood the swollen river demanded fat lobworms, while bread paste trotted through the faster runs was deadly for dace and roach, particularly if some thinly mixed groundbait of stale bread crumbs was fed in every few casts to bring the fish on the feed. Maggots under the far bank brought the blunt-headed, wide-mouthed chub and multi-coloured perch, dorsal spines bristling. Brandling and red worms were attractive to some of the best quality fish he ever caught, of whatever species.

Besides eels, which he loathed, there was another fish he did not enjoy catching, pike. He learnt, however, that even these highly predatory, alligator-jawed monsters were part of the natural balance of the river. He had watched as young jack-pike lay in ambush in the weeds for the weaker members of a dace shoal, those stunted or injured fish that dragged nervously behind the main group, always doomed to fall to a predator. Once, in an incident which made Johnny leap from the river as when he had seen the swimming grass snake years earlier, he came suddenly on a very large pike. He had noticed a small dead fish by a weed bed. Wading out so that he could see what species it was and gain some clue as to why it had died he almost trod on a huge dark shape he had thought was a log. It moved, a giant fish, mottled with green and brown, perfectly camouflaged against a weed bed dappled in sunlight. As if it had not seen the boy, the pike cruised up to the dead roach and hovered there, like an aircraft carrier above a submarine. Then it picked up the dead fish in its massive jaws, turned it until only the red tail fin protruded from its mouth and swallowed it down in a single gulp. The weeds parted as the pike slid away while there was a ridge, a bow-wave, on the surface to mark the leviathan's passing.

Even snakes, eels and huge pike, were a fascination to Johnny. They were more than a counterbalance to the river life he enjoyed. They were an essential part of it. His father had explained the purpose of nature's more sinister hunters; in that summer he watched them at their work. Without any one of them the Bewl would have been a poorer place. He often wondered if there could be any environment so rich as the rivers which drained the Weald. In books and at the cinema he had seen jungles and forests and great grassy plains, where elephants and lions roamed and wildebeest grazed, more numerous than the cows in Mr Billings's fields. There were snakes in those places too, and brilliantly coloured fish in the rivers, fruit bats in those wet, warm forests; but he could not believe that there was anywhere so rich as those Kentish streams and the green fields through which they flowed.

In other waters, 700 miles north, was other life, other riches, in a landscape which was harder, higher and colder. The life in Loch Bharranch, bathed in light for twenty hours in twenty-four, was at its most vital during this phase of the annual cycle. The young salmon, now a parr six inches long, fed voraciously on the midge and sedge pupae that rose from the silt and sand on the loch floor. Some days, in gravelly areas two or three feet deep, dull olive and brown ephemerids hatched. These were the best prey of all, either the streamlined nymphs which burst from the gravel in their rush to hatch, or the adults, spreading their sail-like wings at the surface. As they ecloded, their nymphal skin shone with a vibrant orange before dulling to olive. This orange, reproduced by hundreds of hatching insects, drew predatory trout and salmon parr. The surface of Bharranch would be ringed over huge areas as the fish competed for the transient food source of ephemerids.

The salmon parr was now the shape and virtually the colour of the closely related brown trout. He had their bronzed flanks dotted in black, though he also possessed the 'finger marks', grey vertical bands, which set him apart from the young trout.

According to the ancient folk-lore of the Gaelic people who lived in the glens of Wester Ross, the young salmon's home, the parr marks were placed there on the young fish by the fingers of a wise sea-god from the high-north. He marked only the fish which he had chosen to make the journey to visit his cold kingdom in the wild, wild sea. So, those fish marked thus were sacred and could only be taken by men when the marks were gone and the sea-god had fed the fish and silvered them. It was then that he sent them away from the kingdom of the sea back to the rivers which drained the glens, as a gift to the people.

The parr's back was a deep brown, like wet peat, and this hid him from the sharp eyes of predatory birds as they hawked across the sky. His belly ranged from buttermilk to pearlescent ivory while his fins held the colour of ephemerids hatching, the translucent orange. He was very fast on the fin now, over short distances, and dashed around as he chased sedge flies which skittered over the surface as they lay their water-borne eggs, or electric blue damsel flies which hovered, tantalisingly, a few inches above calm areas of the loch, near reed beds.

He would leap at them, their iridescence infuriating him, catalysing within him such a reaction that made him throw himself at them, jaws snapping and head shaking. At first he could not catch them, for as soon as he broke through the surface into the air they flicked the chitinous fronds of their wings and whipped off across the loch. He dashed and skipped in their wake, but they were too fast. But then he learnt to allow for the refraction and also to accelerate from deeper water so that he shot into the air and snatched them down before they could respond to the attack.

Every month during that rich summer and autumn the parr grew by almost another inch. Soon he found that he could encroach into the territory of the smaller brown trout without them attacking him. He did not, then, venture out into the deep water of Bharranch, for he had seen the terrible threat that hunted out there: huge, kyped brown trout, *ferox*, blacker than peat, bigger than sea-trout and maiden salmon, cannibalistic and deadly. Sometimes, in late evening and during the night the *ferox* slunk into the shallows, wolfing down smaller brown trout and parr, or any creature caught in the open where the black fish prowled. For the ferox trout, insects were not enough. They needed the flesh of fish, even if it were that of their own young.

That October, almost four years since he had hatched on the redd of the Sgurr Dubh, the salmon parr again began to change. Physically, there was little to see, except that he was growing so much faster than ever before in his life now that he had learnt the optimum compromise between safety and hunting in Loch Bharranch. He and other salmon parr of the same year group began to roam beyond the territories they had known so well. The quarter-mile wide loch seemed smaller than it had ever been, restricting and dull. In the time between dawn and the first glint of sun beyond Beinn Eighe, he would swim across the shallows beneath Sgurr Dubh burn west to the sandy bays, turning away from the dark shadow of the Sgurr, through the reed fringed silty area of the loch and be up on the southern reefs and gravel bars.

He knew the shallows of the loch, every point and bay, every weed bed and burn mouth. Deep within him, from where the real change came, he felt a mounting urge, a need to leave Bharranch and its claustrophobic, dangerous waters. He did not know of the awesome dangers that lay beyond his home loch.

Often, dashing out over the deep, sometimes alone, sometimes with year-group parr, he would sweep over the territory of the black *ferox*. His fins flayed so that he accelerated on the surface, lunging into the waves, through them, momentarily down into peaty darkness, into the terrible danger, then back into the light, a salmon's light where wave and sky and sun meet and dazzle from shining scales and whirring fins.

The *ferox* would not have him now, nor any hunter in Loch Bharranch. On the spate following the autumn rains, the young salmon hung in the building force of water at the outflow from the loch. Others had gathered with him, salmon and sea-trout parr, and they too felt the overwhelming urge to leave Bharranch and run on the swollen waters into the unknown where their fins could bite at mightier currents than they had ever known.

As the water thundered across their flanks and hissed through reed stems around them, the little fish ran with fear, though it was never as strong as the urge to migrate, downwards, with the flowing spate into greater waters.

The salmon, among a group of more than a hundred, nearly all that had survived from the thousands of eggs spawned in the Sgurr Dubh redd almost four years earlier, drifted on the torrent beneath Bharranch. Their tortuous way was hindered by dense reeds, bent and forced apart by the flood, and by boulders where the water drove in a white roar, whipping the fish downstream to the next pool, quickly over bubbling rapids which shook scales from their bodies and flattened their bravely stretched fins.

At last, with one more spin and lurch, the young salmon regained control and found himself among more boulders, but in calmer water where a current replaced the spate on the broad shallows of Loch Clair, central loch in the Coulin chain at the head of the Maree system. The battered shoal gathered around him. Torn fins and quickly working gills told the story of the torrent and now the fish hung, as if lost, in peaty-bronze light, more intense than it had been on Bharranch. Their lateral lines told them that there was enormous space around them and that made the shoal become more wary of dangers. They swam tail to tail, flank to flank, sea-trout with salmon, in a shoal defence, and moved towards the shadows of Clair's western shore where a forest calmed the wind and stilled the loch. There the shoal eased apart and the fish settled among rocks wherever there were no large brown trout or sea-trout to harry them away.

Mr Spence was the English teacher at Johnny's prep school. He was fastidious about grammar and spelling, and liked neatness. Presentation and observation of the rules of English were not absolutely everything he demanded from his pupils, but if they could provide these qualities they were safely in his favour. John Howard did not ever aspire to fulfilling the academic measures of Mr Spence.

Despite that, English was not one of the subjects which Johnny dreaded. His favourite was science, for this meant, essentially, biology with a bit of physical science thrown in, taught by the lovely Emily Tonford. She was a part-time teacher brought in by Hilden Grange to satisfy the stipulations of the Department of Education that elementary general science be taught in primary and preparatory schools. She was also the first woman on whom Johnny had a crush. He performed for her, working desperately hard on the subject both because he enjoyed it and to impress her.

English was a different matter. Johnny did not put much effort into it, but he did not hate it as he did Maths, French and Latin. These, after all, were worse even than snakes, eels and big pike. Mr Spence would tut and moan about his presentation, his grossly untidy left-handed scrawl, his spelling mistakes on every line, his antithesis of correct grammatical procedure. He did not bellow at him, however, or hurl his book across his desk, or make him a regular attendant of the detention room, as did the teachers of the detested subjects. Mr Spence would just run slowly through the pages of Johnny's homework book making his corrections with the occasional vocalisation of displeasure.

Johnny would stand at Mr Spence's desk, usually for longer than any of his classmates, listening to the list of mistakes he had made. Except for the embarrassment, Johnny did not particularly dread these sessions. Mr Spence's tweed jacket always smelled of a particularly pleasant pipe tobacco and he used a tortoise-shell fountain pen with a wide gold nib and rich red ink. The corrections made to each page of Johnny's book were things of beauty, exquisite writing in little columns in the margin, long flowing lines at the top and bottom of each page, precisely circled punctuation marks. Mr Spence was all right.

Best of all, he would encourage the slightest glimmer of effort. Those boys who produced their neat essays and comprehension exercises, on time, would receive a flourish of penned praise for their efforts, delicate lines of comment as to why Mr Spence approved of the work, a high mark out of twenty, ruled off with the same red ink. It was something to show their parents, something to keep.

Wednesdays and Fridays were the only tolerable days in John Howard's week during term-time. On these days the mornings at school began with Maths on Wednesday and French on Friday, but then came the increasing pleasures of English, Science and, after lunch, games. Friday was best of all, because there was the weekend to look forward to.

It was on a Friday in November, almost a week after Johnny's eleventh birthday, that he had the best day he had ever had, and was ever to have, at school. That day was to shape his life almost as much as his treasured times on the Bewl.

The morning was cold and clear, a slight, fingering mist rising quickly as Johnny walked the footpath to the bus-stop, his exhaled breath white and thick in the sunshine. The grass was crisp underfoot, the frost becoming dewy and glistening as soon as the sun's warmth touched it. In Tonbridge the Medway flowed with a blue clarity below the bridge where Johnny peered into it and could see a shoal of big roach hanging downstream of a weed bed which was dying down in the cooling waters of late season.

French went by in a blur and Johnny spent the time more profitably than usual. Spread out on his lap beneath the desk he re-read his English homework and checked it for mistakes. It was an essay entitled 'Holiday Adventures' and it was one of a very few English homeworks for which Johnny had made an effort. In fact he had spent almost a week working at it, writing it and rewriting it, checking the punctuation and spelling and even asking Charlotte to help him with the grammar.

The catalyst for this grand effort had been a pen, given to him by his mother for his birthday. He had often spoken to her about the lovely pen with which Mr Spence produced his wonderful script, the corrections and comments, all over Johnny's English exercise book. She had seen his admiration and had taken the hint that if Johnny owned a beautiful pen then he might, just might, be tempted to do some work with it.

The pen was a Parker, glossy black and cigar shaped with a metal band where the cap screwed on to the barrel, and an arrow and stud for the clip. The nib, like the band and arrow, was gold plated and shone with the same warmth and radiance as Mr Spence's pen. Johnny saw in that pen something of the grace and beauty of his fishing rod. The one produced the means to contact fish in his stream, it shone and flexed and felt balanced and good in his grasp. The other possessed the shape of a craftsman's tool and from the sweep and cut of its nib ink flowed and the magic of words could be created. Johnny, with care, with practice,

40

could use his pen to produce those words, meanings in Quink Royal Blue, glistening at first, then dried and permanent, and made by *him*.

By chance, Mr Spence's homework that week had been the essay entitled 'Holiday Adventures'. It was a title which lent itself to Johnny's imagination and, even better, to things he knew about, his own adventures on the Bewl. He spent hours every evening remembering the summer before and, for the first time in his life, he set down his thoughts in words.

In the last half of his Friday lessons, while the boys did an exercise in comprehension, Mr Spence always chose three homework books to read and mark, leaving the rest for the weekend. He would have each of the three, in turn, stand at his left side facing the class, while he marked their books and muttered his comments.

Williamson and Jones Major were the first two to be chosen and they each went through the non-event of their particular marking sessions. Johnny watched them standing there self-consciously, a slight smugness about Williamson since he was sure he would get his usual fifteen out of twenty, which he did. Jones Major came away with a 'satisfactory' thirteen and a remark about 'lack of content'.

'Howard.' It made Johnny jump to hear his name called out and to see his grubby book held aloft. He stood up and walked over to Mr Spence's desk. Williamson and some others sniggered. Johnny was more nervous than usual as Mr Spence began reading and almost immediately began to make his red marks correcting spelling and punctuation. Then, just as he seemed poised to make a further correction in the second paragraph, he paused and stopped muttering. He continued to read and Johnny could feel the tangible tension in the class.

Something extraordinary was about to happen.

No one was fidgeting and Mr Spence was curiously still as he read. Suddenly, even as Johnny's nervousness was beginning to make his knees wobble, Mr Spence looked up from the book, glanced at the boy at his side and looked back at the page.

'That, Howard, is a lovely image.' He paused as if he was finding exactly the right way to express what he thought about Johnny's work. 'You have made your usual mistakes, or most of them, but the picture you have painted of your river is ... very,

41

very good.' And he wrote it down in his wonderful red script at the bottom of the essay against his mark, sixteen out of twenty. *Sixteen*, and he had never before achieved more than eight. Smashing sixteen! He tried not to smile, conscious that everyone was looking at him, but he could barely keep still as Mr Spence wrote the best comments Johnny had ever seen in one of his exercise books.

'You have put a lot of time and effort into this, Howard,' said Mr Spence in a voice which would be heard even at the back of the class. 'In fact, if you had paid a little more attention to the rules of English, this essay would be excellent. Keep it up, boy, keep it up.' And with that Johnny returned to his seat, casting a triumphant look towards Williamson, and the rest of that lesson slipped by in a euphoria which made him tingle. He could hardly wait to show Mum. He picked up his pen and looked at it with pride.

In his next lesson, the last before lunch, games and the weekend – double Science with Emily Tonford – Johnny stared and listened and tried to understand. She looked so warm and comfortable. The boys did not play her up as they did some of the other teachers, those that were not feared.

In the science room the tables were spread out and there was no particular area for the teacher. Instead, Miss Tonford wandered around the boys demonstrating whatever scientific experiment or principle her ingenuity had dreamed up from the Department of Education's loose syllabus. That day they were studying fir cones. They each had a collection of various species to examine and draw while Miss Tonford explained what they were.

Johnny had already arranged his pile, and written at the top of the cream-coloured cartridge paper 'fur cons', carefully underlined and unsmudged, when Miss Tonford came over to him. He drew in a deep breath. She always smelt so nice, of wool and a sweet, flowery soap or perfume, and he always thought of it as her smell, the smell of her skin and hair.

'F–*i*–r, Johnny, the other sort is the fur on animals,' she said quietly.

'Oh, yes, miss.'

'Do you know what sort of trees fir cones come from?'

'Fir trees ... And pines, coniferous trees.' Johnny started to fidget with his Parker as he thought about fir cones. 'Like the trees in the forests all over Scotland.' He thought of the film he had seen a few weeks ago at the Classic in Tunbridge Wells, with Mum and Charlie. There had been coniferous forests in that, where German and English soldiers fought in the snow. 'And other cold places, north . . .' His father had told him about those forests as well. He had said they lay thickly on the slopes of mountains and grew right to the edges of deep lochs in northern Scotland and other wild country, like in Scandinavia. They gave shelter to the wild animals from the cutting winds of winter and autumn's heavy rains. They formed calm oases in the rushing storms. Daddy had told him about red squirrels, and the elk in Norway; he had described the mighty Spey and Tay in Scotland, flowing from forested country, and about the salmon that swam those waters. Some of this he told Miss Tonford.

'Very good, Johnny. Yes, class, fir cones come from coniferous trees, usually evergreens, which means?'

'They don't lose their leaves in the winter, miss,' shouted Williamson before Johnny could reply.

'Yes, and, as Johnny said, coniferous trees often grow in cold, northern places.'

He was happy. He thought about the forests where the cones came from, and snow, thick and crunchy underfoot, weighing down the sagging branches, dropping from them with a satisfying thud. Beyond were mountains, white and blue, high and huge in the air so cold it made your breath white.

High, high above Loch Clair, the craggs of Meall an Leathaid Mhoir to the south and Beinn Eighe to the north were whitened with the first heavy snows of winter. The last black clouds, stark against the dazzling mirrors of loch, ice and snow, were shredding away from the highest peaks and drifting south-east on cold, dry air. The Allt na Luib burn, draining the Clair forest, was almost stilled, flowing only beneath a thickening coat of ice.

Five feet beneath the loch's surface, in slightly warmer water, the eight-inch parr swam. Energy was in him, making him hunt for food which was at its least abundant, forcing him to circumnavigate the loch's perimeter, tasting the inflowing waters and listening to the exciting outflow along Clair's eastern shore. He swam swiftly over deep water, where *ferox* lurked, and followed ghostly sea-trout, the runners of the rain, which he had learnt not to fear despite their size. The sea-trout were questing fish, seeking particular areas of the loch where they felt most secure, close to the breeding burns. They would hang in large shoals, over deeper water than brown trout or salmon. One of their number would suddenly burst from the group, powerfully slipping up into the shallows, whipping up shingle with the shovel of its tail, and launch into the air in a high, cartwheeling leap.

The sea-trout activity excited the salmon parr. Their wandering spirit was in him, though he knew not where to wander and there was always fear, finally making him still his fins in the cold water even as he watched the acrobatic grey fish, and felt the shock-waves of their leaping.

Then the greatest wanderers of all arrived, the huge autumn-run salmon. Driven by the power of the grey-black forks of their tails, the salmon pressed up into Clair. Their number was few, fewer than it had ever been. One fish bore a ringed scar around her girth, just in front of her dorsal fin. No scales grew there and a white fungus, which even the cold waters could not kill, had established a hold. She hung behind the great bronze fish with which she had run, instinct alone giving her the strength and the will to drive her tail at the loch's waters. Some of the other salmon carried strange scars, and a few of them had been injured more recently, and not by the rocks and spills of their hazardous passage up from the sea.

The salmon parr watched the shadows gliding overhead, their glorious angles silhouetted against the bright mirror of the surface. Where the sea-trout had excited him, the sight of the salmon lent a ferocious energy to his fins. Fearlessly he rode up towards them, among them, where he could feel the pressure of water as they passed, a tingle along the nerves of his lateral lines. The vortices at their tails could stop him and even force him backwards, so great and smooth was the power in them. Those were fins and tails that had spread against titanic tides, fins that had mastered the wild, wild sea and driven the wanderers far away, and home again to cold, mountain waters.

He too was a wanderer, at last without the fear which had prevented him leaving the high lochs of the Maree system. He eased himself down towards the outflow from Clair, from which the big salmon had materialised. Alone he gave himself to the water's will, keeping his head into the current and dropping tail-first to where the stream, the boulder-strewn A'Ghairbhe, one branch of the Kinlochewe, would take him.

From glide to pool to rapid, the building river rushed. The water was very clear, without much of the peat stain it carried after a heavy flood. The pools were a blue-brown, turbulent and hissing with oxygenating bubbles while the rapids howled over his back, as much air as water. They foamed and left him stunned for a few seconds, then ended as suddenly as they had begun, beneath great boulders where there was brief shelter for a salmon parr's frayed fins.

That autumn had changed the young salmon's appearance, just slightly. The parr marks were less well defined while his golden colour, like a brown trout, was now more silvery, his brown back greyer. While he had grown so quickly his fins had lengthened, his tail becoming increasingly forked. But within him, hidden, was the great change. That change abandoned the fears of a salmon parr. That change put fury into his fins and the lean muscle of his flanks. It made him run with the waters of the A'Ghairbhe down into the unknown, where the huge Sgurr Dubh fish bravely ran, and from where so few returned, carrying with them the terrible wounds inflicted upon them during their journeys.

6

After the stillness and peace of winter, the snows and rains, the frozen hush, the spirit of the Weald stretched its lush green from meadow and hedgerow, creeping up towards the tips of oak and ash. The fluorescence of anemone and the sunshot yellow of primroses exploded from the banks of ditches and lanes. Already, in the coppiced woodland and in the open space between great beech and chestnut, bluebells prepared to thrust their flower heads from the protecting fronds of their deep-green leaves.

The landscape metamorphosed, suddenly awake, suddenly vibrant, hiding the worst excess of man with thickets of hedge and foliage, softening the ploughed fields with seedling green, concealing brick and concrete with webs of living tissue. Nature fought, and with the warm rains from the west and the sun higher in its zenith, it seemed, then, that it might even win.

John Howard always remembered the weather during the Easter holiday of his eleven-plus year. It arrived harsh and blustery, heavy showers swelling the waters of the Bewl and colouring them with clay and debris. In the flood conditions he did not fish very much at first but, instead, spent hours wandering and watching, exploring farther upstream, beyond Mr Billings' farm.

It was the official closed season for coarse fishing, though the trout season was open. A trout, to the young boy who had rarely seen them in the river and had never caught one, became an elusive and mysterious animal. His father had told him about them and he had read about them, admiring pictures of their shiny camouflage-marked and streamlined bodies. They looked somehow *fast* to him, an impression which had been strengthened by his few encounters with them on the river. Well, they were related to the salmon, Daddy had said, the fastest and most powerful of all fish. Like the salmon, trout were game fish and had evolved in the coldest of rushing streams. While coarse fish had their beauty, their purpose, their niche in rivers and lakes, they were apart from game fish. The magnificent *salmonidae* had been graced with ferocious speed and elusiveness as their prize.

In the stream he had seen flashes of bronze, a flicker of motion which never looked like a roach, still less a perch or chub. The fish would be gone in a whorl of water leaving him with half-seen, half-imagined fragments of the fish's shape and colour; black and red spots, bronze back and sweeping tail.

As he wandered upstream he mostly waded, or stayed very close to the water. This was partly to avoid being seen by the owners and farmers of the land through which he trespassed. Sometimes a farm worker would see him and stroll over to discover what a young boy was doing on the quiet river. No one ever said that he should not be there but they warned him about the deep pools.

He knew about the pools. He had been in some of them, either on purpose during the heat of summer, or by accident as he leaned too far from the bole of an ancient willow in his struggles to reach some big chub which lay in the water below.

So, he travelled on the freeway which is a river, cutting through people's land, not around it like roads and railways, but coursing where nature intended, not man. It was a lush, rainbow-hued world within the Weald. Ducking down beneath canopies of cow parsley, nettles and overhanging alder, Johnny was close to the waters bubbling over clean gravel, surging up over his boots.

Two miles upstream from Mr Billings' farm the river had shrunk, fed mostly by springs rather than the feeder streams lower down. The water felt cold and Johnny noticed that it was always clear, even when downstream it was coloured and rushing with flood.

His great discovery that spring, at the source of his river, was of the fish which had eluded him for so long, and of the wild, inaccessible places where trout lived their secretive lives.

The first one he saw appeared as he crept along a quiet,

shallow glide towards a gravelly run. He saw a ring on the surface, just where the water became smooth. Still as a heron he strained to see into the water, to make out the shadowy shape lying there. He shifted his position just slightly so that he was looking at the surface against the darkness of the far bank rather than the brightness of the sky. There was the fish below the run; long, lean, hovering. Again it rose, the neb of its nose barely breaking into the air as it sucked down a fly.

Like a portal into the unknown, the ring of its rise opened on the surface and drifted down on the current, away from the fish that had made it.

Johnny recognised the flies on the surface as ephemerids from what Miss Tonford had described. He had seen them before and knew that fishermen called them olives, because most of them were coloured in various shades of green and brown. These, the flies just hatched from their water-borne nymphs, were known as olive duns.

The glide in which Johnny stood was about ten yards long and no more than four yards wide. Clumps of ranunculus grew there, short with spring growth and intensely emerald green. The run above glistened as it rushed over the pebbles which produced the rapidly flowing water.

Very slowly he inched his way up the glide, keeping low against the bankside foliage to hide himself, until he was barely two yards downstream of the beautiful fish. And it *was* beautiful. His eyes had adjusted to the light now and he could make out details. The tail swayed and wafted, maintaining the fish's position in the stream, while its pectoral and ventral fins were splayed, then withdrawn, stretched again as the fish shifted slightly from side to side. Its eyes watched and Johnny thought how remarkable it was that those eyes were so obviously focussed on the surface, just upstream of the fish where the rapid ended and where the olives first appeared from the rough water. Its stare was intense and concentrated, a hunter's stare, like Johnny's own.

Its head into the flow, its stare upon the space below the rapid, the trout was most vulnerable from behind. It was preoccupied with feeding on the olive duns and only the nerves on its lateral lines were sensitive to movements and vibrations from downstream, where the boy stood, motionless and staring. He admired its feeding and its grace, the bronze and gold of its flanks as it rose and flashed in the light, its thick black and red spots peppering the scales. For a moment it was easily visible, as it rose, turning to suck down a fly, and its markings shone, as if with their own intense light. Then it lay almost invisible, the marbled browns, blacks and golds of its back indistinguishable from the gravel. Only its vague, finned form stood clear of the river bed, and only Johnny's concentration enabled him to follow its slight movements until, for a flash of time, the light shone from its twisting curves and it possessed shape, purpose and beauty.

Leaning and pressing ever nearer, Johnny was aware of a change in the fish. It had stopped rising and hung deeper in the stream, very still. The merest scrape of the boy's boot on gravel had sent tiny messages of unnatural vibration to the fish; danger hinted at by minute compressions. Its colours seemed to dull and fuse with the stream bed. Pushing nearer still, Johnny knew that the trout had seen him. Suddenly its body sprung from the gravel, its tail whipping up a trail of silt. The water surface was ridged with the trout's motion. It drove up towards the rapid for a moment, then twisted and shot off downstream and across to the far bank. Then there was only the silt and debris it had kicked up, flickering in the clear water. It was like the vapour trail from one of the Comet jets Johnny had seen in the sky, other things which were fast and sleek.

Glacier-carved Loch Maree lay unusually calm in the spring sunshine, so calm that the mountains surrounding it, great Slioch and Beinn A'Mhuinidh to the north, Druim Grudaidh and Beinn Eighe to the south, were mirrored in the smooth surface. The loch stretched over thirteen miles from south-east, where the Kinlochewe river entered, to north-west, here divided from the sea at Loch Ewe only by the short River Ewe. It was in the south-east, farthest from the sea, that the loch thinned as it struck into the mountains. Here there was tremendous depth, 400 feet of darkness, and also bright shallows along the shores where most of the fish swam.

This had been the young salmon's world since dropping down from Clair. Compared with his home loch, and any in the Coulin chain, Maree was massive, a single bay reaching to the north of the mouth of the Kinlochewe being larger than Bharranch. For a time this expanse of fresh-water loch had satisfied his need to wander. And he would not quest farther until his body was ready.

In Maree he had learned and would learn more of this place which drew salmon and sea-trout back from far distant Atlantic feeding grounds. Maree gathered the waters from Bharranch, Clair and Coulin, from the mountains that ringed the high systems, from the burns that ran off the high moor, from A'Ghairbhe and Abhainn Bruachaig, the Kinlochewe's sister branches. It gathered the taste and essence of the land, of the creatures that lived and died in that remote country, and, carried on the waters, that essence ran across a salmon's tongue and through his gills and became a part of what he knew. In Maree's depths lay the secrets of what had happened on Slioch's highest fells, and far, far up on the moor above the Coulin pass.

Maree was the mother water, the loch which the Gaelic speakers had given a saint's name, a sacred loch, a place for pilgrimage, both for man and wild beast. For some men the place was a dream, for others it was still to become a dream. This, the salmon's home, which men had called in more recent times 'the Queen of Scottish lochs', its black depths a secret to all who gazed over them, was understood only by a salmon's nervous system, and his fins sweeping across its vast, cold waters.

At the edge of the inhospitable darkness of its depths the loch's waters shone with light on shallows, like a halo about the abyss. It lit weed beds and big rounded boulders, reefs that jutted far out into the loch, scree-fall beneath cliffs which reached up towards Slioch, and vast sandy bays littered, here and there, with the wreckage of trees and branches washed down the Kinlochewe in winter floods. The dead wood was doomed to remain for centuries, preserved in the peaty water; but, like the sands and reefs, it would be shifted slowly by the wind's equinoctial force and by rushing floods.

The salmon, now eleven inches long and streamlined to the extent that he was lean, his fins disproportionately large, his tail a lilac-grey fork, had become a smolt, his body making ready for the sea. His scales were now like polished pewter, his back grey. The Gaelic people would have said that he wore the sea-coat given him by the sea-god and that he had grown his fins until

50

they were ready to take on a force of water far greater than anything he had known before, in the kingdom of the wild, wild sea. Those people understood that the smolt lived in Maree while he learnt to cope with the big waves thrown up by the storms. In Maree he would be prepared for the journey to come, even as he learnt the secrets of the place where he had grown thus far, the place a salmon knows to be home by its taste and essence, by the magnetic lacework of valleys and peaks.

He wandered the great loch, as he had the Coulin chain, as spring brought melt-water from the hills and a green fringe to the shoreline. Life surrounded him, some of it tiny like the previous year's fry, parr and small brown trout. Even smaller were the insects on which he preyed: caddis in the sandy bays, olive ephemerids over gravel, black and claret chironimid pupae over silt. He even hunted dragonfly larvae among shallow weedbeds, a day's feed in a single, crunching gulp.

Out over the deep, the salmon smolt found the strange, elusive char. They rose from the gloom into the light, their shoals enormous though no individuals were longer than the smolt. As an orange and pink amorphous mass they rose, frenzied in a moment as they fed on deep-water chironimids or terrestrial insect windfalls, then almost motionless again, hovering on their delicately coloured fins. They were preparing to breed, in spring rather than autumn like other *salmonidae*, and were migrating into the shallows. They were the most secretive of all fish in Maree, without the quick spirit of the brown trout, the mysterious migrations and spectacular acrobatics of the sea-trout, or the ocean wanderings of the powerful salmon, nor their silver flesh which men hunted. The Gaelic people said that it was the char which carried within their strange shoals the loch's deepest secrets.

The shoals of smolts, by contrast with the char, were tiny, sometimes no more than groups of three or four. Often the salmon was alone, for Maree's hunting areas were large and in preoccupation with feeding or the search for food, he would drift away from the others, and they away from him. Dull silver in the tumble of waves, or the mirror of a calm surface, he would maraud across the shallows, picking off whatever insects were there and then moving off to the next area where he was likely to find food.

But other life in the loch was larger and considerably more deadly than a salmon smolt. It too shadowed the char shoals: *ferox* trout, the most dangerous fish in Loch Maree, some of them four times the length of the smolt, with deep, muscular girths and huge, toothed heads. But only the largest or swiftest *ferox* saw the young salmon as potential prey, for he was far faster than char, over the greater distances, and his colours and shape were as fleeting as combing waves. Here for a flicker of fins, he was airborne as he dashed from the hooking jaws, then skittered off towards the weeds. He taunted, his fins danced on danger, he leapt above the crests so high that it seemed he flew, re-entering with a hiss into the troughs, swerving round boulders where the spring winds blew smothering waters. In that effervescence the salmon smolt could be lost, silver among silver, white motion on invisible fins.

It was in the calm that the smolt was in greatest danger. Even when he hid down among the boulders there were animals which could find him, by feel and by sight, when there was no wash and turbulence to hide him. He had learned to keep well clear of a heron's poised wade, but there were other birds, ones which could dive and swim.

Cormorants roosted on some of the boulders which jutted out of the shallows in the bays. Their droppings had whitened their favourite stances so much that even storms could not clean the rock where the birds stood. Their gaze took in the movements of fish, the tell-tale rises of brown trout and char as they rose at surface-trapped insects, the whirring leap of sea-trout and salmon smolts. They saw, also, the bow-waving and shouldering of early run salmon, or the stale fish from last year's breeding run not yet returned to the sea, kelts. These big fish the cormorants knew to avoid, for big salmon, either fresh-run or kelt, could not be held even by a cormorant's wickedly sharp and hooked bill.

When the cormorants knew that brown trout or smolts were near they would curl themselves into the water, allowing their webbed feet to trail and act as rudders while they flapped themselves along, underwater, with their wings. In seconds they could be thirty yards from their stances, twisting their outstretched necks from side to side. The first a young trout would know of the danger was the lightning-flash appearance of a yellow bill and gash of white at the bird's throat from the far side of a rock, or suddenly darting out of the gloom. The full, hideous, distorted shape materialised only in the instant the bill snapped across the fish's flanks.

His scales having silvered, the smolt's camouflage against pebbles and rocks was not as good as it had been. His colour was adapting for life in open water. Now he hung in the mid-deep and at the surface. Instead of relying on not being seen he was ever alert, sensing and hearing the cormorants' dive and thrumming wing beats. Even before the birds came within twenty feet of him, before any part of them was visible, he could feel them, his lateral lines triggering him into motion, away from where danger had sent out tiny pressure waves and betrayed itself to him.

There were birds which did not give audible or vibrational clues to their approach as the cormorants did. Herons and divers were quieter though more of a threat to smaller fish than smolts. There were very few ospreys left working the Maree system. They, like the Gaelic tongue, had dwindled until, above Loch Maree itself there was only a single nesting site, up in the birch woods beneath Slioch. This site was not a permanent roost and the pair whose territory it was roamed across more waters than Maree, up as high as Fada and Fionn lochs to the north and Glen Torridon in the south. But when they came, soaring above the loch, their white undersides were almost invisible as they gyred against a pale sky. Any fish on the surface large enough to warrant a stoop and a flash of talons would hear and see nothing as the birds stole in from behind, from where all the most deadly hunters came; lower, sleek, a part of the clouds, spray from waves, a gust of the racing wind ...

Diana Howard stared at her proud son. He stood at the back door of the cottage, wet and dishevelled, a wide grin on his face, a river's light in his eyes. In one hand he held his fishing rod while his tackle bag hung untidily from his shoulder. There was mud on his boots and on one leg of his trousers. He looked as if he had walked miles and, indeed, he had been gone since just after breakfast and it was now tea-time. She looked at the object in his other hand, there for her to see, to admire. Held by his bent forefinger through its gills was a brown trout.

It had been the end of a great campaign. Since seeing the trout near the source of the river, he had seen many more, having learnt what to look for, and where. He had discovered those places which were more likely to hold trout than coarse fish like roach and perch. They liked the fast water, or lies very close to rapids, best of all near a food source, a weed or gravel bed, perhaps beneath the draping branches of an alder from which terrestrial flies and grubs would fall. They did not frequent the deep, sluggish pools where roach shoals hung, nor the roots and crevices where perch hunted. They were, Johnny concluded, creatures of the light, for, like the quick, brassy-scaled dace, they were never far beneath the surface or the bubbling, sparkling areas of the stream.

The more he had seen of these shy fish with their sensitive poise and lightning-fast reactions, the more he had desired to catch them. They were, however, extremely difficult to approach. The slightest shadow falling across the water, or scrape of a boot on gravel, even the blue-orange flash of a king-fisher overhead, was enough to make them bolt.

He had tried trotting maggots and worms through the areas he knew the trout would be, but the stream so high above Mr Billings' stretch was inconsistent in its flow and bits of weed or stones would catch his hook or line and drag the float down. He legered worms in the glides, using a small barrel lead on his line to roll worms over the gravel, but all he caught were the dreaded eels, or, sometimes, fat chub. He would poke his rod through the bankside foliage above where he knew there to be trout, drop-ping the weight and bait into the stream, feeling for the bite of a fish with the fingers of his left hand on the line. Occasionally, when there was not that sickening slow build-up of writhing weight on the line, which was an eel swallowing the bait, Johnny would feel a thump, so heavy and fast it was like an electric shock, different from the take of any other fish in the river. He knew these to be trout, but he could not hook them.

Frustrated by the fish he could not catch, he observed them for hours, watching them feed as a hatch of flies lifted them to the surface or some nymphs or shrimp dropped from a weed bed where a trout waited, darting to the side to intercept the tiny insects and crustacea before the current whipped them away. He read about them, working his way through the Tunbridge Wells library stock of books on the subject of trout. Most of the books covered fly-fishing for trout and salmon. He would study them for hours, trying to understand the strange techniques which fishermen used to pursue 'game fish'. It seemed, then, far more complicated than catching coarse fish and that, in some particular way, annoyed him. The puzzle and challenge of it also excited him.

He looked at the diagrams and photographs in the books. They showed epic scenes – long rods bent against the backdrop of mighty rivers in Scotland; silver fish leaping from tumbling waters far bigger than the Bewl, or even the Medway. The pictures in the books married with the fading memories of his father's descriptions and became the images of those places Dad had promised he would one day take him.

Gentler scenes reminded him of his little river – photographs of the legendary chalk streams of Hampshire, Wiltshire and Yorkshire, where fat brown trout rose to the extraordinarily delicate imitation flies of fishermen casting upstream. The rivers were all lit with a rich, summer sun. Great trees lined lush banks which stretched out into water meadows thick with flowers, where cattle roamed and tweed-jacketed, plus-foured fishermen stalked.

There was the wide Avon, the Test, Driffield Beck. He saw, in yellowing black and white photographs, glorious views along Yorkshire's Wharfe, the big Eden flowing powerfully from the Pennines down into Cumbria. Rivers of quite incredible size, their tumble and race frozen by the camera, were there on the glossy pages; the Tay, Spey, Helmsdale and Thurso, Scotland's glory running through those pages that captured a boy's imagination.

'A fly line and some flies?' said Mr Holsworth in Corner Pets. 'Well, it just so 'appens that yer might be in luck, if yer don't mind 'em a bit second 'and.'

'Is two pounds enough?' asked Johnny tentatively. 'It's all I've got saved.'

'Well, I s'pose it might just about. I don't stock that sort of stuff mind. There's no call for fly-fishin' gear round these parts. 'Appens I got some gear of me own that an uncle left me. I'll never use it now so you might as well 'ave it.' As he spoke the pet shop man's brown-overalled figure disappeared into the back of the shop and Johnny found himself alone, watching over the animals. He was aware of the smell of hay and feed, a dustiness always found in pet shops. Little stirrings surrounded him: budgerigars flapping, some kittens playing in a big pen in the window with the spring sun warming their fluffy, exposed tummies, and a hamster noisily chewing sunflower seeds.

'Here y'are, Johnny,' said Mr Holsworth as he reappeared. He was carrying an old but expensive-looking canvas bag, stuffed with tackle and a rod in a khaki-coloured partitioned cloth bag. The bag was in good condition and bore a label displaying the rod maker's name and address: Hardy Brothers, Pall Mall, London. 'You might as well 'ave the lot – but I want to know 'ow you get on with it, mind, and I want it looked after.'

For the sum of two pounds Johnny had become the proud owner of a Hardy Palakona built cane fly-rod, two Hardy Perfect fly reels on which were wound Kingfisher silk lines, and some leather wallets containing flies and old nylon monofilament and gut casts, and a box like a tobacco tin on which was written 'Loch Leven Fly Box'. Inside were little clips which held delicate and subtly coloured flies, some of them dressed on single hooks, some on doubles.

The tackle was in remarkably good condition except that the lines were very sticky and clogged. Johnny had read in one of the fishing books how to care for silk lines by soaking and rubbing with linseed oil. This he did among all the other absorbing tasks over the next week as he learnt about his new fly tackle.

Every day he took his tackle to the river after doing his compulsory hour's holidaywork, which was more usually done with a fishing book open on his lap, hidden from his mother if she happened to look in on him. It was all so different from the coarse fishing tackle with which he had become so dextrous. The casting was the aspect most difficult to master, for the only weight was that in the fly line itself. It seemed inadequate. He had read the chapters in his books about casting, and read them again, but reading was no substitute for the feel of a fly line in the air, pulling at the Palakona rod.

At first the line, nylon cast and fly landed in a terrible heap upon the stream. Then, in his effort to cast farther, he put too much power into the process and whipped the line against the water or hooked the grass and branches behind him. Only slowly, borne from frustration and long hours of practice did he begin to learn the secrets of timing, allowing the flex of the rod to do the work, pausing as the line unfolded behind him before bringing the rod forwards, like a spring, for the final delivery. Then he watched, delighted, as the line unfurled with the fly touching down gently on the surface.

When this happened, inconsistently at first but then more regularly as he strived towards his private goals, he began to understand why it was that men wrote whole volumes about the magic of fly-fishing. Out there on the smoothly running water, the fly floated, hypnotic, drifting down on the current, angler watching from above, fish from below. He could lift the fly off the surface, whip the line back and shoot it forwards, all the time becoming more accurate. Bankside foliage multiplied the problems, but overcoming these was part of the challenge and the pleasure. It was all a mysterious and enthralling strategy. At the end of it all lay the fugitive trout, waiting on the fleet fins of the *salmonidae*.

Then, one rainy day, almost at the end of the Easter holiday, it happened. Only a hundred yards downstream of where he had seen his first rising trout was a pool, just large and clear of foliage enough for him to cast. And there was a trout near the head of it. He had seen it rise, just once, a trout's rise, not the brief splash of a dace or the clumsy lurch of chub. The water ran smoothly and, from his position on the bank well below the pool's tail, he could see little below the surface, like rolling silk, unmarked except for the one rise. It was a windless afternoon and a drizzle was falling, so fine that it did not mark the smooth water.

He had dared go no closer. So many trout in the last few days had seen even his most careful approach and had fled the open stream for the cover of weeds and overhung bank, or skulked down into the dark depths.

Very slowly he unhooked the fly he had already tied on the cast from its keeper ring above the rod handle. He pulled line from the reel and laid it in neat coils on the grass at his knees. He pulled some of the line through the rod rings, smoothly and without the jerky movement which was always seen by the wary trout, until there was enough hanging there for him to begin casting.

Just as he was thinking that he might have imagined the trout's rise, it flinched again in the stream and he could hear a distinct sip as the fish sucked down a fly from the surface. Johnny looked closely at the water nearer to where he knelt. In a moment he saw the sail-boat shape of a pale-olive dun drifting by. It had just hatched, the three prongs of its tail erect above its upturned abdomen, its wings a translucent slatey-grey. He looked at the fly he had tied on to the cast, a Greenwell's Glory it was called after Canon Greenwell who had designed it, long ago, to imitate roughly the olives of the broad River Tweed. It was more bulky than the natural fly, but it looked somehow right, especially in colour.

The fish rose again, its rise seen, its sip heard. Johnny began casting, flexing the rod and extending line. It swished above the pool and the fly landed two yards short of the trout's lie. 'Always cast short rather than long,' an expert had written in one of the books. 'You will not frighten a trout by casting short, but if you "line him" he will be gone . . . ' It made sense for these sensitive creatures, Johnny concluded. One flicker of light, one stab of unnatural vibration would send panic to their fins. The next cast was longer so that the fly was only a few feet short of the lie. The trout had not risen again and Johnny had wondered if, even with his extreme care, the fish had been alerted to the danger.

Yet the boy had sensed something. Deep down he knew that the moment he had dreamed of had arrived. Almost detached from his physical self he made the next cast, delivering the fly mere inches above the trout's lie. It drifted while Johnny tensed, gently pulling the line back in to take up the slack, his stare absolutely rigid. Then it was gone – a rise, a sip, a bulge in the stream, and the Greenwell's Glory was gone.

Up went the rod, the line hissing over the pool and Johnny felt the electric thud and writhe of the fierce fish beneath the surface. The trout leapt, in a dazzling, arcing motion which would be fixed for ever in the boy's memory. He saw the fish's body shake, water thrown from its fins, the colours, gold, red and amber, iridescent despite the clouds and drizzle which had dulled the light.

In those moments he could remember nothing from the books he had read. Instinct told him what to do as he felt the wild force at his arm, as he watched the rod bucking and the line streaking and stabbing around the pool. Later, much later, when he reminisced about the battle, he had been surprised by his own control, but such thoughts did not come to him then as the fish whipped its tail on the surface. It seemed to be pure energy, ferocious, and Johnny watched, all his senses focussed on the pool, within the pool where the fish dashed, within the fish to its life force. He sensed what it would do, knowing that he had caught it, even before its last dives, its last leap, its last drive for freedom. And then its head was up, exhausted at last and slithering on the gravel.

Johnny could never remember the long walk home, stumbling through the fields as the rain fell heavier and heavier, rod in one hand, the fat brown trout in the other, his bag wet and dripping on his back. But he could remember standing in the doorway of the cottage, the look on his mother's face, then her slight annoyance at the mud on his coat and trousers, then, at last, her gaze resting on the fish he held up for her to see.

'Oh, Johnny,' she said finally. 'That's a *beautiful* fish. I think that's the most beautiful fish I have ever seen.'

That evening, as rain pattered heavily on the roof, the house warm as the spring storm blew outside, Johnny sat down and began his holiday essay for Mr Spence. His exercise book lay open on the table. The fresh page was like the river surface. It too held secrets which he could uncover, which he could unleash. Unscrewing the lid of his Parker pen he began writing carefully and neatly. The river's energy tingled in him again. He underlined the title without a smudge: *The First Trout*.

Great winds blew across Loch Maree, piling waves against the north-east shore and the sound of rain was lost in the roar of the gale, fresh and vicious from the Atlantic. The salmon smolt, like all living creatures in the loch, pressed himself down among the boulders in deep water, well beneath the rolling and tearing maelstrom. Strange lights danced above him, lightning caught and magnified in the giant waves, phosphorescence in spray and foam, glare before darkness.

Then there was the sudden blue-silver light of the moon, briefly exposed between racing banks of thick cloud. It was a full moon, and it unsettled the smolt's instincts, for a full moon meant big tides in the sea below Loch Maree, a sea which called him now. The last change of his youth had happened and the wild, wild sea called incessantly, the place which the smolt had never known yet had always known, in genetic memory.

Beneath the stampeding echelons of waves the silver fish turned down the loch towards a place he could neither see nor hear, though he felt its pull, as the rocks feel massive tides. His first sea run was beginning.

7

Smolts and kelts ran together across the flats of the River Ewe, dropping quickly in swollen flood waters. They had been pushed by the great weight of water from Loch Maree, down into the mile-long confluence at the north-western extremity of the loch and into the building force of the Ewe. The kelts, stale fish returning to the sea after an exhausting breeding run, barely had the energy to hold their heads into the current. At least, after so many miles and months fighting into the stream, they could now travel where the waters took them, always down towards the sea. Sea-trout and salmon travelled together, collected from all the burns and lochs of the entire system, gathered now in this one, narrow route away from fresh water.

The sea run was always confused, always intense. It coincided with the first warm gales of spring when the river rose above its bones and gave migratory fish the drive and urge to follow the rain to the sea.

On the flood the salmon smolt hung while the gaunt figures of emaciated kelts ran past him. They hungered for the sea, for its richness of feeding which would rejuvenate them and rebuild muscle where now hung loose flesh. Some carried injuries from the breeding run and the winter, scars of rocks, otters and cormorants. Even as they dropped on their final descent to the sea some of these fish swam on their sides, faltering and then turning belly up, death stilling their fins. The kelts were misshapen relics of the magnificent fish which had run the previous summer. The smolt shied away from them as they lumbered down the stream, their size still awesome, the kypes on the males' jaws still dangerous to a young cock-salmon, even an immature like himself.

The first taste of salt, the first in his life, ran over his tongue and through his gills. He was in the most confined part of the Ewe, where the water deepened considerably as the river thinned, running beneath a road bridge, at a village called Poolewe, and into the sea-pools. At high tide the salt water pushed against the flow of the river. Then the sea-pools, the last of the peaty outflow from Loch Maree, were brackish.

Here the smolt hesitated, for his body was new to the salt. All his life had been spent in fresh water with minimal salt content. His gills and renal system needed time to adjust to differing osmotic demands. While in fresh water he had drunk very little, the salt balances within him easily maintained. From now on he would have to drink a quarter of his body's weight every twenty-four hours. His kidneys would never be able to deal with the quantity of salt he would be absorbing into his blood. Only his gills could actively transport the salt from his body back to the sea.

In moments the smolt's world had changed. The heavy down-stream push of water, rich with the taste of the high moors and mountain screes was gone. Now it was salt and a confusing mixture of scents. A whole new array of magnetic impulses swept over him. Where there had been bare boulders and gravel there was now sand and encrustations of barnacles and splays of mussels. Some bladder wrack waved across his flanks, bulbous black-brown fingers teasing his fins. There was a terrible thud which had him spinning down towards the sand, searching his new environment for sanctuary. Above him, against the light he saw a shoal of strange, dark-bronze fish, immature pollack, being set upon by some ravenous sea-trout kelts. Each pollack that died ended its life beneath the heavy blow of a sea-trout at full speed.

A shore crab reached out its claws in the smolt's direction, the flash of light from his silvered flesh enticing the crab to strike. Then, he felt the weight of water pushing at his head, a roaring smother of water, heavily salty, building, deepening, sucking, then falling away, pulling at his tail, turning him in the sea-pool with its force.

The first pull of the tide, of immense power, ran across his virgin fins. It was the power he had felt on the shallows of a windward shore of Loch Maree in a storm, waves driving and surging over boulders that moved under the combined energy of wind and water. Except that now, as the smolt pushed away from the Ewe's peat stain, into the sea's brilliant, translucent light, that energy was everywhere, behind, pressing at his back, full at his head.

He was adjusting, every moment, to the new demands of his environment. The shapes of other smolts whipped across his vision, their silver abruptly lost in the sea's greater intensity of light, the sounds of their fins overwhelmed by the rumbling of the tide. Fear made him press down towards the white sands, where some kelp reached out a protective roof. There he lay at the head of Loch Ewe, the waving fronds of weeds above him, alternately letting the morning light dapple his back and then cover him in shadow. He waited for the fears within him to subside and for his body to prepare for the chemical and physical demands of his wanderings and journey in the wild, wild sea.

Loch Ewe, an eight-mile-long inlet from the sea, quietened as the tide ebbed. As Loch Maree had been the gathering place for migrants in fresh water, so Loch Ewe was the collecting area in the sea. Now, in spring, fish came from the river, smolts and kelts, and also from the open sea, fish that would soon run the river to begin a breeding run. First the salmon, mostly maiden fish, grilse, and then the sea-trout, the mysterious, grey-tailed riders of the tide.

Some shoals of grilse were already in Loch Ewe. Three times the smolt's length, yet only a year or two older, they wore their sea coats of rich lilac and glaringly bright silver. Their young bodies moved quickly at total ease with the sea's capricious turbulence. Their flesh was very firm, their bodies deep, strengthened and developed on a food source far richer than anything the smolt had experienced in the Maree system. The long journey from that food source had not weakened them and they were ready for months without food, for when they returned to fresh water their only food would be what they carried in the protein of their flesh. Their alimentary canals would cease to function until they found their way back to the sea. The food sources in the fresh water lochs and rivers were so sparse that they could support only the fry, parr and slow-growing brown trout. Even the smolts had been hungry which had contributed towards the urge to make the first sea run.

There in Loch Ewe the salmon smolt began to discover some of the sea's abundance. The waters were sheltered from the open sea by two broad headlands, Rubha Mor to the north and the hilly country to the south-west leading up to Maol Breac and Cnoc Breac. The two-mile-long Isle of Ewe, almost in the loch's centre, broke up the heavy seas from the western approaches and formed rich feeding grounds along its shallow shoreline and skerries.

The smolt became preoccupied with feeding. On the sea-floor he was attracted by the scampering of small soft-backed crabs. He chased them, confused slightly by the tiny puffs of white sand kicked up by each one of their legs. But their limbs were his targets. He would nip them between his jaws and lift the crab, shaking it so that all its legs and claws rattled. He found that he could tear them apart, gulping down the soft-shelled body.

Shrimps enticed him, elusive grey-brown clouds in very shallow water. The creatures hung, moving with the tide's flow, up and down, into the crevices of boulders, materialising and then disappearing among shore weeds. The paddle-like appendages of their tails flickered, their bodies curling into little hooks, then straightening, their antennae trailing behind them. He would catch them in the open, rushing into them and grabbing them as he passed, feeling their softness crushed in his jaws and their sweetness explode in his throat. He could kill and swallow fifty on each tide.

He and other smolts, together with a few large sea-trout, would swim over deeper water as they hunted in a shoal. In the Ewe's wide bays they found jelly fish, their tentacles hanging down in deadly curtains, concealing the prey the smolt wanted. Young whiting, each no bigger than the smolt's tail, swam within the venomous tentacles, immune from their sting but protected by them from predators. The jelly fish arrived in varying numbers. On some tides there were thousands, many of them sheltering a population of whiting, while on other tides there were none.

When they came it was as a pulsating orange forest, their tentacles drooping downwards, sometimes six feet down, peach coloured, living stalactites. The mushroom mantles of the drifting creatures would drop into the sea, taking their whiting with them, then they would lengthen in an amoeboid motion, stretching and slithering up towards the surface. Their colours were never constant. In a moment they could change from an opaque white to a translucent pink, then, with the light of a setting sun upon them, they glowed with a scarlet aura.

The young whiting were not invulnerable. They had only to leave their tentacle sanctuary for a moment, by a mere inch, for a smolt or sea-trout to slice it from open water and snatch them. When there was a big wave on Loch Ewe the tentacles would waft and spread, giving a hungry salmon smolt many chances to weave through the venomous jungle in his pursuit of the succulent white fish.

Along the western shore of the loch was a series of bays, formed by rocky headlands and bedded by shifting sands and silt washed down from burns. Here the smolt was drawn, not by the tang of peaty water from the burns, which did not possess the taste of the Maree system, but by elvers, young eels, millions of them, more on each tide. Each eel was a slither of brown, like the peaty waters they quested, as small as a single frond of wrack, but in their shoals they merged into one homogenous mass.

Only in the very turbulent water would the waves break up the gelatinous shoals and individuals become detached, space and light appearing between them. Their size belied the fact that they had journeyed so far, across three-quarters of the North Atlantic from the warm sea north-east of the Caribbean where they had hatched among the thousands of square miles of floating Sargasso weed. The elvers were food for countless predators, fish and bird. Big sea-trout harried them almost continuously, reducing the shoals' mass but never, it seemed, making serious inroads into numbers.

The smolt followed the grey sea-trout, excited by their speed and by the way they flayed into the elvers, gills and jaws spread, fins whipping, bodies jolting and bucking. The sights and sounds of killing and frenzied feeding drove him on, the scent of blood and torn elvers rich in the sea. His belly grew tight with elver and whiting and he grew four times faster than ever before in his life.

Feeding on its food, the smolt had the energy of the sea within him. He needed it, for while he preyed on the fish and crustacea of the sheltered loch, so larger predators sought him. In Loch Maree he had learnt to recognise the thrumming, clumsy approach of cormorants. There were more of them around Loch

Ewe, joined by large numbers of shags. The solitary birds on Maree were far less dangerous than the flocks on Ewe. Several birds would home in on a shoal of smolts from all directions, restricting escape. Almost every day the young salmon would hear and feel the birds and would dash in the direction where the vibrations of danger were least intense only to see the black shapes sprawled in the water ahead of him. Frequently he had to avoid them by leaping at the surface. In a curious theatre of hunter and hunted, where the true elements of each became confused and swapped, the birds swam deep in the water and the fish leapt and cartwheeled through the air.

Most dangerous of all the predators in Loch Ewe, silent in their approach, heavily camouflaged and more manoeuverable than cormorants, were the grey seals. Sleek and swift, the seals could turn in a tight pirouette and lurch to full speed with a kick of their broad tails and foreflippers. They also possessed the hunter's most fearsome quality: mammalian intelligence.

All his slippery speed and sensitive reactions were necessary to escape the grey seals. Even as one in a shoal of smolts he was not safe, for the seals hunted as family groups of up to a dozen; twelve sets of jaws only appearing in that last instant, sweeping out of the grey void. In open water the chase would be long. If he had been feeding he would often regurgitate as he fled, his whole body tight with effort. Seals could run up into very shallow water where he would skitter in the surf, their bodies grinding on to sand and rock as his escaping form infuriated them and enticed them back into the deep or within the folds of kelp. He would dash into a shoal of codling, safe as the seals turned their attention on the slower, heavier fish.

Many of his year group died, broken in half by snapping teeth. Scales, shaken from the smolts as they met the heavy blow of a seal head-on, would glitter and spread in the water. A tail would fall towards the busy sea-floor where lobsters and crabs, or conger eels, scavenged on the rare flesh of *salmonidae*, fish that had journeyed down from the high Coulin pass, even some of those from the Sgurr Dubh.

When seals hunted, salmon and sea-trout died. But there was a more insidious death in Loch Ewe. It was extreme and devastating. It did not choose and in its indiscriminate nature it killed salmon and seal together. It took cod and even enmeshed the cormorant, gripping the bird until it struggled in panic, then entwined about it as it sagged, defeated and drowned by a silent, motionless enemy. It had no intelligence which could be overcome by speed and instinct and no limit to its hunger. The death was netting, staked out in the loch or left hanging from buoys at the surface.

Set close to the shore during times when the migratory fish were running, nets intercepted their homebound or seabound voyage. The sea-trout, which did not wander so far as the salmon, but remained inshore most of their lives, were even more susceptible to the fixed nets, placed to intercept their feeding patrols. The young fish escaped, but only when the mesh size was not illegally small. The salmon smolt, relatively large from his successful feeding in the fresh-water lochs and heavy from his feeding since entering the sea, was big enough to be held by illegal nets if he encountered them, but could swim through the mesh of an older hemp net.

For now, the smolt was to escape the nets. It was late June and the netsmen were near the River Ewe end of the loch, making ready to intercept the heaviest runs of sea-trout and grilse of the year. Every day the smolt was working northward, even venturing within sound of open sea. Others were with him, hunting the shoreline for shrimp, sand-eel and elver. In those waters, where there was so little darkness and the sun was hardly set before it was rising again, instinct told the wandering fish that their long journey was before them. The distance from the high, inland lochs to where they had come so far was nothing. Now, out in that rolling void, somewhere in its deep blueness, was where they would wander. The call that only a salmon hears was at its loudest, the energy within them at its peak. If there was fear in them, it was stifled by a far more intense need to quest, to set fins bravely on ocean currents.

Several hundred smolts from throughout the Ewe–Maree system swam close together as the shoal rounded the point of Rubha Reidh, following the line of the evening sun. Instinct drew them that way, north-west, and they would be able to adjust for the sun's position, even to maintain their direction at night, until they found what it was a salmon needed in the open North Atlantic.

They swam on the invisible paths of their ancestors. Ten feet below the summer-smooth surface, on streams of magnetic flux, they left the land beyond their tails. As the dusk light faded over Loch Ewe the miracle of another generation of salmon escaped the dangers of inshore waters and met the first heaviness of wave motion which was the open sea.

8

'But we can't, Mum, we *can't* leave here.' They were leaving Stocks Cottage. This was to be their last summer holiday in the Weald, their last even in Kent. His mother had decided to move to London.

'Look, Johnny,' his mother had tried to explain. 'I must be nearer my work and you and Charlie will be near good schools.' Though Johnny rebelled, and argued with his mother for hours on end, he had watched her as she had made her decision and he knew that she wouldn't change her mind. Her journey every day to and from work in London took masses out of her, he could see that.

Charlotte was doing well at school and had passed ten 'O' levels, most of them with top grades. Everyone said that she was destined for great things. They must have been right, thought Johnny, because when Auntie Viv or Uncle Robert came over, which was quite a lot these days, they never stopped praising his sister and showering her with presents following yet another success. There was one more good reason for their move to London his mother said: Charlotte would be close to one of the university colleges.

'Have we *really* got to go, Mum?' Something in the way she looked at him then, wordless, her features weary, her eyes sad, made him stop. He left the room in silence, picked up his fishing tackle and walked quickly away from the house.

Down by the river he would be able to think more clearly. But there, by the first gnarled oak of what he called Roach Pool, his eyes filled with tears. It was the way she had looked when she told him. She was so tired.

Johnny could not imagine that life away from the Weald had

anything to offer. Were there streams in north London? Were there fields? He could not conceive of a beauty greater than the country around Stocks Cottage, so how could London, a city crammed with people and houses, be a place where it was worth living?

'There are parks, and all sorts of things to do,' his mother had suggested. 'There's the Tower of London, Madame Tussauds, lots of cinemas and theatres ... And we can drive out into the countryside at weekends. We'll be near Hertfordshire and Essex which are lovely counties. We can explore.'

They were going to live in a place called Muswell Hill. He had looked at it on the map. To the north was a county called Hertfordshire which looked tiny on the map compared with Kent and was marked with masses of roads and red hatching which Johnny knew to be towns.

Years later, it seemed to Johnny that all the terrible things that happened to the county in the ensuing years related back to the period just after they left. It was not that he ever blamed his mother, at least after his childish outbursts had subsided, but he grew to hate the demands on people which could take a family from the green fields where clean streams flowed. Even when, much later, he understood those things which the city could provide, he never forgave – for those things, to him, were inconsequential. With them went car-exhaust fumes and traffic jams, mindless crowds and concrete which always flowed and set outwards, towards and upon the green places. Johnny knew, or sensed, that once such places were taken they were never given back.

During that painful August, their last month at Stocks Cottage, Johnny saw the countryside blooming with an intensity of life which once had thrilled him to his heart, yet now he could feel no joy in it. He was going to lose it, perhaps for ever. It would remain, fading gracefully and dramatically into autumn and cold winter, while he would be gone, immediately into the winter of the city.

Two days before their move, the cottage untidy with teachests, the walls and cupboards bare, the soul gone from the place, Johnny visited his river. He did not have a fishing rod with him. Walking upstream as he had done countless times before, instinct rather than a wish to do so made him look into the water and at the bankside life. There were the quicksilver dace in the streamy water fleeing from his shadow. He saw some reeds move and knew, almost uninterested, that a pike or perch was hunting near the roots. For a while he stood by an eddying pool which was the best place for roach in the whole river. He had discovered that they hung in ranks, the little fish up ahead, eager to grab at a little bait before it ran through them to the bend of the eddy where bigger fish hovered. Behind them, where the water curled for a few feet back upstream, swam the best fish of all, the elusive 'pounders'. These were very difficult to catch because of their shyness and the fact that a bait had to run the gauntlet of the smaller roach before it reached them.

Higher upstream, a mile above Mr Billings' stretch, where the river shrank and ran sparkling and cold over gravel, Johnny sat on a fallen oak branch. He had often sat there, for the position gave him an unbroken view of the stream for almost sixty yards, and he would watch for rising trout.

Now, he hardly noticed the rings of their rising. What he had come to believe was the subtlest and yet most intensely exciting sight in the world was, then, almost unseen. He had held some of those trout, stilled their flight in the current, and then given them back to the stream. But now the river had lost its magic, because it was not his anymore. He was leaving its rough, overgrown banks, its little populations of fish, its waving, wandering peace, and so its magic and essence were lost to him. Then, the ghost that had been at his side, guiding and guarding him by the river, was no longer there.

Sedge flies were hatching and the trout were almost frenzied with feeding activity. As he sat on the oak, the fish chased the adult flies across the surface, swerving and splashing noisily. He had seen it before, but when it was over one could never believe it had been so spectacular while the fish abandoned themselves to all but the pursuit of skittering sedges.

Johnny would remember and believe, because he would not see it again, not there on the Bewl.

And what of the people he loved? The people of the Weald: old Mr Billings popping his head over the foliage for a chat and to see that Johnny was all right; Mr Holsworth who had given him the Hardy Palakona, the lovely reels and silk lines, for *two* pounds. He thought of the pet shop man's dumpy, brown-overalled figure, his hands, big and muscular from hard work, his face so kind. Would Johnny ever see him again? Would he see any of those people who had shaped his childhood and coloured it with some of its happiest moments?

In that place where a grazing meadow ran down to a small, clean stream and an oak branch, sheared from the bough by an autumn storm, lay on the grass among clumps of camomile and deadnettle, Johnny cried. He cried for the river he was about to lose, for the years during which he had known and loved it, for the ghost he had now lost completely, for the love of those who had loved him, for the fears he had for his beloved Weald, and his fears for himself marooned in a place he dreaded, so far from where life had shape and purpose.

There had been light almost all the way. The few hours of each night had had the relief of star- and moonlight, a gloaming in the southern sky and brilliant, flickering phosphorescence in the foam of waves. Calm summer weather had not hindered the salmon shoal's progress. The fish had crossed the warm push of the North Atlantic drift, as their ancestors had done, and had pressed on towards the north-west, where there was light and the magnetic flux lines converged. A primitive voice within them told them that there was a place where a salmon should be.

Out on the open ocean they had relied on a shoal sense, each individual adding to the collective information and structure of the others. What one salmon had felt from the buzz and vibration of the surface currents, so they all had felt. As some aligned themselves with the sun's position, the electromagnetic map or the push of the drift, so the shoal was aligned. When the hunting crackle of porpoise sonar had rasped across the sea, so the shoal had opened to confuse any sonar image it might produce. It had lifted into the roll of the groundswell where its echo would merge with that of wave noise and so confuse any hunter.

Enormity had surrounded them, emptiness for tens of thousands of fin beats. Since leaving the sheltered waters of the Hebrides after the dangerous passage through the Sound of Harris, the seafloor had dropped away and the shoal had been marooned at the surface, or always within a hundred feet of the surface, above the colossal deep. Their passive sonar told the salmon of the distant waters below and beyond where their eyes could see, where the purples and blues were extinguished by impenetrable blackness. On the calmest days when the noise of the swell was least, they heard and felt mysterious vibrations. There were chirpings and rattles, frightening thuds, screams and roars: the ocean's creatures talking to one another, predator and prey, inorganic sounds in the vastness, organic mutterings. It was the voice of the wild, wild sea.

Days on the open ocean became a full moon's cycle, while the calling of the high Atlantic grew stronger and the fish grew accustomed to the volume of their world which had lost its limits. Where there had been fear of its size there was now a need for its light, the oxygen richness of its surface sweeping through their gills.

Weeks passed when there had been no food. Since leaving Hebridean waters, there had been far less food than along the island coasts and in the sea lochs. They had found only occasional shoals of young herring on dull days or towards evening when the plankton clouds, on which the herring fed, migrated from deeper water towards the surface.

In their millions the little fish would sieve through the plankton while the young salmon would feed upon the herring. But the bait fish were very small, virtually larvae, and their shoals would disappear as the light intensity grew and the plankton dropped into deeper, darker water where the salmon would not follow. Then, for weeks at a time, even this transient food source would not appear and the ocean remained quiet from sunrise to dusk and through the short nights when salmon fins beat with greater urgency.

The sea had been suddenly colder as the force of the drift had weakened. Instead of holding more promise for the result of their long migration, the Atlantic had grown more threatening; cold, deep and barren, the light harsh. Winds from the north-east had chilled the surface and had pushed the salmon into the empty gloom, fifty feet down. There they had swum, into the third month of their sea journey, August.

Then there was more noise, an intensity of sea-row that they had forgotten existed. It was the noise of an embattled coastline, of sea on rock, of currents suddenly constricted by shallow water, of billions of tons of sea water slurping over a continental shelf. It was, also, the sound of life. This sound had been dim along their lateral lines, but now it burst upon them with a dash and tingle.

They had crossed the 60-degree latitude, turning almost due north into a current at their heads. The first sounds of a coast were off to starboard, a rocky peninsula: Cape Farewell. This was the southern tip of Greenland jutting down into the Atlantic from the high Arctic. It was mantled by ice sheets and it had been from here that the cold winds had blown, cooling the Atlantic's surface. Now, however, the water was slightly warmer than it had been farther south. Upwellings, borne on deep currents from the tropics, 5,000 miles distant, surging beneath the north Atlantic drift, had met the great northern shelf and escaped the constriction by venting towards the surface. Here, beside the ice fingers of the Greenland coast, the sea's surface was warm and water vapour rose, condensing in the cold air and wreathing columns of ice in a ghostly hold.

The light was more diffused than it had been below the 60-degree parallel, the sun shrouded by a milky light while columns of clouds miles high towered up over Greenland, leaving the sea open to the misty sky.

The salmon remembered the enormous heave of water where the sea meets land, for it was the same angry force he had felt back in Loch Ewe and the Hebrides. It was the force to which all living creatures had to bend and be subservient, for it could not be overcome. It could be joined, coupled with the power of a salmon's tail, and it could be survived if it was not met with inertia. Motion, with the tide and currents, the pull and flood of cold energy, was stability.

Though it possessed the force the salmon recognised, this place was different. It was what had called him and drawn him across 1,500 miles of ocean. Here was where he wanted to be, for the time being, even though it was so far from home waters and what he understood of survival in his endlessly dynamic element.

The warm water upwellings were enormously rich in phosphate and it was this that attracted all the living creatures to what would otherwise be a desolate sea. The phosphate fed a food chain which began with phytoplankton and ended with the great whales.

74

Invisibly it began, in the glow of bright light when a plant cell absorbed phosphate in a complex chemical reaction which gave it the energy to photosynthesise, to convert carbon dioxide and water into oxygen and sugars. Cellular matter grew, fed from that richness of phosphate and the perpetual light of summer. It grew in a billion, billion cells, an infinity of plant matter bursting and reproducing upon the sea's surface. It was seen only in the green cloudiness of the water, a plankton mass consisting of coccolithophores, nanoplankton and larger diatoms and peri-dinians, all fuelling greater organisms with their abundance.

Still invisible as individuals, though the plethora of numbers made a haze in the sea, zooplankton fed on the green matter voraciously and yet removed but a tiny fraction of the cellular abundance. Greater planktonic creatures fed on the smaller ones. Creatures whose life was held in a single cell were preyed upon by multicellular organisms. Radiolarians and copepods, micro-scopically savage, patrolled the drifting harvests, themselves being sought by larger hunters. The plankton moved at the mercy of sea currents, the less small being driven by figmentary fins and brushing cilia, or by undulations and squirts of water. Fish and crustacean larvae, minutiae, grew upon the phosphate wealth, the sea blooming in a flowing, heaving field of green, brown and orange.

At the peak of the plankton pyramid were the shrimp-like krill, easily discernible as individuals, being up to three inches in length, but in their feeding and breeding shoals they cast shadows across the sea. As the light intensity grew after sunrise, the krill, like most of the zooplankton, dropped deeper in the water, up to 600 feet down where no light from the sun penetra-ted. Here they fed on the dead and decaying planktonic matter that had rained from the surface. At night they rose into the eerie noise of the shallows, where the luminescence of their own bodies lit the sea in a shimmering blue-green aura. Their own noise was a whisper as they sieved smaller plankton and shuffled in mating dance. It was this sound of their swarming that attrac-ted the salmon.

Feeding havoc in the dawn, before the krill dropped from the surface, 200 young salmon knifed into the abundance, ten miles off the Greenland coast. The krill, jittery motion curving into commas and straightening in a streak of trailing antennae and shed eggs, were no match for the silver fish. Only their vast numbers confused a salmon's eyes as they bolted in every direction, lacking the harmony of a shoal of fish.

In the feeble light, their own luminescence lit the sea with their scattering, like sparks. The cock-salmon rushed at them, the lights shooting around his head. His speed was such that he had barely to twist from side to side to catch his prey. A hundred danced past him, though at almost every snap of his jaws a krill was broken across his tongue, each one nudging the one before down his throat. For a full hour he would gorge himself until he felt the tightness across his abdomen which reduced his ability to manoeuvre. As the krill dropped deeper into the sea, their lights dimmed into a homogenous, faint carpet of electric blue. The cock fish and his shoal would abandon them, sated, and rise up towards daylight and higher oxygen concentration.

Within another hour, the tightness would ease and hunger again would dominate their passage through Greenland waters. But it was the ability of those waters to provide for giant appetites which had drawn the salmon, in the wake of their ancestors over millions of years. Ice ages, pushing the ocean's fringe farther south, receding again in the thaw, had shifted the feeding grounds, although the information of the rich feeding was passed on, generation to generation.

Other harvesters swam enormous distances to feed on the summer plankton. White fish, cod, haddock and saithe, had travelled from south, east and west. They fed in strata, the haddock grazing the sea-bed, cod above them while the saithe remained in the light, sometimes even among the salmon when feeding on krill was at its most intense.

Among them all came baleen whales. Humpbacks, black of body with long, noduled foreflippers, lumbered noisily through the seas in little family groups, while triangular-headed minke jostled and jumped in schools of fifty. Sleek and very fast, the colossal finbacks rode the ocean swell, parting it, gulping at it with jaws that fell open to reveal caves lined with baleen rakers. They sieved the sea, expelling water but trapping thousands of krill in a single mouthful. In a day an adult finback could swallow three million krill weighing nearly two tons. It took a shoal of a hundred salmon a month to harvest the same. And this was a single morning's feed to the biggest of all, the giant blue whale; 100 feet and 130 tons of blue-grey mammal, alone, almost unheard and unseen, despite its size, along the fjord-indented coast of Greenland where it led its secretive life.

The salmon, migrating northwards through Davis Strait, saw all those creatures, large and small, which, like them, had been drawn to this ancient feeding ground. It was late September and the light was failing, even at that high latitude above the Arctic Circle. The fish had doubled their size since their arrival in Greenland waters, growing faster than even during their intense feeding along the Scottish coast.

Sometimes far offshore, more usually within sound of the coast, they hesitated in their northward journey. Then, in heaving equinoctial seas, made wild by the cold winds from Baffin Bay, they turned until their prevalent direction was south-east, where the light was strongest. They rode up desolate fjords on the tide, in among crevices in ice cliffs which ran down into the turquoise depths.

On grey shingle beaches they chased capelin shoals, tightly packed fish, themselves as silver and sleek as miniature salmon, though in shoals containing tens and hundreds of thousands of individuals. Here too, in the fjords beneath the Sukkertroppen Isflade, a giant glacier attached to the main Greenland mantle, the salmon joined their shoal with others. With the Maree fish swam smaller, younger salmon from Newfoundland and Labrador. Icelandic smolts also joined them.

The shoal was discontinuous and transient. One day it would number thousands, with fish ranging from twelve inches to giant adults which had made several sea runs. Huge Norwegian fish, and those enormous specimens from England's southern chalk streams, added their awesome girths to the shoal's numbers. They would glide as a single unit against icy walls, always hungry, always hunting and using the acute shoal sense to listen for danger or the murmur of food fish or krill.

Small maiden fish arrived from Ireland, others from the Faroes archipelago. The greatest numbers of all, and the greatest range of sizes, came from Scotland. There were smolts and maiden grilse from a hundred different systems, and some hen fish from the larger Scottish river systems, Tay, Tweed and Helmsdale, that carried their long, heavy bodies with a graceful power. Among them all were a few, a very few, of the Sutherland and

Ross-shire giants, masters of many migrations. They came to the shoals of smaller fish rarely, appearing on a high tide in a lagoon of ice-strewn water, then gone, gorged on capelin, into the vortices of an ebb and the open blue of Davis Strait.

Then, in the night, when minke and killer whales hunted, when storms tore the surface waters and drove the salmon deep, or into the lee of southward travelling icebergs, the shoal would split. Some fractions would turn back into the krill-rich north, others would quest the fjords. Some remained in the void of the strait, easing out into the Atlantic on the Labrador current. Many turned for home after the summer's feast which had packed protein on their glistening flanks.

Salmon swarmed, apparently in confusion, in the bays and by the islands off the southern tip of Greenland. In the secret blindness that is instinct they made their unconscious decision, as shoals and individuals, to run for home or to stay in the rich seas.

Around them were the sounds of encroaching ice, a cracking of sheet ice, broken by the sea's swell, a gargantuan splitting of an iceberg from glaciated fjords, of ice avalanches from the higher slopes of the islands into the churning sea. The warmth of the sea fought the cold of the air and dense mist shrouded the sea and ice and banished even further the shortening hours of sunlight. In the water was a greyness, far removed from the opalescent clarity and the startling light that had infused the summer seas. Now, the salmon's world was twilight. Where he swam, even near the surface in open water, was in shadow. But still the phosphorous upwellings brought a richness of food. Capelin and krill abounded and the cock-salmon had felt little urge to leave.

His shoal was smaller than it had ever been. Just twelve fish stayed with him. The rest had turned for their home systems in Labrador, Iceland and Faroes; in Norway, Ireland and England. Many had already fled the wild seas of Greenland and set their fins upon the great journey back to Scotland. Some, destined to be the fresh, silver spring-run fish, would even find their way to the Maree system beyond the Hebrides. These, though the fish of his own territory, were not of his ancestry and he would not travel with them. His path was with the few, with those from the high system above Maree. They, like him, would know when to gather, and when to leave the richness of southern Greenland. He would not make the journey alone, not yet, and not with grilse or fish from other runs and systems. When he travelled it would be in the immediate company of fish of his own ancestry, the salmon from the Sgurr Dubh and Coulin.

He could not know these things, for it was written invisibly in his genes. It was the extraordinary wisdom of nature to make the races of salmon distinct, even those from the same home system, in order that any one race could be protected from the disasters which befell another. The awesome dangers that faced salmon were episodic and numerous, and it was only in the diversity within this resilient species that survival was ensured.

And yet, even as the cock fish turned towards the half light of deep sea, out into the Davis Strait, having overcome any urge to return with so many others, the greatest test of his species' resilience was unfolding. A time of devastation had arrived.

PART TWO

Wanderers before the storm

9

Well, that was how it had been. Johnny remembered it all very clearly. The unhappy parts were as vivid in his mind as were the halcyon memories. Only the mediocre was lost and confused.

It was strange, though, how your childhood caught up with you. Actually you never really got away from it. Those early years remained a part of you; and childhood's legacy lasted until the grave. The events which might have happened many years earlier generated the adult. The memories persisted, the best and the worst of them. In life there was never any escape from the pains and joys – the ghosts of the past.

Cycles, a man's life was governed by them as much as a salmon's; you went spiralling round, picking up new information on every loop, learning how to cope better with the next. No escape.

Johnny was packing on that humid August night after the telephone call from his friend in Wester Ross. Memories crowded in on him, some from his childhood and some from the times after his family's move to London. Somehow they all had a bearing on what he would do next. It was almost predetermined, yet unexpected. 'The salmon are back,' Iain had said. Extraordinary. Johnny had thought he had seen the last of them, the last of the truly wild fish in northern Scotland, just as he had seen the end of the Weald as a beautiful, living landscape. Here was another chance, in the Loch Maree system.

As he packed he looked casually through a file of papers, taking out what he would need to take with him and what would need Anna's attention while he was away. An old school report came to hand, and he could not help reading through it.

Hereward House Preparatory School for Boys.
Report on John S. Howard, Christmas Term.

We have not had sufficient time to learn very much of John's qualities. He has contributed to his class as a whole, though his academic standard is weak. He appears to be at least a year behind the average, though I am pleased to see that he has some grasp of science and geography and feel that, perhaps, this is the direction he might take in future years.

Our greatest concern is Mathematics, on which John has no grip. If he is to pass the Common Entrance next term he must be brought to a far higher standard. Highgate, or any other public school, will not consider him unless he achieves a satisfactory mark in Mathematics. He will find that more advanced science is dependant on a command of this subject.

John is even weaker at Latin and the languages, though I am pleased to note what Mr Firth has to say about John's use of English in essays. Comprehension, however, is going to need as much attention as French, Latin and Mathematics.

He is bright but lazy, unless the subject particularly interests him. We have noticed that he is quiet when playing with the other boys, though it has been brought to my attention that he quarrels with some of them and has had one or two fights.

Holiday coaching is to be thoroughly recommended. There is not much time left until the Common Entrance.

Colonel (retd) D. Brewster, Headmaster

He remembered it so well, his hatred for those subjects which had bored him, and his growing realisation of the power of words on a page. His mother had nagged him endlessly. Tired from another day at her job she would shout wearily at him to do his homework.

North London had been a frightening, soulless place. Where there might once have been woods stood a row of stunted chestnut trees, aligned not by nature but by those people who had planned the ranks of houses, roads and railway lines. Where there must once have been open fields where cattle grazed, were houses – the roads were flanked with them, line after line of semi-detached houses built in the thirties, with little front gardens and long, narrow back gardens where their owners

84

established a fragment of individuality. Where detached Georgian and Victorian houses stood Johnny noticed a greater number of London planes and chestnuts, even the occasional, isolated oak, and a hint of open space, parkland.

Instead of an overgrown footpath, or a grassy verge to a winding lane, or hedges and worn and tumbling fences, there were pavements and walls, zebra crossings and man-made routes. Home, one of those semi-detached houses half-way up a hill, 149 Priory Rise, became a sanctuary. Stocks Cottage had never needed to be that. The cottage had been part of the environment which Johnny had loved. The entire Weald had been a sanctuary to him. But at number 149 he could shut the door on the constant groan of traffic climbing the hill in third gear. He could sit in his room overlooking the jungle of the back garden and try to forget that a thousand, a million houses surrounded his, rather than fields and woods.

The world had turned grey and brown. He re-read all his fishing books and surprised his mother by asking to visit the local library. She soon discovered that he was after only fishing books which the libraries in Tunbridge Wells and Paddock Wood had never possessed. At least, she thought, he would be reading something.

Again he saw the lovely southern chalk streams where fat, golden trout swam. Again the pictures enticed him with the overwhelming appeal of sunshine upon water meadows. Images he remembered, pictures into which he projected himself. A photograph would have him staring intensely as he examined its every detail, a stillness and a longing about him.

It was the beginning, really, of a dream. It was the dream that was inspired and ignited by those worn photographs of distant places. That magnificent view across Loch Assynt, islands and great, open space, and giant Loch Affric where water stretched towards the distant, empty hills and a boat drifted, a mere speck in the enormity of wildest Inverness-shire. And there, at the foot of a long glen, was Loch Maree beneath the high, broad spearhead known as Slioch. Under the picture was written, quite simply: 'A sea-trout fisherman's dream – Loch Maree, Wester Ross'. And it *was* a dream to the young boy in 149 Priory Rise.

There would have to be escape, freedom again after this. Perhaps it could no longer be in the intimacy and gentle beauty of the Weald, but, surely, it could be by that wild, wild loch reaching through the mountains towards the sea, in a place called Wester Ross.

'Actually he is a bit of an enigma,' explained the Colonel to Mrs Howard when she went to visit the school to arrange extra coaching. 'Mr Firth has shown me John's exercise books and they reveal quite the most extraordinary contrasts. On the one hand he shows us the most infuriating lack of effort. Like this, for example ... ' He showed Mrs Howard a particularly sloppy piece of comprehension homework which was smudged and had no margin. Reading the untidy scrawl revealed that John had not correctly understood the questions, or even bothered to try. 'But then look at this, where was it now? Towards the back I think, oh yes, here, an essay he did about a walk in the country.'

Mrs Howard laughed. 'Yes, he would have put some effort into that. He likes the countryside, you see. We lived in Kent, until last term.'

'Look at this paragraph.' Colonel Brewster pointed: 'The leeves were falling more quickly onto the water. On the blue rush of the streem they were like an armarder of boats. when they got to the eddy they all gathered in a huge brown and golden raft. It was so thick in places that a kingfisher could stand on it.'

'If you ignore the spelling ... Well, it's as if two different people did those pieces of work,' suggested the Colonel. 'I think that we need to relate everything to those subjects that really interest him. Where possible, that is. If we can show him how important Maths is to science then he might put more effort into it. And English ... if we could just convince him that English Literature and comprehension exercises would improve his essays. He obviously enjoys those. He might be tempted to give them a little more attention.' He frowned. 'Mind you, I don't know what we can do about French and Latin.'

They discussed Johnny's coaching programme. As Mrs Howard was leaving, the Colonel suddenly said, almost absent-mindedly, as if to himself: 'You know, among all that awful mess in his books is something quite special. As Mr Firth says, those essays can be full of observation and imagination. If only we could point his mind in other directions ... Well, Mrs Howard,' he was abruptly matter of fact and pragmatic again, like the army officer he had been, 'we shall do our best to coach him up to par for next term's examination.'

'It's easy, you idiot!' Charlotte was frustrated with trying to show her brother some simple algebra. 'If x is twelve and y is three, and if x equals yz, then z must be four. Mum, there's no point in trying to explain it to him, he's too thick.'

'Shut up, Charlie. Just because you understand doesn't mean it's easy ... '

'That's *enough*, you two,' shouted their mother. 'Come here, Johnny. I'll explain it to you.' Johnny picked up the books and slouched over to his mother's chair. He looked depressed and tired. It saddened Mrs Howard to see her son like that. So rarely nowadays did he reveal the laughter and free spirit she had loved to see while they lived in Stocks Cottage. Had it been a mistake to move to London? Yet, if they had not come to the city where her children could be properly educated, what future would he have had? There was no business for him to inherit and no father in whose footprints to tread. He would have to achieve something in his studies, like his sister. There was a future in that.

But as she explained the basic algebra to him again, his head hung as if there was no vitality in him, and there was no understanding in his eyes. She would have to do something to bring him out of it, something to replace the Weald and the Bewl.

'Come on, Johnny, up to bed now. You've school in the morning.' They climbed the stairs together to his room. 'What book do you want?' He looked at the bookcase at the end of his bed.

'*Loch Trout*,' he said. She found the slim volume, sat down on the bed and turned the pages. It fell open naturally at a black and white photograph, slightly out of focus, of a calm loch with hills climbing from the far shore. There was a man in the foreground wading and fishing, his cast frozen by the camera. Johnny was peering over her shoulder, obviously captivated by the photograph.

'What does it mean?' she asked, referring to the caption 'dry fly in an almost flat calm'.

'Oh Mum!' he glanced at her, surprised. 'Colonel Oatts, he's the author, the one fishing there, is fishing a dry fly. You know –

one that floats. And the water's so calm. That's when dry fly is best on Scottish lochs.'

She did not see. She could not even begin to understand this subtle and strange thing which captivated her son's imagination. Fishing, for goodness' sake. If only it was algebra. Yet ... She could see the beauty of the loch, set against those Scottish hills, the open peace of the place. She had an idea.

'Listen.' She shut the book. 'I'll make you a promise. You pass your Common Entrance and we'll go there, to Scotland. For a holiday in the summer.'

'Do you mean it? Promise?'

The dream came just a little closer then, and she saw energy flowing through him, lighting his eyes with a runaway happiness. She dared to hope for the first time that he might, after all, just pass that wretched examination. It seemed so important – it was important – but she was beginning to understand that his life was to be interwoven with things remote to most other people. No matter what he eventually achieved academically, his course would not be like Charlie's. His career would not be measured in the usual way, prepared for or predetermined. She hoped only that it held happiness for her only son.

Danger was close, a fearsome danger which could only be seen at the last moment. The cock-salmon, with only four others, had been chasing capelin among the ice shelves and walls of a deep fjord. Now, the salmon were being pursued. The ice distorted the vibrations which, in open water, would have told them exactly from where their pursuers were coming. The changing light and scattered shadows among the sheet ice confused them. There it was again, the thrumming beat of a large, fast-moving animal close by. From out in the grey-blue emptiness of the fjord came discontinuous vibrations. There was more than one hunter out there and the salmon sensed only that they were exposed to the animals which sought them.

Then, sleekly sloping out of the gloom, a female harp seal materialised, her own eyes seeing the glint of salmon flesh. She spun up towards them, her pale fur and strange harp mark across her neck and back camouflaging the huntress amidst the dapple and fragmentation of light. Five caudal fins thumped in reflex at the water, though the ice prevented the salmon swimming farther into the fjord and they were forced to turn. The cock fish was the first of a group to face the swerving attack as the seal flew at the shoal. There was ice above and behind him and he could only lurch away to the side or down into the darkness. In the moment that he saw the seal's eyes and jaws he chose the darkness. There lay open water where he could thrash his tail and gain speed. His companions all chose to remain in the light. They broke to the right and the left and each was snapped up in an instant by the female seal and her companions which had been following her, lethally invisible among the fjord's treacherous ice-fields.

He heard them die, a crunching and tearing of flesh, and he heard, also, the thrumming sound of a chasing seal, just one, though she was very close. He dived deeper, his swim-bladder compressing and adjusting to the depth for which he strove. In near darkness he sped, water rushing through his gills, his heart racing and forcing oxygen-enriched haemoglobin to the muscle of his flanks. His tail was spread in the weapon-like fork of the *salmonidae* and the seal could feel the vortex thrown off the beating fin in front of her face. Her own tail-flippers drove her in pursuit.

The plummeting wall of an iceberg barred their passage. Suddenly, it lit the sea with the prismatic light it had refracted and reflected from its many surfaces. The salmon swerved and aimed himself at the place where the light was strongest, thrusting his tail with a strength which ignored the pain in his muscle. Lactic acid, the waste product from his exertion, was building up rapidly. Unless he stopped soon, so that the acid could be metabolised out of his system, it would still the muscle it poisoned and it would kill him. Unlike the seal, his kind could not sustain a very high speed for longer than a few minutes, though a salmon has other qualities which enable it to survive against greater size, stealth and stamina.

In the dim light of the Arctic afternoon, the great spectacle was unseen. *Salmo salar*, the leaper, launched himself high above the bulging lunge of the harp seal. As he leapt his tail still swept, his body curving back and forth, and the seal desperately snapped her jaws at the swirl and blast which had been his body but was now spray and air. For a moment she lost him in the confusion of surf and wave. With a crash he hit the water, his tail still sweeping. In a loop he dived twenty feet and again shot up to the surface, leaping, hanging and bucking. All the while the seal lurched after her elusive target. She would be almost on top of him, his death just a quick bite of her jaws away, then his silver had streaked before her eyes and he had found the brief sanctuary of the air.

The lactic acid bit at his muscle. He made one final, desperate leap, eschewing the tightness along his flanks, the fear of the big animal behind him giving his tail one last thrust and then, after a heavy thud which knocked the strength from him, he lay still and was aware only of light and silence.

The seal had fired herself in rapid pursuit, pausing briefly only to suck in air at the surface, pauses which had given the salmon the moments he needed. His leaping had made him a difficult target, but with each one he had grown weaker and she better able to judge where he would re-enter the sea. On his last jump, as she manoeuvred deeper in anticipation of the strike she would make when he crashed back down through the surface, she was aware of the ice surrounding her, confines of blue, white and grey. And the salmon did not fall to her jaws. She spun around, hunting for the fish, furious at having lost him. She dragged herself out on to an ice shelf, breathing heavily after her exertion. Again she slipped into the sea, searching and listening. Then she slid farther out into the fjord where she could hear her family group. She heard the happy sounds of feeding and knew that another salmon shoal had been located. The frustration she had felt shredded away from her as easily as the bubbles from her nostrils and she kicked out towards the hunting party.

The salmon lay where his last jump had taken him, into a shallow pool upon a ledge of ice. Waves broke over a lip of ice and into the pool which was heavy with slush. The fish lay half on his side while his gill plates worked quickly to feed his deprived body with the oxygen it needed. The lactic acid had cramped his muscles and sapped his energy almost to the point when it might have killed him, but for the fact that he was held at the surface by the ice under his belly, among the little wavelets that washed the oxygenated water through his gills.

When later, in near darkness, the acid tightness in his flanks faded and strength returned, he pushed himself through the slush and flopped out of the pool and back into the sea. Alone he sculled through the gloom among icy pinnacles and caverns. His lateral lines felt the sea, felt for that throbbing of seal flippers, but there was a silence and emptiness in the Greenland night.

The struggle, the tears, the fighting, were all over. Johnny had passed the Common Entrance examination and had been accepted by Highgate School. He would never know precisely what had made him do the work. He understood how his mother's hard-earned money had been poured away on his education, and this gave him a feeling of guilt if he wasted the time when he should have been working at his books. The guilt was barely enough to overcome the boredom of simultaneous equations and the kings and queens of England.

Among the stacked pages of boredom, however, much to Johnny's relief and surprise, there were discoveries and even sources of fascination. There was the king who wore a brilliant red cross upon a white tunic, Richard the Lionheart, who led armies from England far away across the sea to desert lands. His cause, the crusades, sounded so courageous and exciting. And at a place called Battle, Sussex, not far from where John had lived, great armies had assembled, English and Norman, in 1066. He had gone there with his mother – *there*, to the place where the fate of England had been cast for centuries. All you could see was rolling pastureland below a village where there stood a walled abbey and most of the shops seemed to sell antiques. His mother had bought a car in the village, a Mini Clubman, from Styles Garage. But history had been made there.

Geography had held more fascination than History. Maps were a wonderful invention, thought Johnny, with their condensed details of the land, the symbols which showed where a church stood or where a railway line ran through a cutting. You could even see the highest points of the hills and read the contours below the surface of a lake or the sea. There were facts too, in Geography, which caught a boy's imagination and made him remember them for ever, like how there was a place called the Amazon Basin where the biggest forest in the world grew. The forest was being cut down, an area the size of Switzerland every year, so that coffee could be grown. It covered millions of square miles, the teacher had explained. You could fit England into it many times over. By the time Johnny had children of his own the Amazon rainforest would be virtually gone.

Then he learned about the fishing – the North Sea – firing his imagination. There was the herring from that, one of the richest fisheries in the world. The tonnage taken each year threatened to wipe out the stocks. Governments of countries bordering the North Sea were getting worried about the overfishing.

And most fascinating of all were the great whales. Nations had grown strong upon the back of the whale, on baleen, on sperm whale oil, on blubber and meat, until the whale species were threatened with extinction, like the herring, like the Amazon. It all seemed so massive, so final.

From the haphazard collection of facts, he had grasped enough to scrape through the Common Entrance requirements, though he failed the French section dismally. His best mark was in the combined History and Geography paper, followed closely by English, almost entirely on the strength of his composition. In Mathematics he obtained the pass mark of 45 per cent, with perhaps a little kindly marking from the examiner.

So it was that Johnny's mother received a letter from Highgate School telling her that her son, at the age of thirteen, had gained a place, although it was recommended that he be given extra tuition in the basic subjects before he began in September.

'I can't afford that, Johnny, not on top of the fees. You'll have to read plenty of books this holiday – Charlie and I will help with your Maths.'

Passing the dreaded exam gave Johnny a sense of euphoria, a pleasure which he felt mounting when he discovered that, despite the cost, his mother really intended to honour her promise to take him to Scotland if he passed. One evening in July she showed him an advert in a country magazine: 'Wester Ross, croft cottage, sleeps four, village of Kinlochewe, two miles Loch Maree, sea-trout and brown trout fishing available, some salmon . . . '

They were to have the last two weeks of August there, Loch Maree; it was said to be one of the best sea-trout fisheries in Scotland. Johnny studied his fishing books for every scrap of information he could find about the mysterious migratory trout, the sea-trout, and anything about Loch Maree. He stared even more intently at the few photographs he came across of the loch.

They revealed a great water flanked by mountains and wooded hills. The place was beautiful, even on the hard, still gloss of a photograph without colour. Sea-trout and occasional salmon of immense proportions swam those waters. Fly-fishermen from around the world came to catch them. They came too, so the books explained, to marvel at the scenery, 'Queen of Scottish glens', to see the eagles, ospreys and red deer, and to walk in the mountains.

At last, after so long without feeling its flex and familiar, friendly weight, Johnny took Mr Holsworth's Palakona fly-rod from its bag. It stretched across his bedroom, an extension of himself, while in his imagination it reached out into a wide sky-scape where heavy clouds came in from the Atlantic and fierce winds blew. It reached over the pitching waters of Loch Maree. He moved his arm and wrist, his grip firm on the cork, and heard the lovely swish the tip made through the air, remembering the feel of a fly line cast over the Bewl's gentle rush. His mind's eye did not see those Wealden brown trout. Instead, mightier, silver-white fish exploded through the surface waters of his imagination while the Palakona strained against a ferocious power, the power of a fish that had known the wild, wild sea.

The Mini Clubman, laden with whatever Diana Howard thought they might need during the holiday, laboured on to the A1 and the beginning of the long journey north. Johnny sat wedged between suitcases in the seatless metal interior of the back while Charlotte enjoyed the comparative luxury of the front passenger seat.

In the gloom of daybreak Johnny saw signs to Potters Bar, St Albans and Hatfield, though there were only brief moments when green fields, small copses and hedgerows broke up the concentrated clumps of houses. This, Hertfordshire, was supposed to be outside London, but it seemed to Johnny to be just an extension of that vast city. It was certainly not what he thought of as countryside, not like the lush Weald.

Then, as the roundabouts and road intersections became less frequent, the towns and villages thinned out and bands of open country drew his eyes towards the freedom of distance. Past the sprawl of Stevenage and the undulations of north Hertfordshire they drove on into the wider vistas of Huntingdonshire. He felt that he was escaping and his excitement grew as the miles increased between himself and London. There, with the flatness and space of Cambridgeshire strangely comforting, followed by the big folds of Rutland and Leicestershire, he felt he knew the route. It was more than the fact that he had studied the map of Britain so much in the past few weeks, marking in pencil all the roads to the county of Wester Ross. He was on a path which led away from what he feared. It ran towards the exciting, the extra-ordinary, and hope. That thought made the terrain through which they passed somehow warmer. It was like a corridor which wound through a dusty old house, ultimately to an open door and sunlight.

Cities and counties were not so much landmarks to Johnny as the rivers, all with name plates by the bridges that spanned them. The rivers which had geographical meaning for him. He knew them all from accounts in his books, and the library collections through which he had avidly worked. He knew of the fish they held, their character and the country they drained. They had passed the Ivel and Great Ouse within an hour of leaving London. John had craned his neck to obtain a better view of the reed-fringed banks and sluggish sections where lily beds grew, mysteriously shrouding the blue-brown water. He saw a boat marina on the Ouse, the little pleasure boats all silent and motionless in the early morning stillness. It was not difficult to imagine the roach shoals and fat chub which swam in those meandering rivers.

Farther north they crossed the famous bream waters of the east Midlands; the Nene, Welland and Trent. Much wider than he had imagined it to be (from the descriptions by the great Nottingham angling writers), the Trent presented its enigmatic challenge to a young fisherman. Here, so they said, were roach in their millions and fat bream roaming the muddy river bed; but it was not an easy river to fish with its long, straight banks and the difficulty of locating the largest shoals.

The character of the rivers changed again in Yorkshire. Here the Wharfe and the Swale gave a hint of the nature of their upland sources. They were swifter rivers, boulder-strewn and sparkling, flecked with white rapids and bubbling streamy sections. This was his first sight of a new domain; that of the *salmonidae*, of trout and grayling.

Any softness in the landscape and its water systems disappeared in North Yorkshire and on into Durham and Northumberland where the Tyne, Tees and Tweed flowed; big rocky rivers draining a big, rocky land. There was a wildness here, east of the Pennine ridge where the waters of these mighty rivers sprung from a catchment area of high, flinty hills.

Later, and on all the journeys to Scotland Johnny was to take through the years, the miles were marked out by those rivers. Each one was a measure which told him how far he was from London or his destination. The Great Ouse was fifty miles out, the sparkling Wharfe a hundred and fifty ... And in Scotland he was to grow to love the sight and sound of the great rivers flowing towards the east coast; the Tay and Tummel, fast Spey and glorious, tumbling Findhorn; powerful Ness, short, but carrying the waters from huge Loch Ness. The Beauly and Connon, secretly flowing along tightly curving valleys, were the last east-flowing rivers he would see before the last stage of the long journey. From Dingwall, north of Inverness, the route led into wonderland, towards the west coast, Wester Ross.

With the evening sun ahead of them, warm orange and not unpleasantly glaring, the mountains rose and the single-track road threaded its way through gorges, beneath heather-clad slopes and over rough moorland. Charlie was asleep in the back, while Johnny, in front for the Scottish part of their journey, watched the landscape unfolding. Neither the descriptions in books, nor the photographs, had prepared him for the awesome sight of the mountains and wet moorland. The lochs were more spectacular the farther west they lay. First, Loch Garve, then enormous Luichart. The long, loch-studded River Bran wound near the road through a desolate moor, draining from Loch A'Chroisg. Mountain slopes stood steeply above the valley and the road itself steadily climbed, it seemed, up into the sunset. Mrs Howard navigated the endless bends with the Mini in second and third gears, wondering if they would reach their destination before nightfall even though they had just passed a sign which showed that Kinlochewe was only another ten miles ahead.

Then, around yet another bend, they saw it, far off in the distance, beneath the apricot glow of the evening sky, Loch Maree. She stopped the car in one of the passing places and she and

Johnny got out. They stared towards the bottom of the long glen, eight-miles distant.

'Look, Mum, it's *beautiful*.' He could say no more, and she said nothing. It was simply that, beautiful; a long, vast loch reaching down towards the sunset and the west coast, islands scattered down its length with massive mountains towering above on both sides. Mrs Howard looked from the view to her son. As never before she understood what it was that drove him, what meant everything to him. The evening breeze ruffled his hair and she saw the glint of the sunset in his eyes. The joy he felt in the cool wind and the glorious vista of the loch and mountains was etched in every part of his face. He was strangely still, as if concentrating deeply. Indeed, that first sight of Loch Maree was for ever to be fixed in his mind. It was the first image that would come to him in later years, after all the joy the loch would give him, after everything it taught him, after the terrible, unbelievable sadness of its greatest loss.

The cottage was tucked neatly away on the edge of the village of Kinlochewe almost at the foot of the glen two miles above Loch Maree. Johnny ventured from it into his paradise, returning each evening laden with memories of mountain, river and loch. Built of stone, it was clean but damp and his mother said that it would be uninhabitable in the winter. Johnny thought it would be cosy, warmed by its two fireplaces. He could imagine them stacked with the black peat the local people used, smouldering through the night while snow shut out the rest of the world. He could remember winters like that in Stocks Cottage in the Weald, except that the fires there had burned coal and logs.

In the Highland summer, however, when gentle winds blew from the west, from the sea, Seun Cottage with its whitewashed walls and blue-slate roof, resting in a poorly kept grassy field where sheep grazed, was not the fortress against the wild environment which Johnny imagined it would be in winter. Instead, it was an essential part of the glen.

It had rained heavily for several days before their arrival, but each day since had been warm and calm. Johnny was gone from dawn to dusk. It reminded his mother of earlier years when he would disappear into the green fields around Stocks Cottage and she would know only that he was somewhere along his river.

Instinctively, she had known then that he was safe. It was the same now, even though this country was massive and awesome to the eye, and the River Kinlochewe ran furiously in flood, unlike the Bewl's gentle meander. It was curious how she trusted him to be careful when he was by water and in the countryside. In the city she worried, because there Johnny was not so sure of himself, there he knew fear; but by the torrent of a wild river, on the boggy moorland and scree slopes, she felt that no harm would come to him beyond scratches and bruises.

The river ran with a bubbling, roaring freshness along its rocky valley. Upstream of Kinlochewe, Johnny could see, away to his right, the grey and white upper slopes of Beinn Eighe. The scree up there was so shattered that it looked as if it had been quarried, though only ice, frosts and summer heat, had formed it. Lower was the heather moor, criss-crossed by burns which were white with heavy flow, though slowly fining down as the moorland's sponge dried. Along sections of the river's banks there was woodland, mostly Scots Pine, though there were some young plantations of spruce and larch. In Kinlochewe itself were some massive beech trees, peculiarly anomalous amongst the area's flora and betraying a freak underlay of calcium-rich rock. It was the acid moor which dominated, however; brown, glistening peat where heather and bilberry grew. Pale green spagnum moss carpeted the wettest areas and Johnny soon learnt, after a few bootfulls of water, that the dry-looking moss hid nasty stagnant pools and soft peat.

Close to the river's banks, and on the hills above, he came across squat little clumps of a succulent-looking plant quite unlike anything he had seen before. He knew it was unusual and when he found a picture of it in one of the books he had brought from home he was fascinated to learn that it was insectivorous. It was called a sundew and its sticky pink protrusions fingered the air, seemingly dripping nectar to entice unwary tiny midges towards the glue-like trap from which they would never escape.

Johnny liked the sundews because they ate some of the terrible biting midges which to him were the only great menace in the Highlands of Scotland. Sometimes, when the air was still, the midges would descend on an exposed area of skin, apparently in their thousands. He scratched the poisonous little bites until they swelled into red and white bumps. Sometimes the itching would not stop until the bites bled with his scratching. The sundews could do no wrong. The sundews were especially excellent because Charlie thought they were creepy and if she was winning an argument he would threaten her with putting one in her bed when she was asleep. That always ended the arguments, usually with Charlie in a blind rage, screaming at him as he fled with his fishing tackle and lunch box.

There was a chain of brown-trout lochs, 1,200 feet up on the hills to the south of Kinlochewe. It took Johnny an hour of hard walking to reach the first loch from which he had a view of the most westward arm of the Kinlochewe river between Loch Maree and Loch Clair. On the map he could see that Clair was joined to another loch which was not in view, Coulin, and another which was just visible as a crack of light in the mountainside. Johnny did not know how to pronounce its name; Loch Bharranch, small and compact beneath a big dark peak, Sgurr Dubh, and dwarfed by comparison with mighty Loch Maree to the north. From his high-altitude stance, Johnny marvelled at the way the waters were connected, how they lit the pastel browns and greens of the landscape with glaring blue and silver. Loch Maree itself lay massive in its hollow between the great mountains. From this distance its surface appeared peaceful and its many islands like becalmed, fairy kingdoms.

On his climbs to the high lochs, Johnny was always turning his head to look back over the magical loch. He would pause as he caught his breath for the next fifty feet of his ascent and stare, wishing that he could paint it the way he saw it each time, constantly changing, endlessly enthralling. When Loch Maree fell away from view beneath the brow of a hill, he would glance towards the west where Clair and the strangely named loch glistened. He wished to paint it all, so that he could always watch and admire and so that others would see what he had seen. But in his staring he was painting the colours and forms of hills and lochs deep within his mind, not for others to see, perhaps, not yet, though one day he would paint them in his own way.

Then came the chance of a day on Loch Maree, on the great loch itself. Iain Sutherland, the owner of Seun Cottage, had a boat on the loch and had offered to take Johnny out.

'Oh, don't go on,' Charlie had moaned the evening before the hallowed day. 'It's only fishing again. You should be bored with it by now. You've done it every single day we've been here.'

'Well, it's much better than sight-seeing,' he had retaliated. 'Sitting in the car all day. Anyway it's not the usual sort of fishing, it's for sea-trout and on Loch Maree.' It meant nothing to Charlotte who, at seventeen, found even the sight-seeing boring and her brother perpetually irritating. Wester Ross was not her idea of a holiday. But then it was not exactly Johnny's idea of a holiday either; for him it was an idyll, one that he wanted to keep for the rest of his life.

A wind had blown up in the night and the loch's surface was marked by foam lanes and a scatter of white-topped waves. Iain held tight to the Seagull outboard engine which drove the heavy wooden boat noisily along while Johnny felt the powerful roll and pitch of the big water. The boat road up the crests and then stamped jarringly down, throwing spray into his face. They crossed the loch and came under the shelter of a grassy headland where a burn entered.

A wide bay lay before them, three-quarters of a mile across. In the lee of the headland there was only a ripple, but on the far shore, where Johnny could see a birch wood sprawling up the hillside, there was a white line of breaking waves. The sun shone intermittently through a thickening bank of cloud, now lighting the surface in yellow and ochre, then gone and casting grey and blue shadows.

'Now, laddie,' announced Iain suddenly, 'while I hold her nice and steady, you just stroke the flees through the waves like I told ye. Not too fast.'

As they drifted across the bay the water became wilder and the boat rolled and lurched. Johnny found that controlling his fly line and flies in the wind's force was difficult. He was fishing a traditional team of three flies, casting them ten yards downwind, lifting his rod until the first fly was skating along the surface, like the tantalising motion of an escaping insect, then the second fly, then the third, each hanging a moment before the final lift and re-cast. John knew this to be classic loch-style sea-trout fishing, developed on the most famous waters of Scotland and Ireland, and it was said by many to be the most exciting method for catching sea-trout. Johnny did not doubt that, even before a fish had come to his flies. As he settled to the rhythm of Loch Maree, casting and watching the flies and for signs of sea-trout in the maelstrom, he felt a mounting thrill, an expectation of a momentous event.

It came with the fury of the *salmonidae*. On the wall of a wave, near the downwind shore of the bay where Johnny could see the boulders of the loch-bed and hear the waves hissing on the beach up ahead, his top fly appeared momentarily. There was an explosive whirl in the water and the briefest of silver motions, more imagined than seen or heard. The fly was gone while John instinctively lifted his rod higher and felt solid resistance. In that moment the Palakona dipped in an alarming bow and the line was almost wrenched from his hand. A power beyond anything he had felt before, stronger by far than the little brown trout of the Bewl, surged off into the spilling waters of the loch. Trying to regain some control, John held the fly line too tightly, despite Iain's warning, and the speed of the fish he had hooked tore the line off so fast that it burnt his forefinger. Then, with a deep swirl and lunge, the fish leapt high in the air, shedding itself of the surface turbulence. For seconds it seemed to hang upon the crests, shaking its head and its silver-girthed muscle. In the boy's mind it hung for ever, a beautiful, savage fish, the first fish he had hooked which had known the wild, wild sea.

Later, looking at the curves and thick-set flesh, feeling its smooth shape, opening its mouth to see the scissor of jaws, the wickedly sharp teeth and tongue serrations, spreading the fins with their dark-grey sweep, especially the tail, like a shovel, which had given the creature such power, Johnny felt guilt at having killed such a creature. It was only a fish, people said, but it had been alive once and now it lay dead in his grasp. It had come home from an unimaginable journey through tide, storm and danger. Then, fatally attracted to a dancing fly on Maree's surface, it had unleashed a lifetime's energy in minutes. Just a fish, starkly measured by its weight, two pounds and six ounces, but to John it was both magnificent and terrible. It epitomised the landscape of Wester Ross, the wilderness atmosphere that pervaded the place, the fierce aura and the elusiveness that surrounded all the animals of loch, mountain and sky.

Even then, as a boy learnt of the magic of north-western Scotland, ancestral stronghold of the *salmonidae*, a sinister force had begun to grip the fins of the great fish. It came at their species from all directions. It came as a hunter infinitely more deadly and indiscriminate than a boy and a Palakona fly-rod, and from within as weakened fish became susceptible to fatal disease. It came in drought and the final, deathly relief of sour rains and devastating poisons. It came with the cunning of silence and deception and threatened to still the salmon's fins for eternity.

10

Adolescence brought new restrictions to Johnny's world, but also new challenges, values and fresh measures. His memory of gentler days in Kent had dimmed and he was left only with the startling image of Loch Maree from his recent past, the last dream, the knowledge that there was somewhere left which was pure and beautiful, somewhere to which he could always escape.

Other things had beauty, like Sarah Hammond, Charlotte's best friend. She brought out in Johnny an enormous desire to touch her and to be with her. There was an aura about her, something which gave you a heavy feeling in your stomach, which made you look from her lovely smile to other parts of her; young and energetic yet womanly. Her face haunted him. He searched innocent remarks for greater meaning. It would keep him awake at night or drift into his waking mind.

On Charlotte's eighteenth birthday, shortly after she heard that she had been awarded two A grades and a B in her 'A' levels and had gained her place at the Royal Free Medical School, there was a party at number 149. All her friends from school came, some of them with rowdy boyfriends, but John was delighted to see that Sarah came on her own.

During the afternoon, when most of them had had too much wine or lager to drink, they played what they called rugger in the little back garden. It consisted of hurling a partially deflated rugger ball to one of the girls and then chasing her and grabbing at it, and her, until it could be torn from her grasp. When Sarah was thrown the ball she shrieked with excitement and ran towards the back fence and temporary sanctuary. Johnny was first to reach her. She hugged the ball tight to her body and Johnny was oblivious to the other boys thumping into him. He was on her. Just for an instant he felt her breast, strangely not so soft as he had imagined, and the rigidity of a little nipple across his palm. He squeezed, briefly, among the tangle of arms and hands and sweatiness, and heard her yelp and then laugh.

He staggered as the mêlée disentangled. Suddenly he was the only one not laughing. He looked at her while the others ran off after the next victim. She had been kneeling. Now she stood, her cheeks flushed and an engaging smile on her face. He was right in front on her, almost touching. They were the same height, faces so close together. There was nothing else in the world but her. He began to mouth some words, but she brushed past him.

'Come on, Sheila's got the ball.' She was gone, back to the game, but he did not turn to follow her. The heaviness seemed to fix him to the spot so that he dared not, could not, turn. The crowd swept past him and was suddenly overwhelming. Then he was running, into the house, away from this new feeling he did not fully understand. Running now – yet moments before the fiery headiness had stopped him dead.

Now there were two preoccupations in Johnny's life. Sarah and the gigantic sprawl of island-strewn Loch Maree with its silver-white trout hurtling through big, dangerous waves. School fell a long way short, but even so there were moments, distinct and memorable punctuation marks in an education.

George Sellick, 'Old George' as the boys called him, taught general science to the younger school and biology at 'O' and 'A' level. To Johnny, Old George brought a meaning into whatever lay on a microscope slide or the colours in a test tube. He had a way about him which arrested rudeness and disrespectful behaviour from his class. The frailness of his ageing body was quite overshadowed by the wisdom and understanding in his face. Johnny thought that he was one of the few masters who could enthuse about a subject in a way which brought it to life. You could remember fascinating little details from Old George's classes. Like details in the cells they saw under the microscope and how there were billions of such cells in a body, *billions*; or the fact that most copper salts were blue, while the colour of a flame when crystals of copper sulphate were held on a wire in a bunsen-burner jet was green. The way Old George taught it you remembered. He would joke with the boys, spending as much time with each of them as they wanted. Johnny took considerably of his time. The boy's clumsiness demanded it, as did his interest in the subject.

George Sellick encouraged any effort, even the untidy diagrams and drawings in Johnny's exercise book. He painstakingly repeated basic scientific facts which the boys would need to know for major public examinations. Johnny could not, at almost fifteen, successfully translate three successive sentences from a simple French exercise, but he knew that carbonates effervesced to give off carbon dioxide when a dilute acid was added to them. He knew that potassium was a soft, malleable metal which had to be kept under oil, for when it was exposed to air it tarnished rapidly and a vaporous cloud streamed from it. When Old George dropped a little chunk of it into water it fizzed like a wild mad thing, emitting pops and hisses and a strong violet flame of burning hydrogen.

'Hydrogen is the gas which was used in airships like the Zeppelins,' Johnny remembered Old George explaining. 'It is lighter than air, the lightest gas that exists. So why do you think it was abandoned in favour of helium?' He showed the class a photograph of a wartime Zeppelin in flight – a great, grey, German battle airship, like a whale in the sea.

'Because it would burn, sir,' shouted Johnny. 'If it was hit with a bullet, or there was a flame, the hydrogen would burn ...'

'It would, indeed, Howard, and it did.' He showed them a photograph of the burning Zeppelin in New York, the terrible, massive fireball dropping from the sky on to running figures beneath. Johnny remembered about hydrogen, as he remembered much that the elderly science master taught.

It had been obvious from the start, however, that Johnny would not ever enjoy success with languages, ancient or modern. French annoyed him. He could not master the oral contortions necessary to produce the distinctive nasal sounds. He was embarrassed by his own attempts when he had to read to the class. He had received a detention when the French master had overheard him remarking that the language was meant for girls to speak, not men. German was not so bad. At least that had edges to it and it did not sound as if you were trying to sing a sickly ballad when you spoke it.

George Sellick kept what was known as an 'open lab' in which he encouraged the boys to come and look at the biological specimens and all the paraphernalia of the main science laboratory. Among the dark wooden corridors and rooms of the Old School, the laboratory became Johnny's favourite place. Usually it was empty or occupied only by one or two sixth-formers studying quietly for their exams. Sometimes Old George would be pottering about, cleaning slides and test tubes or generally tidying up while he hummed to himself.

One morning during the last period before lunch, when Johnny should have been at French, he strolled into the laboratory. Sunlight caught the dust particles and shone in long, warm beams from the south-eastern windows. The oak bench tops shone and smelled of polish. To Johnny's delight the room was empty except for Old George whose lab-coated figure was busily engaged in assembling some chemistry apparatus for an afternoon sixth-form practical class.

'Hello, Howard. What are you doing here?'

'Free period, sir,' Johnny offered as he usually did when he was asked the potentially embarrassing question.

The master frowned slightly and looked back at the sprawl of connected glassware. 'You get quite a lot of those, don't you?' He knew that John Howard was 'skiving off' from another lesson. It had been brought up in a staff meeting when several masters had commented on Howard's increasing absence from their lessons. George Sellick, the boy's form master and also the person who saw more of him than any of them, was charged with the task of tackling the problem.

'Quite a few, sir. What are you doing there?' he asked, changing the subject.

'Hm, organic synthesis. Now look here, young man, I think it's about time we had a chat.'

'About organic synthesis, sir?'

'No. About your education. About sciving your lessons and telling me lies about free periods.' He watched the boy's eyes widen and then look down towards the floor. Johnny knew that he was cornered and seemed abruptly to deflate. 'Don't you think that we should sort that little lot out?'

'Yes, sir,' came the quiet, almost whispered reply.

'Right then. Now you sit down on that stool, I'll sit here and you can tell me all about it.' The boy did not speak, his eyes downcast. Gone was his nonchalance, his usual questioning, his enthusiasm for searching out interesting specimens from the draws of the laboratory. But Old George knew about boys whose misdemeanours had been found out and he knew how to communicate with young minds. 'Now, let me see. You like science ...'

'Oh *yes*, sir.'

'And Mr Wilshaw tells me that you show great promise in English, though he feels you should pay more attention to the rules of grammar. But *great promise* is what he says ... Well, that lot's fair enough. Then we run into a bit of trouble, don't we? Like French, for example, which is where you should be now, I suspect?'

'Yes, sir,' he whispered.

'You know, I was never any good at French either. Mind you, I got my head down and scraped through the exams. It's expected, you see. You have to do it to keep everyone happy. You'll be taking your "O" levels in a year or so and unless you pass enough of those you'll not be able to go on to the next step, you see?'

'"A"' levels,' said John.

'Yes. Your passport, young man, 'A' levels. Look, you're interested in animals and fishing, aren't you, as well as science?' Johnny nodded silently. 'Now I happen to believe that you could do something in life with your interests. I don't know what and neither do you yet, but one day you will want to do something really important with your life. To do with your love of nature, I expect. When that time comes you don't want to be held back by not being properly prepared. It all catches up with you, you see. Your "O" and "A" levels will matter.'

'But I can't do the French or Maths, sir.'

'Ah, but I know you have the backbone to have a go at them. You're not dim. Just a touch idle at subjects which don't interest you.' Old George's tone became conspiratorial. He leant towards John. 'Why don't you have a damn good crack at the Maths? It's an important subject. You could never do "A" level sciences without passing "O" level Maths.' He winked at the boy as if to say that he did not give a hoot about the French so long as he went to the lessons.

Johnny never knew quite what it was about Old George that

inspired him to pay more attention to the subjects he found boring. He felt he had an ally in that dark school where the smell of books and polish and boys pervaded. He knew the old man understood him and that if only he could really pass a subject like Maths then he would repay George Sellick's confidence, which was a great thing to have.

And he did have the man's confidence. Old George watched the boy as he crossed the laboratory, on his way to the French lesson. Johnny was not a 'waster' as some of the masters suggested. You could not have that much hope in your eyes, that much enthusiasm and passion in you, and be a waster. If Howard failed it would be the fault of the school for not harnessing and channelling the boy's energy. You could not let that energy run away without direction. That would be a waste. Boys from Highgate made something of themselves. They went on to university and into the army. They became politicians and powerful men; scientists, doctors, lawyers and financiers. Howard was unlikely to do anything like that. Despite his keen interest in science, there was much more of the artist in him. An odd, enigmatic mixture, thought Old George, a mixture which his masters did not know how to handle adequately. Few of them would even recognise it. Their energy and imagination was but a placid pond compared with Howard's raging sea; a wild, wild sea.

Mr Wilshaw was a young Australian teacher on a two year contract with Highgate School. He taught English to the lower sets in the junior school. Mr Wilshaw did not like to stick resolutely to a syllabus. He wanted to catch the boys' attention and had found that the only way of teaching English to rebellious boys was to avoid routine. Instead, he read to them, and made them write essays on subjects which interested them. Apart from Old George's lessons, Johnny looked forward to English the most, especially when the book being read thrilled or intrigued him. He began looking forward to the next chapter. Mr Wilshaw would sometimes get them (though they should never use the verb to get) to write an essay for homework on their version of the next chapter.

It was through Mr Wilshaw that Johnny developed a love of books, late in his adolescence but the more passionate for that.

A class reading of *Journey to the Centre of the Earth* had him searching out other Jules Vernes titles. *The Invisible Man* began his H.G. Wells phase. John Buchan's *The Thirty-Nine Steps* thrilled him. The descriptions of Richard Hannay, an innocent fugitive, on the run through London and Scotland, burned with such intensity. The chapters entitled *The Bald Archaeologist* and *The Dry-Fly Fisherman* were quite the most compulsive episodes Johnny had ever read. He could see himself as Hannay, dashing across the great hills and moors of Perthshire. Then again he saw Loch Maree and the high hills encasing the Kinlochewe river, Glen Torridon and the Coulin pass, the places where people like Hannay, like Johnny, could survive best, where their true natures were unleashed.

The most wonderful find of all, however, was Gavin Maxwell's *Ring of Bright Water*. It was a discovery which Johnny later realised was as important to him as the hints of the joyous mysteries of Sarah Hammond and the sight of Loch Maree pitching under a strong wind from the west. He was intrigued with the idyll Maxwell described: life in a cottage on the shores of a remote bay in western Scotland. Camusfearna, the Bay of Alders; even the name ran liquidly off the tongue and through his mind. It would not be so different from Seun Cottage at Kinlochewe.

Johnny cried when he read how Mijbil, the otter, died at the senseless hand of man. He understood the subtleties of what Maxwell wrote and revelled in the descriptions of the western sea. He visualised the Sound of Sleat, the Hebrides and the deep-cut sea lochs of the mainland where basking sharks and sea-trout, mackerel and eels swam, while the skies and the white-sanded beaches were alive with the sights and sounds of the life Maxwell portrayed so vividly.

Maxwell had escaped the burden of life among the crowds. He had found his paradise and had revelled in its richness, giving it, through his writing, to anyone who cared to look.

Walking down Hampstead Road between the main school and the sports grounds and dining hall Johnny heard his friends' constant chatter and the stream of passing traffic. Here, on the edge of London among the roads flanked by exclusive houses set in park-like gardens, it was difficult to visualise places like Camusfearna and Loch Maree where there was the sound of rain and wind and not the noise of human beings, where the horizon was closed only by distant hills and forest, not the regularity of buildings. Those places seemed to Johnny to be so far away now, brought a little closer by *Ring of Bright Water*, yet through those same pages, made more precious and far more difficult to attain.

So it was that as Johnny began his 'O' level year he found himself in a world cut off from most of what he really treasured. He made a refuge in several series of books which provided a key, a standpoint, to the world in which he desired to roam. After *The Thirty-Nine Steps* he read the other Buchan titles, *Greenmantle*, *The Three Hostages*, *Prester John*, though only one, *The Island of Sheep*, could match or even surpass *The Thirty-Nine Steps* for adventure and the vision of remote and wild landscape.

Ring of Bright Water led him to Maxwell's first book, *Harpoon at a Venture*, the astonishing story of the establishment of a shark fishery on the Island of Soay. With anger and bitterness, Johnny watched the disintegration of Maxwell's idyll with his otters at Camusfearna in *The Rocks Remain* and *Raven Seek Thy Brother*. There was a desperate call from those pages, a man with the nightmare of tragic loss constraining his life as he watched and wrote about the destruction of the natural world, epitomised by the crumbling of his own cherished lifestyle in a remote setting by the western sea.

From Maxwell's lyrical and beautiful fact to the fiction of J. Meade Falkner's *Moonfleet* and the shorter Hemingways, especially *The Old Man and the Sea*, Johnny strayed into fantasy, into the magical world of Tolkien where evil and ultimate good clashed over another sort of ring.

It was a time for fantasy, with the Rolling Stones playing their charity concert in Hyde Park and older boys humming tunes from Sergeant Pepper, growing their hair longer than Highgate School's regulations formally allowed. Johnny sensed a new era sweeping away the old, and he felt that he straddled both. Very dim, almost lost, were the images of his childhood – Kent and lonely days by the stream and in green meadows. This new era crowded in noisily with talk of Vietnam and Monty Python, of Mick Jagger and flower power. Fourth and fifth-formers talked knowingly and excitedly about mysterious drugs which gave you portals to new worlds. They were words on everyone's lips, amphetamines, LSD and cocaine, and Johnny did not yet know how they destroyed the lives of young people. The boys talked too about sex in this new age of freedom. Johnny heard the lurid description of things he yearned to do. Yet he felt a love for a girl he would never have or with whom he would never share the things about which boys spoke. Sarah came to him only in his fevered imagination. She came, glistening and fiery and wanting him, just him, and his desire swept away the French master's monotone and had him hoping that the bell would not go too soon to reveal his embarrassment when he stood up.

With his head full of images from the stories he had read and the memories he cherished, he often wrote, making his first exploratory, adolescent steps into territory where few among his peers ventured. He went far beyond the limits of Mr Wilshaw's set homeworks, lovingly translating the things he saw and felt into forms and structures in English. There, on paper, in sentences and paragraphs, some smudged and straying above and below lines, or into the margins, were Johnny's deepest feelings, what he loved and admired, what he hated and feared. Naive and swamped with adjectives, his collection of essays, stories and poems in exercise books and on foolscap paper became something of which he was enormously proud. It was something private and special.

The Sgurr Dubh salmon was enormous now, after months and years of rich feeding off the west coast of Greenland. He migrated north during summer, into the abundance of krill in Baffin Bay, and south during winter where capelin shoals massed in the fjords. At over a metre long he would have weighed twenty-five pounds in the air, though he was only half that weight in water. Still he was a virgin fish, having never felt a strong enough urge to head east into the void, where, somewhere, lay the islands and sea lochs which led home.

For weeks at a time he would be alone before finding and joining the security of a great salmon shoal. Mostly, the fish he found were those in their first or second sea year, a quarter his size. They were fast moving and haphazard in their migration. Danger ran with them. The way they remained exposed in open water close to the surface made the big cock fish nervous. He hung beneath them, on the periphery of the shoal.

There was a hum across his lateral lines. Sinking deeper, away from the hiss of the shoal, he felt the sea for its messages. The hum was now a thud and it came from the direction in which the salmon were heading, slightly off to his left flank. It was passing, a strange, menacing noise in these seas; yet it was falling away behind the fish.

On the surface the Danish high-seas trawler *Christiensen* furrowed the easy swell. Following instructions from the bridge, men busily worked winches and fed out the long net. The sonar had picked up the signal of a dense shoal and the helmsman was sweeping round behind it, tightening the fish, while the net tracked and its wide mouth yawned open, like a monstrous, feeding blue whale gulping at the krill-rich seas.

They had to work quickly, while the weather held and before the salmon dispersed. And they had to stay ahead of the other trawlers in the area. There was fabulous wealth in these seas, made richer by the recent discovery that it was the main feeding area of the Atlantic salmon. The Danes, with the advantage of having Greenland as a Danish territory, had taken the first and greatest steps into exploiting the magnificent find of salmon grounds. At first no one had realised that the Greenland salmon were actually the fish from every Atlantic sea-board where a salmon run existed. Only after the catastrophic decline in numbers of fish returning to these countries was the full scale of damage created by the Danish high-seas salmon fishery realised. The quotas came too late, only after the species was severely depleted in numbers, often to the extent that an entire year's run from a particular system was netted out and lay in the freezer compartments of a trawler fleet.

So quickly the meshwork jaws came at them. They had ignored the hiss and thud of its approach, always safe, as they had been, in the tight formation of a shoal. Now with a shadow reaching around them, they turned and dashed, only to see the shadow and the jaws up ahead. The big cock fish had been beneath them as the net had engulfed them, constricting their progress, forcing them to turn up into the light. As he turned and set his wide tail to the sea he glimpsed the panic that had gripped the fish, even as the netting touched their flesh and their fins. He saw the glitter of loose scales as the fish flayed and churned. They dashed to right and left, and down towards the deep. Some rushed towards that ultimate escape of a salmon, the air, driving towards a high, arcing leap. But the shadow lay above them and only their heads lunged through the mesh, their gills and girths caught in the sharp, abrasive netting. More quickly even than it had stretched around them the net had closed until it was not merely a shadow, but a wall, a curve of solid mesh, clamping down upon its prey. Few of them could even move now as the weight of the net and their companions pressed against them. There was no room, no liquid energy at their fins, no chance for a dash and leap at the surface. They spun, each feeling a relentless pressing, each spending the last of its energy on a non-directional, panicked thrash of a tail or tearing twist of body.

There were so many salmon that the trawler staggered as it ran up against the full weight of the load. The winches strained and the boat's speed fell away. To stern was a heaving bulge in the waves, the packed trawl, writhing with £25,000 worth of salmon flesh.

As he fired himself away from the panic and carnage and sound of heavy machinery under strain, the salmon noticed others with him. Six fish, the only survivors from the shoal, had followed him to escape. In him, in the fish from the Sgurr Dubh above Loch Maree, in his great girth and powerful fins, they saw something to follow as, instinctively, they knew that he would lead them to safety.

They were all fish from the west coast of Scotland. One of them, a hen on her second sea run, was from the Loch Maree system. She had descended as a kelt, a spent fish, from the River Ewe earlier that year, having successfully spawned on the redds of the Coulin pass. Though smaller in the head she had his recognisable shape and markings, the thick shoulder ridge and deeply forked tail, the scatter of dots behind the gill plates and the distinctive spread of muscle over the long body. These marked them both as fish from the Maree system, just as the shape and characteristics of all salmon held true for any particular system.

The others were maiden grilse, having been at sea for less than a year. They were from various northern Scottish rivers, one from the Hope and Strath More, another from the River Ailort and Loch Eilt, two from Skealter on North Uist and the last a vagrant from Loch Damh above Torridon. Behind the large hen and the huge cock-salmon they were small, like little satellites. They had survived only because they had seen and followed the escape dash of the two larger fish. In such a short time they had changed from being part of a homogenous shoal, feeding and migrating northwards, to being the only representatives of their systems within a hundred miles.

There would be others, somewhere along the thousand-mile-long arc around western and southern Greenland, and out into Baffin Bay and the Labrador current. They too, though, would be under attack from the Danish trawlers ruthlessly exploiting one of the world's great and exclusive food sources, a fish for which people would pay ten-fold the price of cod.

Now, at the mouth of an iceberg strewn fjord far up the coast of Greenland, the seven-strong shoal hovered, listening to what was a quieter sea. Beyond the crackling of ice and the tide's shiver and surge, there was an ominous silence. Where there might have been a familiar sound, no salmon fins whispered across nearby currents.

11

Even Maxwell's world, Johnny understood, was not sublime. There could not be any perpetual peace, though an instant could be utterly beautiful and gentle. Camusfearna lay in ruins, burnt out, like the dream it, and Maxwell, had cast. If that could happen in north-western Scotland then, surely, there was less hope elsewhere.

His mother watched adolescence laying deep wounds in the child he had been. Much of his childhood had survived into his seventeenth year. This quality struggled with the new and energetic brashness of the young man. As his peers developed the crude brutality of early manhood, or settled for the apparent calm of bespectacled and book-entombed study, Johnny fell into neither niche. He was atypical, afforded labels such as roguish, enigmatic, defiant and disdainful from his masters. Old George and Mr Wilshaw spoke of promise, but one for which they would have to dig deeply, or one which would surface only when the boy allowed it.

In the struggle through his 'O' levels the promise was barely to be seen. He scraped through five of them, including Mathematics, much to Old George's and his own delight, and was retaking some of those he had failed, including History and French. But he had passed enough to be allowed to undertake an 'A' level course and for that he was studying the three sciences; Biology, Chemistry and Physics, even though George Sellick had suggested this to be the wrong mixture. He knew the boy was good at science, though he was no scientist. He felt there was something else that Highgate school should be able to draw out of him. The science master had little idea, however, that Johnny was drawing it out of himself without their help – with the exception of Mr Wilshaw who had been so good for the boy's writing.

Mrs Howard knew more of this side of Johnny. She knew of the exercise books and bundles of foolscap and A4 he kept in his room. He hid some of the books behind his desk or beneath piles of books in a corner. She sometimes discovered them as she cleaned his room, always replacing them where she had found them, after glancing through the pages, reading some of the poems and parts of his essays. She noticed how his child-like qualities persisted through his most turbulent years, strong in his writing. Many, if they had read his private thoughts on paper, would have called them immature or naive, an impression exaggerated by the mistakes in grammar and the frequent, all too obvious lack of care he put into the structure of his work. The images he created, though, were rich and full of passion. She could see the green of his countryside, the whiplash of salmon tails on cold, foaming water, the intense beauty of the places he loved. He had painted Seun Cottage in a way which revealed that he knew every one of its weathered stones, and Stocks Cottage nestling in autumnal mists by the silky, magical flow of the Bewl. His writing made her yearn for the summer evenings she had spent in their garden, listening to him approaching across the field in the dusk, seeing his grinning face and dirty knees at the gate, his happiness. Nowadays she saw it only in their summer trips to Loch Maree and in his memories of the Weald, trapped in his writing.

She saw, also, the intensity with which he felt the images that hurt him. These were the moments when the child and the young man were in deepest conflict, when he stepped further into manhood, into a world which was cruel and in which you had to be strong to survive. Sometimes she saw in him a mood which upset her more than anything else, times when her boy seemed to lack all the hope and enthusiasm which he had possessed in Kent. There were moments when a shadow was thrown so darkly across him that it shut out even the brilliant light of what he had loved. One day in the summer term of his lower-sixth year she saw it as a gigantic burden on his shoulders, crushing the last morsel of dazzling youth from him.

He had played truant again, unexpectedly after almost an entire half-term during which he had attended every day and every class. It was a Tuesday in June, warm and hazy, when other boys sat in classrooms in shirt-sleeves and loosened ties, concentrating with difficulty on the Nitrogen Cycle and Ohm's Law. Johnny had not planned to 'bunk off', but as he had walked towards school that morning, his jacket slung over his shoulder, the thought had seeded in him. He knew he would be discovered, though it would be worth it. How many summer days like that one had he spent by the little river in the Weald? And he had thought, when they moved to London, that there could be no more. Well, why not? Summer had arrived and the Bewl would be flowing. He had five pounds in his pocket, enough for a couple of doughnuts from the baker in Highgate village, the tube fare down to Charing Cross and a return ticket to Paddock Wood. He could almost walk it from there, or hitch a lift ... Impetuously he decided. He would do it. He *would* see his river again, and the summer Weald: bugger double Physics and Practical Chemistry, bugger school.

The telephone was ringing as Mrs Howard stepped through the front door that evening. It was Mr Chapman, Johnny's housemaster, who was inquiring why Johnny had not been at school though the office had not been informed that he was unwell. Even as Mrs Howard was about to reply, the front door again swung open and Johnny stood there, staring at her. Something about him was wrong, desperately wrong, so that she said: 'I'll call you back soon, Mr Chapman. Johnny's here but ... I'll call you back in a minute.' She put down the receiver and hurried over to her son. 'Johnny, what is it?' She pulled at his arm and guided him into the kitchen. 'What's wrong?' He was pale, despite the hot day when everyone was red in the face. His eyes and expression were as if he was dazed, a slight frown creasing his forehead. His voice, when it came, was quiet and shaking. He was almost in tears.

'Oh Mum, I'm sorry, I ...' He looked at her, lost, confused, battered by something awful. 'I bunked off today, didn't go in to school. I ... I went down to Kent, to Paddock Wood, to Stocks, except ...' His eyes were red against the tight, pale skin and they were filling with tears. 'It's not there anymore.'

'What's not there anymore?'

'*Stocks Cottage*. It's gone, and the garden and most of Mr Billings' field. It's all gone and there's hundreds of houses there.

And men building more. Mum, it's terrible, they've destroyed everything, even the river.' And then the tears burst from him, the last of his childhood dissolving in long, choking sobs. Diana Howard hugged him. He shook in her arms, and she understood what had happened. Mr Billings, who had always complained about not being able to make a good living from his little farm, must have sold up to the man who had bought Stocks Cottage. Of course. That was it. A property developer.

It was incredible. She could barely understand the mentality which could destroy the idyllic cottage and surrounding fields. Could the clearing of those lovely meadows be justified, no matter how much money the man would make? Not for the first time she regretted selling Stocks Cottage, but now her regret was more bitter. She hated the man who had bought and destroyed it. He had told her that he was buying it for his grandmother. It must all have been lies. And what lies had he told poor Mr Billings? How on earth had he gained planning permission to perform such a ghastly act against nature and beauty? How could councils and planning departments allow such things to happen?

That it was all so terribly wrong she felt with a venomous intensity, viciously clawing at her heart as she tried to comfort her son. The wrong of it was there in her arms, shaking, sobbing in a way she had forgotten, as she had done in the weeks after his father died.

Only later did she manage to extract from him the facts of his trip to Kent. Some of it he never told her, though she found it in his writing, even months and years and decades later. There was more detail and more pain as his ability to express himself increased with age. It was the destruction of the river which was the greatest agony to him. Its flow had been reduced by an Artesian borehole drilled upstream for drinking-water abstraction. There was now the barest trickle between stagnant pools which were littered with building rubble, some of which it later occurred to Johnny would have been pieces of Stocks Cottage. There were old tyres, bottles, cartons and all the jetsam of 'property development'. The reed beds were all but gone and what alders remained now stood far back from the water's edge. Where there had been a dangerous, swirling eddy, threatening to undercut some oak roots, was now a mere puddle. Johnny had caught his first big roach from that pool, a pounder. Now it could not support sticklebacks. Its life was as still as its flow. The run where he had caught trout, where the scent of water mint and cress had filled the air and the stream had flowed tinkling and tumbling over gravel, was now a muddy mire, also littered with man's waste.

Now there were so few. In the years he had spent at sea, the cock fish had watched his species dwindle. The high-seas nets were strung and trawled the length of the Greenland coastline in their insatiable hunger for salmon flesh. The noses of propellers and diesel engines were heavy during the long summers, pushing ever-farther northward. Even in the darkness of winter they came, in calm weather: thud, thud, thud, and the splash and swish and hush of nets, the whirring and clank of winches, the intense thrashing of a thousand salmon tails, while immense shoals were enmeshed and hauled from the sea.

While so many had been taken, ever fewer returned from their home-river systems. While maiden fish, grilse, had suffered continued decline, the loss was enormous of those fish which had spawned and returned to sea as kelts, the great salmon from Norway and Scotland which had survived earlier migrations. These were the most sought after of all prizes in high-seas fishing, one of the most valuable of the sea's commodities.

It was not only the nets. Some fish which had managed to return to Greenland waters bore scars which had not been produced by the abrasive cut of nylon mesh. They were the marks of healed and dormant ulcers and flesh infections. These fish came from coasts off to the east and west, though mostly from Europe and Scandinavia, where the episodic diseases of the *salmonidae*, ulcerative dermal necrosis and furunculosis, were infesting stocks already ferociously reduced by netting. Most infected fish died. A few, those lucky enough to be swept by spates out to sea, where the diseases lay dormant, survived until their next attempt at ascending their home system on a breeding run. Then the viruses became active, laying flesh bare for fungal attack. The glorious silver scales dulled, while white patches of disease grew about the eyes, jaws, gills and shoulders, and down the back, the fungal roots eating like a cancer at the flesh. The weakened fish abandoned their breeding quest and fell into the slack water of river pools or skulked in the shallows of a loch until weakness stilled their fungus-encrusted fins.

Clean and enormously powerful, the cock fish and his vagrant shoal, along with the big Loch Maree hen fish, had turned south, running towards the growing light of summer. There was a strength within him, coupled with a strange desire. This he vaguely remembered, deep within the genetic messages and absoluteness of the salmon-mind. The urge to migrate was overwhelming. It would not be a simple migration in pursuit of a food source. Now he felt the need for his home system. As if mirrored in her dazzling flanks, the desire was also within the hen fish with which he had swum for two years. He saw it in her, for he had grown, learnt and waited with her. Together their great fins had sliced tides, while the other, smaller Scottish fish followed. And again they would follow, over fantastic distances, all the way home.

The weight of water at his head threatened. It surged, stinging, across his lateral lines, daring him to swim into it. He knew its currents, its sounds, its temperatures, its voice and its threats, and he feared none of it. Knifing into the titanic rush of water, the salmon put Cape Farewell at his tail. Only disobeying instinct was to be feared. A salmon's fins were made to be united with the wild, wild sea.

Dear Mr Howard,

Many thanks for your recent letter and accompanying article. I thoroughly enjoyed the piece and am keeping it for publication in *Trout and Salmon* in due course. Your writing has a lovely blend of facts, which our readers will find useful, and evocative description.

I have never been to Loch Maree but have to admit that after reading your article I am sorely tempted to mount a fishing expedition to those parts.

If you have any other articles on the sea-trout and salmon fishing in Scotland (or England perhaps) I would be most happy to see them and consider them for publication.

Yours sincerely,
Ian Holmwood
Editor

Johnny read and re-read the letter. He could scarcely believe it. *Trout and Salmon* was going to publish one of his articles, the first one he had sent. He had spent weeks planning and writing it, discarding paragraphs and pages, even whole drafts. A determination had grown in him to show the reader the special things he had seen on Loch Maree, to show other fishermen the beauty of those northern lochs where swam the wildest fish of all. It had been a frustrating task, easy in its concept, because the images and pictures were so clear in his own head, yet shaping them with words in a structured article was a technique he had never learnt. Anyway, how on earth did you trap Loch Maree in words? You could describe a field, a wood, a mountain, but how could you adequately lay Maree's vista across 2,000 words when there was so much beauty, so much passion which it generated in those who knew it? So he concentrated on the sea-trout run and how these world famous Maree fish came at a fly, savagely on the surface, and how they leapt and tore line off the reel when you hooked them. He wrote about the flies that caught them and gave only glimpses of the great loch where they swam. Oddly, though, the brief descriptions of Maree in his final draft gave it a mystery which it always possessed for those who gazed over its dark and formidable waters. More than anything, his article showed how Loch Maree had become a dream to a young man and it invoked a yearning in others to experience something of its strange atmosphere.

Mrs Howard came out of the kitchen to see her son staring at the letter.

'Johnny, you'll be late for school ... What's that you've got?' He showed her, saying nothing. She glanced over his shoulder, then pulled the letter towards her and read it through carefully. '*Good grief*. I had no idea ... Accepted for *publication*. Oh Johnny, that's wonderful.' She hugged him and saw the pride in his eyes. 'Are you taking it to school? Show it to Mr Chapman and Mr Sellick. You should. They'll be delighted.'

It was extraordinary, she thought, how there could be such utter extremes in her son. She had seen him in such anguish, the day months ago when he had taken himself off to Kent, and now so happy that he was speechless, a massive grin bisecting his face. Suddenly they both laughed while he jumped and stamped and whooped for joy, gripping his letter in both hands.

So some of those thoughts he set down on paper and kept hidden away in his room were to be published. They were to be read by people other than his mother and his English master, and in their release he would gain in confidence and, perhaps, find a channel, a direction, into the cruel, outer world. He would instinctively forge his own direction. His adolescent fears were dispersing, though she hoped his growing-up and his career would lead him some way back towards the sublime happiness he had possessed in Kent, or on towards the new passion he had developed for northern Scotland.

She was also delighted that now, at last, some of his masters at school, other than George Sellick, would take some notice of him. How many other boys from Highgate had had articles accepted for publication in a magazine? That, surely, would prove that John was no fool.

The gathering had lasted for ten tides, each one bringing another small shoal from the Atlantic wilderness. Out of the terrible void they materialised, ghost-like and silent. On one tide there would be a group of three or four, a dozen on the next. Each fish tasted the sea, sometimes catching snatches of scents they remembered from earlier life in fresh water. The trigger of familiar taste told them that they were close to where they needed to be, close to home after so long away.

The huge cock and hen fish from Loch Maree had both been away for longer than the others. It was the hen's second return, while it was the first time her companion had sought his home system. Yet they knew this coastline, beyond the Hebrides where the tides ran with a roar, was theirs. Like west Greenland, the coast was indented with large, sinuous channels, sea lochs, though here there was no ice. Where there would have been capelin there were mackerel, and among the predators to be watchful for here were grey seals rather than the ubiquitous harp seals of Greenland's waters.

Scattered they came across the Minch, spreading and fragmenting further as each coastal system claimed some of their number. It was September and they were the last of the year's salmon run, the famous autumn migrants, largest of the season. The grilse had migrated before them, through June, July and August. All that remained were these mysterious few, greatest among all *salmo salar*, the autumn leapers.

There it was, almost hidden along the folds of the battered Scottish west coast, the opening to Loch Ewe and the Maree system. The cock fish gyred away from the shoal, followed closely by four hens, including the huge fish which had been his companion throughout recent years and the long sea migration. Two smaller cock fish recognised the Ewe's sound and taste and followed the shoal which had splintered from the main group. The remainder pressed on towards the north where their own systems lay; Loch Broom and Laxford, which led to mountain-flanked Stack; then Inchard, and even Eriboll and Loch Hope, beyond Cape Wrath.

The seven Maree fish glided across Ewe's surface in early morning, crossing a flood tide. Coastal hills wrapped around them and the volume of sea noise they had felt throughout their journey gradually diminished. Cruising quietly in the calm, autumn sea, they passed the emaciated carcase of a grey seal and they listened to the strangely quiet tide.

Then, abruptly, they felt an old and intense excitement as up ahead they smelt and felt the vibration of a heavy concentration of salmon. Even as the shoal came into sight, however, the cock fish had bristled his great fins and halted motionless in the water. There was a net, but quite unlike the dangerous trawls off Greenland, and there was no sound of fishing vessels. Within the net were salmon, hundreds of them, though none seemed agitated at being held captive by netting.

It was a sea cage, one of four to be placed in Loch Ewe since the salmon had left the system for his years at sea. It contained three hundred salmon, all mirror images of one another, all short, fat and healthy and within a few ounces of six pounds in weight. Each stroked delicate fins on the slight currents which seeped through the meshwork that surrounded them. Some possessed net marks, loose scales and torn fins caused by them being packed in such a confined space. They were caricatures of their species, tragic abominations compared with the rugged race which had so richly colonised the North Atlantic coasts. Not a single one of them had seen the sea beyond Loch Ewe, nor the ancestral breeding redds of their kind. Neither had they swum a distance greater than the confines of man-made vessels.

They were farmed salmon and had been hatched on trays over

which flowed carefully monitored, acid-free water at a constant rate and near-constant temperature. Then they had been grown on in larger tanks, fed regularly and nurtured in conditions which maximised their rate of growth. Within a year they had developed into twelve-ounce smolts, ready for the sea, though they would never know its wonderful freedom. Gradually their keepers, the farmers, acclimatised them to saline conditions by flushing brine through their tanks. Finally, their migration was done for them as road tankers transported them to the rapid-feed sea cages in Loch Ewe.

In their short lives the captive fish had known no predators, no territorial squabbles and no lean times when their food had been scarce. Nor had they ever needed to hunt or to take shelter. Any tiny morsel of instinct left within their battery-farmed bodies, the need to run on cold tides, the desire for a spate at their heads, was suffocated by the impossibility of escape. All had been provided and yet all that was wild had been denied. They were an exotic protein commodity, in tremendous demand which resulted in their flesh fetching higher prices in the market than prime beef. They were far from the wild, though people could not taste the difference.

While the drones inched hypnotically around their cage, waiting only for the automatic feeder to drop its three-hourly ration of feed pellets, the wild salmon stole past, unnoticed by the captives, a strange fear at their fins.

There were hunters in Loch Ewe, bandit hunters. They ventured into the loch on the flowing tide pursuing vague echoes of sea-trout and mackerel shoals. They were porpoises, hungry, adventurous desperados chattering to one another with high-pitched voices and crackles of sonar. Whispy grey and white, they curled out of the deep, tails beating, voices cutting the sea while hunger keened their instincts and lent them a terrifying speed as they homed in on any sound or vibration which might be a food source.

The salmon swam now with a sea-trout shoal which also quested the fresh water from Maree entering at the head of Loch Ewe. The shoal was a magnificent spread of several generations of two species of *salmonidae*. Small sea-trout hovered in a single layer, ten feet below the surface. Above were the lilac and silver shapes of the big salmon, their fins a dark violet. Below swam the largest sea-trout, fifteen feet down, grey backs, white bellies and black fins. The heavier fish were almost all hens, swollen with eggs, their flesh tight with muscle.

The first screech of sonar stilled them all with its rasping intensity. From across their flanks the porpoises appeared, viciously cutting into the densest layer of fish, the small sea-trout. Beneath him the cock fish saw the sea fill with the roll and dash of grey backs, then a shudder of silver scales, sparkling, explosive noise and the dreadful hunters; warm-blooded intelligence coldly killing. From his momentary shocked stupor he lurched into motion, accelerating to almost thirty knots in four seconds. Clear of the shoal and the killing, he dived, along with the other salmon, towards the loch bed. A blast of sonar burnt along his nerves. In open water he was mercilessly exposed to the most acrobatic hunters of the sea, faster than sharks, more cunning than seals, and his size tempted them. Porpoises whose tongues had just tasted the crushing burst of sea-trout ova yearned for his muscular prize. They flung themselves in pursuit, down to the darkness of the loch floor, where their eyes were almost useless, though their sonar could hunt out his form.

The salmon would not leave the relative sanctuary of the loch's floor. Instinctively, they headed towards the shore, into the confines of the loch where there were boulders and weed-beds. The water shallowed. They felt themselves exposed in the light, caught not only by sonar but also by the porpoises' acute vision. Still the loch shallowed, five fathoms, four, a reef; they swerved upwards, bellies scraping against rock, two fathoms, bright light, a swirl of white water, breaking waves. Clouds of sand whirled, kicked up in their wake, blurring their pursuers' sound image. A porpoise leapt above them. They saw a grey belly overtaking them, feet away, then inches, almost touching. The cock fish saw teeth in the greyness, a scything mouth and then an enveloping darkness and disorientation, something clawing at his flesh, unyielding, draining his energy, clamping down on his head, his tail, his hard, pulsing muscle. And at last he stopped, deep in a bed of kelp.

The porpoises, berserk and furious, leapt above the weedbed. They dared not enter the kelp, for fear of being caught in the treacherous and tough fronds which could trap them until they drowned. They brushed against the rim of the bed at high speed, harrying the salmon in the hope that the fish would be startled and bolt from the undersea forest.

The tide was ebbing, making the water dangerously shallow for the mammals. Reluctantly, they turned away towards the loch's deeps. Their sonar crackled, filling the sea with their anger, while the salmon lay in the darkness, cushioned by kelp.

Much later, in the last glow of the evening, and at the height of the next flood tide, any watching eyes might have seen seven leapers hurling themselves into the cool air, not far from the mouth of the River Ewe. Soon the waves and the row of their antics settled and the smooth loch hid the secret passage of the Atlantic salmon. Like silver apparitions they crept close to the loch bed, testing the brackish flow, clandestinely merging with boulders and bladder wrack in the stream.

There had been rain in the mountains far inland. Burns were whitened with the rush of water stampeding down a thousand slopes. Loch Maree had risen a foot in the spate, after the dry months of July and August. The Ewe belched and roared down to the sea, fresh, peat-stained water meeting the blue-black tide beneath the intensely white mats of foam. Beneath these, in the violent force of water, the salmon slid.

In the darkness and noise they lost contact with one another, though each drove into the river together, each picking out routes which would ease slightly their passage upstream through the maelstrom. The cock fish did not know whether the big hen was behind or ahead, only that she too would be running, for the need to reach a place beyond the river, and the loch above that, was intense in both of them. It lay at the heart of the migration force which drove them. Without that force neither would have left Greenland's waters to approach this place of dangers. Although there was a peculiar sense within the two of them, together, along with their companions, as they slipped through the inhospitable flood. The dangers were there to be overcome, so that the fish might reach the ancestral redd of the Sgurr Dubh, above the Bharranch, where lay the greatest sense of all. Any fears of the river's confines and its bellowing voice were as nothing against the call that drew them on towards Maree and the high system. Each swam alone, though with shared purpose. Now there were so few left to carry and encounter the mysteries of the Atlantic salmon.

12

It had rained every day and night for a week. Showers gave way to incessant rain followed by misty drizzle. Then a gash of blue sky and a racing shaft of sunlight – intense colour in the greyness – would be swept away under the assault of another wet front from the west. John Howard had never seen Loch Maree so full. Burns and flash streams etched white scars on the cliff faces of Slioch and Beinn Eighe. Everything dripped, the Scots pines and the storm-battered birch, the bracken and the heather. The landscape glistened with light, like freshly cut lead, glinting off screes and gravel, the bark of trees and the wood of the boat in which Johnny drifted.

Away from the clutter and confusion of Highgate and London, he could think clearly. He had passed his 'A' levels, but with poor grades, barely enough to be accepted by university to read one of the sciences.

This was the first time he had come to Scotland alone. Seun Cottage had been booked as in every other year since their first visit, though later in the season as there would be no new school term for Johnny. Alone on the loch, life in London and the future of a university course seemed inconsequential.

This was where he wanted to be, beneath stormy skies, where sea-trout and salmon ran on September floods. He felt peculiarly safe here, with the comforting familiarity of the mountains and birch woods reaching up from the lovely loch shores. The wild water did not frighten him. After what was now frequent use, he understood the limits of the boat and how much wind the old Seagull engine could battle against. Besides, if caught in gusting winds he could always dash for shelter in the many bays along the north and south shores. Only crossing the loch, over what was in places four hundred feet of black depth, where the surface heaved under a strong wind along the thirteen-mile fetch, did his hand tense on the engine's tiller. His heart raced as the boat thumped and crashed in the white-maned swell. Alone on the big and beautiful loch; this was where he wanted to be.

His decision had been made months earlier. He would not discount a university course, but he needed something else before that. He had glimpsed it in *Ring of Bright Water*, and touched on it in the secrecy of his own writing. As a child he had known it so surely, though it had become confused in early adulthood. He needed open country, like this, and water; to learn about things which other people had forgotten or ignored, or simply had not seen. He yearned for what the Weald had had, and was losing because of what was called development. He could see this quality all around him on Loch Maree, and feel it in the gusting wind off the Atlantic. Most clearly of all he saw it on the fin – a mystery dressed in grey and ghostly shapes, swimming up from the sea.

George Sellick had been right. Johnny would do something with his love of nature. If he was to do that, however, he would have to experience more of it, its marvels, beyond where most people ever saw. He wanted to give shape, with words, to the extraordinary story of the salmon and sea-trout of this wild place.

During that autumn on the loch, an inner peace briefly calmed the adolescence which had been raging in him. The arrogance of his youth was humbled by what he saw. Each time the grey marvel of salmon appeared, briefly and suddenly threatening as they broached from water which had been empty of all but the rhythm of waves, he felt that he was witnessing an event of nature which should be treasured. While he saw many sea-trout, there were few salmon, though that made the sightings all the more remarkable. Johnny knew that these great fish had once been abundant, with the Scottish systems as teeming with the migrants as were the rivers of Alaska with Pacific species of *salmonidae*. It was strange and awesome that even in a huge and remote loch like Maree, where the fugitive fish should have been milling and packed on the shallows, there were so few. Why did they brave the terrible journey from Greenland to return to their ancestral breeding sites? Why was such a magnificent creature part of the most tragic story of migration? Was it all in their instinctive drive to reproduce, only possible in fresh, cold water? But why had nature decreed it so? Their story was beautiful, beset by dangers which were overwhelming their kind. Yet in those dangers was the greatest beauty of all, for survival against such exigent pressures was magnificent.

How could he, John Howard, tell their story in the way it needed to be told? Would people really be interested in such a rarified event as a salmon run? It was people, after all, who allowed the destruction of such natural wonders as the Weald of Kent. If they did not care about something so obviously and tangibly beautiful then there was far less hope for wildlife which existed in a place remote from civilisation. Anyway, it was mankind which was exterminating the Atlantic salmon. Perhaps only a few fishermen would care about the decline. Though frustrated by these ideas, Johnny refused to abandon his desire to paint, in his way, the truth and wonder of it all. People destroyed because they could not see, he rationalised.

He saw. In snatches of grey and leaping silver he saw the spectacle of Loch Maree salmon in the driving rain and tumble of waves. On the edge of the River Kinlochewe's peat stain, where it flooded into the loch, marking the passage of its racing waters from the sodden hills, the few salmon gathered among shoals of sea-trout. Some arrowed into the river, abandoning Maree and making their bid for the high system while there was flow to guide them. Others waited, tasting the water from the hills. They lunged and cruised, the cock fish wielding the weapons of their kypes and sharply pointed tails, the hens swollen, courageously pressing at the powerful currents.

Where the salmon lay at the river mouth Johnny did not fish. He had caught salmon before on Loch Maree, in earlier years when they had been more abundant. Now, it seemed to him that it would be wrong to catch any of these last few of the year's run. Local people had told him that the summer grilse run had been very disappointing and at least half the fish seen had carried signs of the dreaded disease, UDN, and so were doomed to a slow, stifling death. The fish riding the rains of autumn were even fewer, though apparently disease-free.

Johnny fished for sea-trout well away from the river, though each day he spent several hours drifting, or pulled up on the shore, watching for the salmon, hoping that he would see greater numbers venturing into the flood. It was there that he saw the giant cock fish.

The wind had set from the north-west and for a few minutes it had stopped raining. Over his shoulder John could see dark clouds stacking, threatening to bring the next load of rain from the ocean. Ahead, towards where the boat quietly drifted, was the river mouth. All around him the loch's brown waters slurped and sucked under the wind while foam marks rose and dived, split and gnarled like eagles' talons. Flotsam from the hills littered the surface; minutiae from the peat moors, heather flowers and fragments of bark, twigs and whole branches, sheep wool and hooded crow feathers, weeds and grasses torn from river bed and bank. The occasional swirl or leap of a sea-trout marked the waves, exciting in their suddenness and violence. But then, less than a hundred yards offshore, the salmon broached. Heading downwind on the surface, the fish was oblivious to the presence of the boat only a few yards away. To the salmon the boat was just another piece of flotsam flecked upon the loch, drifting where the wind took it.

Johnny was astonished by the fish's size. It was frightening to see the great beast suddenly there in front of him, risen from the darkness. The head nudged out of the waves, itself as big as a sea-trout, then the broad shoulder and wide, long back. The salmon carried autumn colours, a red and chesnut patterning over bronze, with a scattering of large black dots. The fins were colossal. Dorsal fin erect, the salmon rolled through a wave, a motion which seemed so deliberate and slow; then the awesome sweep of tail, so powerful that Johnny could see the vortex spinning on the sloping wall of the wave. The fish was utterly master of his element. He rode the water, elegant despite his size, a perfect blend of fin, muscle and mystery.

There, home from the sea, was the greatest migrant on earth, twisting his deep flanks on the pitching surface. More than a migrant, to the young man who watched. Crystalised there, with that magnificent fish, was a meaning too enormous to express, wonderful as a dream, astonishing in reality. The mauve and black tail fin again sliced into the air; a wave, a wide, forked signal, gone in a sliding curve back into the deep.

The boat grated over rock and gravel, startling Johnny. Had it been that long? It must have been minutes since he had seen the fish, a hundred yards offshore. Now the boat was running broadside on to the beach by the river, spinning out of control in the current. He grabbed an oar and pushed at the boulders until the bows pointed out into the loch. A few pushes and he was out over water deep enough to start the engine. He paused, watching the river. The salmon would be in there now, Maree behind him. He would be shouldering into that smother of water from the hills.

And people did not care. He did. But he had seen that fish.

He was not alone, though he was leading and apart from those which followed, even the big hen fish. She had seen him pushing towards the river and she sensed that the time was right to make for the high system and the breeding redds. The smaller salmon hung behind them both. They listened to the river's voice becoming a savage roar around them as they left the relative peace of Loch Maree. The giant fish, ahead, were lost in the peaty turbulence, though the smaller salmon knew that if the leaders had decided to run the river the time was right to do so. If the fish from the Sgurr Dubh ran, then all salmon, the remaining few, should follow.

Behind them, behind the survivors, was the staggering gauntlet of dangers which had continuously threatened. Greenland's nets, fierce predators and devastating disease. Even in Loch Ewe these few had been lucky. The porpoise attack, the loathsome salmon cages and the flooding waters of the River Ewe, ripe for running, had driven them quickly through the sea-loch. Had they paused too long they would have wandered into one of the many illegal fixed gill-nets which poachers set along the shore, or been infected by UDN or furunculosis from the sick fish in the brackish water of the estuary.

Here, in the spate from the high system above Maree, they followed the ancient path which would lead to the Coulin chain and Bharranch. Despite his size and age, it would be the first time that the cock had returned to the redd from which he had hatched. Yet its taste was familiar to him, unquestioningly his home system, and it drew him more powerfully the closer towards it he swam. The peaty waters rushing across his flanks excited him and he drove into them with insurmountable purpose.

Where the river shallowed over a bar of gravel he shouldered up into the dazzling light so that he formed a wide bow-wave on the surface, his dorsal fin cutting through the air. His passage startled a wading heron, sending it into a croaking flight of panic; and it terrified a hunting bitch otter. She had heard his approach, his thrumming fins as loud as a shoal of sea-trout and, moment-arily, she had turned to attack. His kype had scythed towards her, his head dark and awesome, his hide leathery, dashed with the autumnal scarlet markings and diamond scales. He had rammed into her belly as she turned to flee. She twisted to bite, to defend herself from the largest fish she had ever encountered, but his tail slapped into her face and she was sent spluttering amid a burst of bubbles towards the river bank.

The otter had been but a brief nuisance to his passage. Nothing could stop him now in his need to reach Bharranch, and certainly not otters' teeth. Brown trout and sea-trout scattered from the pools through which he ran. The route opened for him, any hindrance falling away behind his tail. Though he could not see or feel them, he knew that the other salmon were following. Their scattered convoy wound through the sea-bound waters, opposing their journey. Yet the Kinlochewe was a portal to the spawning grounds. A shadow slunk over the river from the north-west, Beinn Eighe, and the river divided. Without hesi-tation the salmon forced his way into the westward flowing arm, A'Ghairbhe, where the current was strongest, though its taste was most familiar. His migration cycle was approaching its end.

Another migration, in its way as complex as the salmon's, was just beginning. John Howard drove his rusting, fifth-hand Austin Mini along the single-track road leading away from Maree. A resolve had taken him. He was determined to take a part-time job on a fishing boat. That, he thought, would be *living*. His friend Iain Sutherland in Kinlochewe had told him that his brother would take him as a crew-man on his trawler based in Mallaig on the west coast.

'Aye, I'll take ye on. I'm a wee bit short of crew these days,' the tired voice had said on the telephone. 'If brother Iain says ye'll do then I'll give ye a trial. We're off for a week or so up to Faroes day after tomorrow. Can ye get here afore then?'

He had telephoned his mother to tell her that he had got a job on a farm and that he would phone or be on his way home in a week or two. She had sounded worried, but had not questioned him too closely.

'You'll phone if you need help?'

'I will, Mum. See you soon.' He had hung up. He would tell her about the trawler when he got back. There was no point in worrying her until he was safely back on land.

The Mini chugged and misfired along the gruelling mountain roads on the elaborately twisting route between Kinlochewe and Mallaig, not sixty miles apart in a straight line, though nearer two hundred by road via Dingwall, Loch Ness and the Great Glen. Still it rained, so that John had to stop twice just to dry out the temperamental carburettor. But his spirit was light and he was thrilled at the prospect of going to sea. Most of his peers from Highgate would now be preparing for university or a job 'in the City', but he was headed for the trawler *Shadow of Skye*.

'I'm John Howard,' he shouted up towards the two figures on the deck. The harbour was busy with fishing boats, most of them small, though there was one other trawler, besides *Shadow of Skye*, berthed along the old stone quayside.

'So ye are,' called the shorter and older of the two men, 'and I'm skipper of the *Shadow*, Peter Sutherland.' He wore an oil-stained blue boilersuit and woollen cap. He grinned at the young man as if waiting for Johnny to say something more.

'We spoke on the phone yesterday morning ... '

'Aye we did that.'

'Yes. Er, can I come aboard?'

'Well, if ye're goin fishing wi' us, ye'd better had.'

With the deck of *Shadow of Skye* under his feet and his embarrassing introductions made, Johnny felt more at ease. Mr Sutherland and his partner, whose name was Michael Muckle (though Johnny could call him 'Mackerel' or Mac, as did everyone in Mallaig), talked in reserved and slightly sarcastic terms to the young man.

'I'll pay ye only half the going rate this trip, seeing as ye've no experience of fish and trawlers, and we'll see how ye get on. If ye're any use at all I might give ye another trip. Ye wouldnae be having a card would ye?'

Johnny looked puzzled.

'A Seaman's Card,' added Mackerel Muckle gruffly.

'Oh. No, I don't, I'm afraid.'

'Aye, I thought as much. We'll have to keep a wee bit quiet about that. Locals would nae like a foreigner fishing out of Mallaig, specially one without a card. Still, there's few enough local lads to employ. If the other boys ask then just say ye've moved up from Hull or some such English fishing port. Best stay on board *Shadow* for now and clear off quick when we get back. If ye're worth another trip we'll work it out from there.' Johnny thanked the two men for taking him on.

'Ach, ye'll no be thanking us after a week up north this time of year,' said Mackerel while he scratched his grey-stubbled chin.

'Aye, we'll see about that too,' put in Peter. 'Now, tell me how's brother Iain in that wee village of his? He speaks well of ye . . . ' He pulled Johnny aside as Mackerel went below to make the tea, muttering something about having an English 'green hand' on board, as if there could be nothing worse than that.

The week that followed was a concentrated mixture of pain, discomfort and exhilaration. It began as the *Shadow* slid out from Mallaig on an almost mirror-calm sea. She was alone in the early morning light, a scarlet glow following her out from the mainland. The islands were lit with deepest red and purple so that they smouldered like tired but active volcanoes. It was not Maree with the astonishing sky of an autumn dawn, but it was nonetheless, he thought, breathtakingly beautiful.

'Ach, Johnny,' shouted Mackerel from the wheelhouse amidships, 'will ye stop yer day-dreaming and get to making breakfast.'

Down in the cramped galley, just aft of the sleeping quarters the noise of the Perkins engine was a constant thud, though somehow reassuring. It had been cold on deck. Down here there was a steamy heat, a comforting cocoon of smelly warmth which Johnny was soon to come to yearn for during a prolonged spell at the nets or the icy fish hold.

As he slapped thick rashers of bacon and kippers into the huge frying pan he surveyed the sleeping men. In the widest bunk, farthest from him, was Peter Sutherland, tufts of white hair poking from beneath his woollen cap which apparently he wore more or less all the time. His blankets were pulled untidily over him and he snored, open-mouthed and abandoned in his own whisky-induced dreams.

The twins, Bill and Hugh Fraser, inevitably known as Bill and Ben, were also asleep on their tiny bunks, one either side of the gangway. As he cracked some eggs into the pan Johnny mused that though they were twins they were not any more alike than you would expect ordinary brothers to be. Bill was smaller framed than Ben and had darker hair. He spoke, also, with a coarser accent, more Glaswegian than Highland.

Besides Johnny's and Mackerel's there was another empty bunk, up near Peter's. This belonged to Hector, 'Little Weed', all six feet and two inches of him, at that moment up with Mackerel in the wheelhouse. Like Bill and Ben, Hector had been a crewman on board the *Shadow* for several seasons, but quite unlike his crew-mates he spoke very little. 'And when he does speak,' Mackerel had explained the evening before, 'it's to say something that makes a bit of sense. Ye listen out for our Hector, Johnny, he's a good man.' Hector was the most enigmatic of the crew, very strong and nimble about the deck, and expressionless for most of the time. Even when the twins began their regular expletive-coloured banter, barely a smile lit his face.

The kettle was hissing away on the stove while the bacon, kippers and eggs swilled noisily in the pan's fat. There was a thumping over his head. It was Mackerel stamping on the wheelhouse floor announcing that he was ready for a cup of tea and breakfast. Johnny ladled out two platefuls of the delicious-smelling mixture, taking care not to crack the egg yolks, as Mackerel had insisted, and carried them up the companionway to the wheelhouse.

'About bloody time too. A man could die of starvation on this deck.' Mackerel had an unfriendly expression on his face as he glanced at Johnny. 'And where's the soddin' tea? I cannae eat breakfast without a cuppa.'

'Yes, all right, Mac, but I couldn't carry the plates and the cups together. I'd spill all the tea ... '

'Will ye listen to the poor lad,' said Mackerel, feigning exaggerated surprise. 'He cannae manage plates and cups together without spilling the tea. Well, ye'd better bloody well learn quick, like all the other duties on this boat.' Johnny fled below for the tea. Mackerel shouted after him. 'And wake the others for their breakfast. Tell Peter we're jist coming around Dunvegan on Skye.' Johnny could not stop himself glancing across the sea before he went below. The light was strong now and the Minch was gently rolling, like a series of foothills reaching towards the mountains beyond. Those peaks belonged to Skye; they made up the jagged range of the Cuillins which towered above landscapes Johnny knew, and lochs where salmon still swam.

'I want that hold so clean it could cure ye of the clap!' Between them, Peter and Mackerel were tough on the crew. Johnny felt they were more especially hard on him, because he was a green hand and they were knocking him into shape. They were also tough on themselves, putting as many hours as the younger men into the pre-fishing chores.

The Outer Hebrides lay far behind them now and the Atlantic heaved with a big September swell. Out of sight of land, Johnny had been sea sick for the first time in his life. Five times he had vomited, until his stomach was empty and his throat burnt with bile.

'Ach, that'll clear the land from ye,' Peter had explained. 'Ye just sit down and work on deck with the nets a while until ye get over it.' Johnny felt ghastly, near death, marooned on that awful, lumpy sea amid diesel fumes and the smell of fish and frying food. 'Ye just have to get the rhythm of it.' Mackerel and the twins had laughed at him and in his grim sickness Johnny did not have the strength to retaliate to their cruelly humoured comments.

'Hey, our green hand's truly green,' taunted Bill. 'Have ye any other colours to show us, Johnny?'

'Maybe we should call him "Green-gills",' persisted Ben. 'Lad's got to have a name better than Johnny. What about "Puke"?' His freckled face looked thoughtful. 'Yeah, Puke, I like that.'

Towards the end of their second day at sea, however, the

tilting and plunging foredeck gradually ceased to be physically disorientating. It was not so much that it had a rhythm to it, he reasoned, as that his muscles yielded to its motion and his stomach and head seemed to sit in their proper places. After many yards of amorphous net had been disentangled and mended, as Hector had shown him, his hunger returned, as well as a deepening empathy, rather than dread, for the open ocean.

John had had no idea that there could be so many jobs to be done by a trawler's crew when it was not actually engaged in fishing. Nets, ropes and trawling equipment were virtually interminable and needed almost constant attention if they were to function at their best. Despite his sickness, Mackerel called on him to take his turn in the galley and prepare astonishing quantities of food and tea. As he found his sea-legs, however, probably because of enforced sessions of work and cooking, he discovered just how it was that six men could devour so much food. The work at sea produced voracious appetites.

The fish hold made him shiver. It was wet and smelly, a steel compartment painted ice-blue, cold to touch and cold to the eye. Refrigeration pipes criss-crossed the walls and ceiling while plastic and wooden fish boxes were untidily stacked in all four corners. It was an enormous, heartless box, like a crypt. He stood with his back against one wall, between pipes, surveying the hold's bleakness under the light of two powerful, wire-enmeshed bulbs. In one hand he held a scrubbing brush, a stiff-bristled broom in the other. As he watched the only glimmer of hope in the entire hold, the half-open deck hatch in the ceiling beyond the steel ladder, he wondered as he had done several times during this, his first working sea-voyage, why on earth he had decided to commit himself to the misery of it.

Ben's face appeared at the hatch.

'Hose is coming down and I'm switching on the pump. So get scrubbing.' No sooner had the hose hit the floor than cold sea water spat from it and snaked fiercely around the hold, drenching Johnny, despite his waterproofs and boots. He grabbed it and pointed it at the pipes and boxes, scrubbing and jetting away the accumulated layers of fish slime and scales and dirty ice from the last trip.

When Ben again flung open the hatch and told him that his supper was ready he was astonished at how much time had passed. He had gone into the hold after lunch and now, as his aching muscles pulled him to the top of the ladder it was dusk. Out of the dank hold he paused to survey the sea, reaching and rolling out towards hidden horizons. The motion of it, beneath the peach and orange of the western sky, a silky swell on which the *Shadow* slid alone, was hypnotic. Just for a moment Johnny thought of other dusks, on Maree, with a falling wind leaving only a groundswell on the loch and the satin glow on the water, while sea-trout and salmon shouldered up towards the shallows. It was extraordinary to think that salmon swam here too, hundreds of miles from their home waters, crossing the sea to find the richest feeding grounds that existed, packing on muscle and learning the wisdom of long-distance migration through this desolate sweep of ocean. So too was John migrating and learning of things remote from everyday experience.

With Peter Sutherland at the wheel the crew sat in the tight confines of the galley and eating area. The air was thick with water vapour and the smells of cooking, blue with tobacco smoke and foul language. Bill and Ben had been arguing and teasing Mackerel.

'Silly sods,' he said looking directly at Johnny. 'Honestly, lad, the rubbish I see coming to sea nowadays. These two are no better than lobster bait and ye'll need a bitty more muscle before ye's much use.'

John smiled at the sarcasm. His attention was caught by Mackerel's hand clasping his pipe. The middle finger was missing.

'How did you lose your finger, Mac?'

'Ach, it's as well ye ask before we start the trawling. Winch got it. Bastard. One on the *Shadow* herself – port-aft winch, it was. I were laying rope off the trawl on to the winch and didn't shift me hand fast enough.' Johnny grimaced.

'Aye, nipped it clean off as the rope bit. So fast as I hardly noticed what had happened till the blood shot everywhere. Funny thing though, I saw my finger flip off over the side. Odd sort of a sight.'

'What did you do – I mean, didn't you have to get to hospital or something?'

'No, lad, there's no point in hospital for a finger that's cut clean off. Ye just tie the stump off and bandage it all up and try

137

and forget it. It's worse if ye just crush it like Bill did in his first season with us.'

Johnny looked inquiringly at Bill who reached out his right hand. It was the first time Johnny had noticed that he too had lost a finger, the little one.

'Trapped it in the winch same as Mac, but the bastard got crushed rather than cut off nice and clean. Hurt like bloody hell, man. Worst thing was these bastards wouldn't take me in to port to have it seen to, even though we were close to Stornoway. They waited till they'd finished a bloody day's trawl. Christ, I was fair bloody screaming with the pain of it.' Ben and Mackerel let out long whoops of laughter at the memory of it and Johnny joined in, despite the macabre nature of it all.

Mackerel wiped a tear from his eye. 'Aye, as I told ye, it's all rubbish coming to sea today. Lads that can't take a wee bit of pain.' When the laughter had subsided the old man looked more seriously at Johnny. 'Anyway, let it be a lesson to ye. Always keep yer limbs moving when the net's out and watch fer them bastard winches 'n ropes. They'll cut ye up or throw ye over-board if ye give 'em a chance.'

When the whisky came out and Hector went up to relieve Peter at the helm, Johnny felt an overwhelming tiredness sweep over him. Those days had been exhausting and he could not imagine how it could get harder when the fishing began.

'Ach, but ye'll find out tomorrow when we go for the first trawl,' Mackerel reminded him. 'Ye'd best tuck yer poor wee self into bed just now while we men does a serious bitty drinking.' Johnny did not need to be invited. He hauled himself painfully to his bunk. Without bothering to take off his clothes, now dry on him, he simply undid the button and flies of his jeans, tucked himself into the coffin-like confines of the bunk and was asleep in moments. The murmuring conversation, the thrumming engine and gentle thud of the bows in the swell were the last, fading sounds he sensed as he slipped into unconciousness.

Peaks of islands stood out ahead, like the summits of a mountain range above cloud. Faint, pastel greens and browns shone through the misty-grey Atlantic like a watercolour. It was midday yet the light was like that of early evening. The sea and islands had the atmosphere of the north – cold and washed out.

Winter lay not many weeks away here and Johnny shuddered as he felt the keen wind from the Arctic slice through his waterproofs. He looked back at the wheelhouse where Peter stood at the helm, glancing at the echo-sounder, then towards the islands or the compass bearing. Johnny and the three other young men stood by the nets and otter-boards waiting for Peter's command while Mackerel leant against the wheelhouse, glaring at his deckhands.

'Stand-to now, m' lads, wait for it, wait till Peter gets a sound of them haddocks.'

For once the twins were silent and the only human sounds to be heard were Mackerel's mutterings. Above the engine thud emerged the sucking lurch of the *Shadow*'s slow passage. The Faroe islands hung surreally ahead and Johnny found it impossible to guess how far away they were. Just one of them, Suduroy, stood out to starboard and he could tell that it was no more than a few miles off, but the others, to the north, were like mirages ...

'Right, lads, that's it, *nets away*.' And so began the tumbling, exhausting work of shooting, working and retrieving a trawl. Johnny had been briefed as to what was expected of him and within minutes of starting the exertion was almost overwhelming so that he took recourse in the routine, shutting out the pain of thought. Everything appeared suddenly gigantic and incredibly fast. There he was in the epicentre of some tumultuous action where the seas parted with a great explosion as the spreader boards hit them and the unyielding net increased in weight beyond comprehension; the ropes, too thick for his twinned grip, hissing out, burning and chaffing through his rubber gloves; the trawler's creaming, spuming wake as she curved across the sea, dragging her net while the propellor revolutions increased until there was a terrible vibration which threatened to tear the *Shadow* apart.

She staggered under her load and the swell caught her. The men had braced themselves for the impact as the net bit at the sea. Except for Johnny; he stumbled and slid across the deck on his back, ramming his shoulder against the port-side gunnel. He rolled over, struggling to find his feet, to meet a wave in his face, sending him gliding across to the other gunnel.

'Will ye stop yer fuckin' swimming practice and get on these ropes,' came Mackerel's lashing reprimand. His fingers entwined in more netting, he pulled himself upright and half ran, half floated towards where Hector was lashing rope on to a ferociously spinning winch.

'Watch yer hands now, Puke,' shouted the big man. 'Watch how I do it.' But then Johnny could watch nothing but the trawl as it bulged in the sea to aft while the derrick stanchions creaked dangerously under the load. 'Aye, now, that's a good first run.' Hector had not once looked back, concentrating as he was on the rope and winch, but the way the trawler had slowed under the weight and the stanchion strain described to him the quality of the catch.

Extraordinarily like a bull's testicles, the trawl net hung beneath the derricks, heavy with a brown and white amorphous mass. Johnny and the twins grabbed at the base of the net and began to exert their combined weight into swinging it above the hold.

'Aye, aye, that's it, break the string now,' called Mackerel. Johnny and Ben grabbed the retaining ropes while Bill macheted the purse rope. The haddock, bulge-eyed and bronze, burst from the net with a roar, their tonnage spilling down into the hold amid spray, slithering slime and scales.

Peter had flung the helm over and the *Shadow* heeled until the seas sliced on board along the port side. In the mist the islands dipped and rose again, like whale backs. Spray lashed into Johnny's face, but there was no cold in him now. He felt a trickle of hot sweat running between his shoulders and down his back and his biceps burnt with their delicious tightness. There was a dull ache in his shoulder where he had rammed the gunnel, but his body and mind were hyperactive now. Pain and fear, even in the wildly lurching *Shadow of Skye* in the deep groundswell, were further away from him than they had ever been.

'Next net, lads,' came Mackerel's order as the boat came on to an even keel and she raced off towards the south-west, now with the islands astern. 'C'mon, lift the fucker up.' Bill and Ben shouldered Johnny from either side and he heard them grunt and puff, teeth clenched, as they all lifted the spreader boards and the first pile of netting. Behind them Hector and Mackerel worked on the other trawl jaw. 'Now, lads, away she goes.' They heaved. And again the wham as the seas met the vast net and apparatus and the ropes whistling and sizzling; again the curving sweep of the trawler and racing vibration shaking the steel and wood of the boat and the men's hot limbs. 'Hang to now, Puke, 'less ye want another wee swim.' He did not need to be reminded. As the deck juddered at his feet and the seas in the trawler's wake were a raging spume and tumble, Johnny held tightly to the stanchion rig. 'The sea's packed with the haddocks tighter 'n Elspeth McKinnon's drawers!' bellowed Mackerel. Bill and Ben sang out with the joy of it all, for thought of their bonus, for their sheer, magnificent pleasure, while Johnny, caught up in the orgiastic thrill of it, shrieked wildly, grabbing for the ropes without needing to be told what to do, laying loops over the whirring, smoking winches.

Much later, after more trawl runs than Johnny could remember, he sat slumped over the galley table. It was dark outside, and had been for the last two runs when the net had come in almost empty. They had lost the haddock shoal, but not before they had half filled the packing-hold. Mackerel was up at the wheel while the rest of them groaned and moved about stiffly after their exertion. Peter did the cooking and hummed a tune, breaking off every now and then to comment on the day's work.

'Aye. That's always a good reef if ye can find it. Always stiff with the haddocks at this time of year and with the cods a wee bit later.'

Johnny raised his head from his arms. 'Reef, were we near a reef?'

'Right plumb above it, lad. Fifteen fathoms or thereabouts. Aye, it's a grand mark and I'll thank ye to keep quiet about it back in Mallaig, else them other fuckers'll be up here soon as the fishing back home dries up.'

'I haven't got very much idea even where we are, Peter. Somewhere off Suduroy, Faroes. How far off the island were we?'

Peter laughed: 'Too fuckin' close so the rules say, but not so close as the Russians go in. Anyway, those Danes don't worry about a little trawl like the *Shadow*. We're in and out again before they see us.' He broke happily into one of his sea ditties. Then, for the first time, Johnny winced at the pain in his shoulder.

'Complaining about a wee tap on the shoulder?' said Bill. 'Take a look at that.' He brandished his forearm for Johnny to see. There was a weeping gape of skinless flesh where a rope had chafed.

'C'mon then, Puke,' put in Ben. 'Let's be seeing yer wounds.' They helped Johnny out of his smock and woollen sweaters, then the wet tee-shirt. Ben whistled exaggeratively when he saw Johnny's shoulder. 'Aye, right enough, he's a one for pretty colours is our Johnny Puke. See, he's got a right lovely blue and purple now!'

With haddock, chips and whisky heavy in him Johnny sat half asleep in his chair. At last his incredible hunger was satisfied and only whisky slipped down his throat. The pain in his shoulder was now again only a dull ache.

'Why do you come all the way to the Faroes, Peter?' he slurred. It had been puzzling him for days. 'I mean, there must be good fishing in Scottish waters.'

But Peter was asleep, his pipe still hanging from his mouth, glass still half full in his hand. It was Hector who spoke.

'There's too many fishermen in Scotland, Johnny. It's not like the old days when there was enough fish for them all. Now they have to struggle. They fish right up to the beaches. Sometimes the fishes they catch are all immatures, poor wee sods, and the herring's almost gone from the North Sea.' He spoke slowly, his voice deep. 'So Peter and Mac reckon its worth the extra fuel to put up to Faroes or Iceland for the cod and haddock. Ye can see how fast the fishing is up here. To get a load like that back home ye'd have to fish more 'n a week. We'll have a few more runs tomorrow and then make for home.'

'Aye with a nice fat pay-off back in Mallaig and my Eileen waiting to spend it with me,' sighed Bill.

'Waiting, my arse,' put in Ben. 'Eileen'll be shagging some dirty sod right at this moment and then she'll spend all of his money.'

'Ach, ye're both silly sods,' interrupted Hector. 'Ye work your skin off on the fishing then spend it all on girls and whisky back home. Where's the sense in it?'

But it all made an odd sense to Johnny as he closed his eyes and allowed sleep and fantasy to play with his mind. There was the girl from Cumbria, Lizzie, who worked the summer season in Kinlochewe hotel. Her dark, flowing hair and her sexy eyes taunted him, forming lewd images in his mind. She had been the first woman he had loved in that way, had actually managed to undress and . . . The memory of it, in the essentially male world of the *Shadow*'s galley, brought a welcome heaviness to him and he pulled himself across to his bunk, drew up the blankets, and lost himself in sleep and dreams.

Six more runs had filled the holds and the *Shadow of Skye* had turned south-east. During the long voyage home, with south-westerly winds creaming the seas across the bow, the four younger men had been occupied with the awesome chore of cleaning and packing the fish. Johnny resigned himself to the wet misery of being surrounded and awash with haddock, either on deck or in the dank hold. The amorphous mass of fish had to be sorted by size and crated. The six-pound class had to be gutted and filleted.

'There's more cash in the fillets,' explained Hector. 'They go straight to market. The rest go to the brokers and processing factories.'

'Why don't we fillet all of them, then?' asked Johnny.

'Ach, that's the housewives,' replied Mackerel. 'They like them just the right size. They don't want sides off them titchy haddocks and a thick cut off the big fellers won't fit in the pan nice. Too big or small and we send 'm for processing.'

After two days sailing the haddock were graded and stacked ready for off-loading. Overcoming his weariness, Johnny felt pleasure and pride in seeing the chore completed and neatly accomplished; the three- and four-pound fish crated and layered with ice, the creamy-white fillets in thick, translucent rows, and the big haddock up to sixteen pounds in weight, only six to the crate, laid side by side, head to tail; a deep-sea trawler's protein-packed prize.

And Johnny had helped assemble that magnificent haul from the sea.

On the morning tide, nine days after she had left Mallaig, the *Shadow of Skye* pondered down the North Minch. At last the work was done and Johnny was free to wander about on deck. Mackerel and Hector were with him while Peter and Ben were at the helm. Bill was below looking at some of his enormous collection of girly magazines.

'He's just warming himself up for that wee lassie,' explained Mackerel with a grin. 'She'd knock anything off if there was a bit of cash in it. Not like his brother at all. Ben now, he's got a nice kirk girl who holds his hand like and maybe allows him a bit of a grope on a Saturday night. Aye, they'll be married in a year or two.'

The Scottish mainland rose off to port and something gripped in Johnny's throat as he watched. The hills beyond Enard Bay and the little summer islands dotting the bay itself, then southwards, beyond Greenstone and Rubha Reidh Points, were the great Torridon peaks which marked the way to *his* place, his most treasured place, Loch Maree. Tomorrow he would drive back to the loch from Mallaig, to Iain Sutherland's house. Like the salmon, he was coming home.

Peter guided *Shadow of Skye* under the shelter of Rona, low and lean like a sturgeon's back awash in the sea, and ran her down the Inner Sound, past Scalpay to Kyle of Lochalsh. The current raced them past Kyleakin lighthouse. Peter and Mackerel waved at the ferry captains and began quipish conversations on the radio with other fishing boats in the area. Johnny heard only snatches of the banter, for as they pressed down the narrow Sound of Sleat he saw the village of Glenelg. He strained to pick out recognisable marks along the coast, for this was Maxwell's country, where *Ring of Bright Water* had been created. He had visited Lower Sandaig, which Maxwell had called Camusfearna, though he had never seen it from the sea.

He saw the skerries, necklaced by white water, within the bay, the Bay of Alders. Johnny could see the mark of the burn, where the otters had played, where it entered the sea, and the bared foundations of the ruined house where the magical book had been written; another man's dream. He was aware of Mackerel at his side.

'Ye know this place, Johnny?'

'I've been here. A man called Gavin Maxwell lived in a house, there.' He pointed at the grass-covered mound half-way along the bay.

'Aye, Major Maxwell and his otters.'

Johnny looked at Mackerel, surprised that he should be interested in Camusfearna and the man who had lived there. But then Lower Sandaig was only a little way up the coast from Mallaig. Everyone in those parts would have known of Maxwell, for in the last years of his life he had become one of the most famous men in the Highlands and islands.

'Ach, he was a strange man that one. Ye know he had a shark fishery?'

'Yes, on Soay.'

Mackerel grunted. 'Damn fool venture, if ye ask me. A shark fishery!'

Camusfearna lay far astern, but still Johnny's stare took in the lie of hills reaching above the bay. The sitka spruce were taller than he remembered. They had not even been planted when Maxwell lived there. How things changed. How quickly dreams became crueller in their passing or in their realisation.

In Mallaig, the unloading was accomplished quickly and the young men on the *Shadow of Skye* hurried to gather their possessions and dash off to their respective homes.

'Be seeing ye, Puke,' called Bill. 'Mind ye don't let yer lass grab that nasty shoulder too tight.' He and Ben rushed off along the quayside.

'Here's your money.' Peter casually lifted a wad of bank notes and pushed them quickly into the breast pocket of Johnny's shirt. 'It's the full whack, seeing as ye was not so useless as I thought ye might be.' It had taken Johnny by surprise. He stood mutely in front of the trawler captain. 'Mackerel and I were wondering if ye'd like the next trip.'

In all his life until that moment Johnny had never received a compliment he treasured more than the one just given him by Peter Sutherland. He knew how hard he had worked, could feel it in his aching limbs and tired muscles; but it meant the world to him, then, that Peter too knew of his efforts. He felt that he had earnt his place as a man in a man's world.

'Yes, Peter. Thank you.'

After making his goodbyes, Johnny walked towards the town where he had left his Mini. Two youths, one a redhead and the other a short, mean-looking character with his hands in the pockets of his jeans, barred his way at the entrance to a narrow side-street. They sneered at him.

'Who the fuck are ye?' asked the redhead. 'Been working on the *Shadow*, have ye?' The other lad made an exhibition of sniffing, clearing his throat and spitting. Johnny looked down at his boots where the thick gob had landed. Something in him was tightening while at the same time he could feel his grip ease on his bag so that he could drop it and hurl himself at the gum-chewing youths. It was not a fear of the two thugs. Rather, it was rage at having to be confronted by them, after all he had been through during the last nine days.

'We hear ye're an English bastard. Me and me mate here don't like the English, see.' He prodded a thick finger into Johnny's chest. 'It's only us Scots work the fishing boats.' The bag fell to the ground and Johnny's fists clenched. Even as he raised his arms to strike there was a hand on his shoulder, pressing him down firmly. It was Hector at his side.

'His name's John and he's a good deck-hand, so why don't ye lad's fuck off and do somethin' useful?' There was a heavy threat in the voice. In an instant the thugs backed down.

'Yeah, well if *ye* say so, Hector,' mumbled the redhead. 'Just asking the lad ... ' They shuffled uneasily into the main street and were soon lost among the crowds of shoppers and fishermen.

'Folks hate change, Johnny,' explained Hector. 'Those lads are too daft to sort out work for themselves. They see a new lad in town as a threat. Scotland's changing so much just now. The fishing's changing, and most of it for the worse.' He patted Johnny on the shoulder. 'I'll be seeing ye in a few days, then.' Johnny watched him walking off among the crowds, his huge frame conspicuous among the more ordinary builds. Of course times were changing and the world was a violent place, as terrible as it was beautiful. He noticed a telephone kiosk and made up his mind to call his mother. He had spoken to her ten days ago. He felt that he had aged ten years.

13

It was late November and colour had drained out of the land until only grey and burnt-out brown remained. The water in the Sgurr Dubh burn above Loch Bharranch ran in a leaden glide until it pressed over the gravel bar where it gurgled and hissed down to the loch. The young man had walked the half mile across the rough moor from the single-track road that wound along Glen Torridon. By the burn he knelt among some shrivelled heather watching where the salmon lay.

They were the biggest salmon Johnny had ever seen, a cock and a hen, the only two fish in the burn. Despite their size, only someone who was used to watching fish would have been able to see them. They lay almost stationary, the giant male slightly above and ahead of the hen, his tail brushing the thickness of her flank. The white gash of their mouths showed briefly as each drew water across their gills, then their torpedo shapes hovered darkly in the flow, the russet, black, and brown patterning of their backs and sides camouflaging them against the stream bed.

Surely, thought Johnny, the cock fish must have been the same one he had seen in Loch Maree, entering the river mouth during the September flood. He had not seen, or heard of, another salmon so large in the system. The hen fish would be a thirty pounder, especially with the load of ova within her which she had carried up from the sea. The male was bigger, perhaps thirty-five pounds, with enormous, weapon-like fins and re-curved kype. He looked dangerous, poised for violent movement, finned muscle wafting against the burn's feeble flow, built for currents greater by far.

So this was where the big Maree fish spawned, above Bhar-ranch. Johnny wondered why they did not run the other arm of the system, up beyond Clair and into the Coulin. But then this arm was more remote, almost hidden beneath the black peak.

As his eyes became more attuned to the slight motions the salmon made, Johnny noticed that the hen fish bore twin scars, well healed, slicing down the lower part of her right flank towards her tail fin. An otter's teeth had layed those scars when she had been a mere grilse on her first spawning run into Maree. On that same run, while still in Loch Ewe, she had swum into a fixed net and escaped only because of a weak link in the mesh which burst as she had struggled. That encounter too had laid a ring of scar tissue around her body, just forward of her dorsal fin. These slight marks made her recognisable. She would carry them for life. The cock fish, however, bore no noticeable scars. He would always be recognisable by his unusual size, of course, and the deep spread of his fins. Large hen-salmon were rare, large cock-salmon were almost unheard of because of the much higher proportion of fatalities among male kelts compared with the females.

At least this fish would not have to fight other males for the right to be on the spawning redd. There were no others in the Sgurr Dubh burn and even if there were they would not dare to contest the rights with the huge cock fish. His energy could be directed towards digging the redds, hollows a foot deep, in the gravel and guiding the female in the spawning act.

Johnny watched. The cold made his teeth chatter and limbs tremble, as the salmon began excavating the gravel. Hanging downstream the female also watched as the male twisted on to his side, seeming to double his size when viewed broadside, and drove his tail into the stones. Johnny could feel the thud of it through the peaty soil and could hear the rattle and crack of pebbles clashing and tumbling. A cloud of silt puffed up into the stream. When it had gone, after the tail had whacked and shovelled a few times more, Johnny could see the hollow that had been dug, flanked and backed by a rim of stones. The salmon curved in the stream and dropped down to where the hen fish swam. He nudged at her belly, forcing her upwards until she was poised above the redd. There she dropped, three-quarters of her body falling into the hollow so that only her head and tail protruded. She arched as the male's kype stroked her flank and a jet of pink-orange eggs shot from her ovipositor. A kick of her tail and she had shrugged herself free of the redd. In an instant the cock fish lay where she had been and the water beneath his tail whitened with milt, gushing across the eggs which lay beneath the current's force. A few seconds later and his tail was again working at the gravel, this time more gently as it dextrously scooped the rim of gravel into the hollow, above its precious cargo.

The first redd of the year was set in the Sgurr Dubh burn, and Johnny had seen its mystery take shape. What remained, after the salmon had together pushed upstream to work on another redd, appeared as little more than a mound in the gravel, though the young man knew what promise lay hidden beneath that insignificant mark. It was more than just fertilised salmon eggs, it was the potential for a race of salmon quite apart from others; huge, heavily patterned, wide-finned giants, as different from grilse as a deep-sea trawler from a lobster boat.

'Ye'll do best to keep quiet about it,' advised Iain Sutherland later. 'There's folk around that would not be content in watching the salmon. Poachers from away down the Glen.'

'But the salmon are going dark now. No one would want stale fish, surely?'

'Not good rod and line fishers, no, but they would do a poacher very nicely. Ideal for smoking. Do ye realise how much they're worth if they're as heavy as ye say?' Johnny knew that salmon fetched high prices, even those that had been in fresh water for a month or two, darkening their sea-coat. As Iain said, big salmon were ideal for cold smoking and selling in Glasgow or London as 'smoked wild Scotch salmon'. There was even a black market for them, their anonymous, traceless flesh sold through the back doors of expensive restaurants and hotels.

'Well, ye'd not see change from five pounds for a pound of that flesh. Say thirty pounds weight in each fish; that's three hundred pounds in a man's pocket for a bit of fishing that would take him ten minutes.' Iain drew on his pipe and pushed his feet a bit nearer the peat fire. The croft was quiet except for Mrs Sutherland pottering in the kitchen.

'My brother tells me that ye've taken pretty well to the fishing.'

'Peter's a good skipper. Everyone in Mallaig likes him.'

'Aye, he's a popular soul,' Iain concurred. 'But he wouldn't have ye on his boat if ye were no use. And neither would Mackerel Muckle.'

Johnny grinned as he thought of the partners and the *Shadow*'s crew. No, none of them would tolerate a fool in their midst. He knew he fitted in among them, despite the fact that he came from southern England. But he would not be with them all his working life. He, and they, knew that.

'Have ye plans, Johnny?'

Plans, how many times had he tried to make those? He was almost twenty years old and while his friends back in England seemed to be settling nicely into university courses or promising careers, he was in northern Scotland, with no structure to his future. No matter how much he loved working on the *Shadow of Skye* a career as a trawlerman was not what old George Sellick at Highgate had meant when he had said that Johnny would do something with his life, with his love of nature. What of his writing, the venturous steps he had taken with his articles for *Trout and Salmon*? Four had been published and another four returned to be 'polished and updated', which, he suspected, meant that they were not really up to standard. *Country Living* had returned an article of his on the subject of the river bank in summer with the explanation that it did not fit in with the editorial plans for that year. But he had made a beginning and felt that this was the direction he should take. Back in his room in London were reams of his writing, going all the way back to his first grammar-defying efforts; his poorly scanning verses and overflowing prose. Here, in Scotland, he had done very little writing, but the images danced around so vividly in his mind, even shaping themselves with words and phrases.

'I'm going home to see Mum for Christmas,' he said. 'Peter has promised me the winter season on the *Shadow* and the hotel say they want a ghillie for the loch when the salmon and sea-trout run in the summer ...'

'Aye, but what plans for your life, laddie? Ye should be thinking about that just now. Once you've left your teens life rushes by too quickly.'

'Next year,' explained Johnny, 'I thought I might go to university, if I can get in, and read a science subject. Biology or chemistry maybe.'

'Now that would sort ye out a proper career.'

'What is wrong with fishing as a career, then, Iain?'

'Nothing, lad, if ye happen to be born to it. Ye love it right enough, and ye know more about them salmon and trout than any man I ever met, but ye are not born to be a trawlerman. It's not that it'd be a waste exactly ...' The elderly man frowned. 'But ye might feel ye have something more to offer than catching cod and haddock for the rest of your life.'

That was the trouble. Right now Johnny felt that life as a deep-sea trawlerman was all he desired. He had his friends in Scotland while those back in England were drifting away from him. The way of life, too, was so much more exciting, more urgent, allowing him to use his body and his mind. He saw things that life back in London barely even allowed him to imagine. And now that they were carving up Kent, laying waste that glorious green richness of the place, there seemed nothing for him down there.

While there was Kinlochewe and the *Shadow*, while there was summer work as a ghillie on Loch Maree and other sea-trout and salmon fisheries in the area – while there was Lizzie who would have him whenever he returned from a trawling trip – so long as there were the mountains and swathes of moorland and the wild, wild sea, all gathering in his mind, one day for him to write about as Maxwell had done ... Well, he knew he was wandering in the right direction.

His instinct told him this. It might also have told him that he was wandering before the storm. The terrible storm was gathering. He had seen it in the decline of the salmon. Even the sea-trout were not so numerous as they had once been, especially the larger fish. He had discovered from Mackerel and Peter why it was so necessary for the *Shadow* to venture ever farther from Scottish or even European waters, up into Scandinavian fishing grounds; Norway, Faroes and Iceland.

'Ach, there's trouble gathering here,' Mackerel had explained when a grey and sinister gun-boat had appeared astern on their last trip to Icelandic waters for the prize of big cod. 'Those boys are getting pretty sore at us lot coming up from Scotland and taking their fish. They want us to stay offshore, where there aren't so many cod.' Mackerel had shaken his fist in the direction of the shadowing gun-boat. 'Aye, it was a different story when those bastards were emptying the North Sea of our herrin's.' The fact that it was the Danes rather than the Icelanders who had been most responsible for wiping out the herring stocks had escaped Mackerel. To him all foreigners, including the English, were to be blamed equally for wrecking the fishing close to home.

It was not only fish stocks. Everything now seemed to be adversely affected by what Johnny saw as man's incursions. Charlotte had sent him some newspaper cuttings on the subject of conservation. One of them was an article called 'Spaceship Earth' and he was quite taken by the concept: the entire planet could be likened to a single spaceship, all systems needing to work perfectly if the mission was to succeed, even to survive; and how the systems were breaking down on earth, threatening the success, the viability and the survival of the massive spaceship. It *was* like that. Maxwell had said as much, Johnny had seen as much.

As corpuscles in the living body of the earth the salmon swam and were threatened by anything which threatened the body. As their numbers dwindled so the body weakened ... Hell, it was happening no matter how you dressed it up. What mattered was whether or not it could be stopped.

The peat on the fire hissed and the wind was moaning across the moorland and through the beech trees in Kinlochewe. Iain Sutherland, a tamer and gentler version of his sea-going brother, was nodding off to sleep while the flickering glow lit his wrinkled, Highlander features. Mrs Sutherland wandered through the sitting room with a pile of plates for the cabinet. She smiled at Johnny as she passed. He loved these people of Wester Ross and Invernesshire. There was a kindness which oozed from them and marked their features with an aspect you so rarely saw in southern England.

There was time; time enough to learn enough and to love enough.

The water slipped beneath the mounting wind, cold and silvered in moonlight. The two big salmon were dropping, slowly and with ponderous effort, down towards Loch Maree. Behind them, high up the glen, above Loch Bharranch, their redds lay still as death, though what the gravel hid was the vitality of embryonic life, sleeping in the silence. It had taken almost the last of their own lives to set those redds, to spawn in the climax of their migration. Now the world spun them, jostled their fleshy flanks, tilted them on rushing, heartless floods. Lesser males, carrying less energy in the diminished protein of their muscles, would allow the exhaustion and the cold to finally tilt their bodies until they scraped and slid on gravel, coming to rest in stiffened, emaciated death. Even the hen fish struggled to retain their balance on the currents, their last protein store burning up to afford some of them enough energy to find the sea.

Two ghostly shapes, side by side, slid into Loch Maree from the river mouth. Here, eight feet below the surface, in stillness, they hung, jaws gulping at the oxygen-rich water, gills and fins splayed. Even so their purchase was poor and their passage down the north-east shore discontinuous. The cock fish lay his wide tail on a boulder, his head up towards the moonlight reflected off the snow-clad slopes of Slioch. His long body was set in a curve, the belly slightly concave, the fins huge but almost completely lacking their great power. Then he might have fallen into the graveyard waters of Loch Maree, but for the hen fish stroking past him, her wash lifting him from the boulder and bidding him again into the salmon's never-ending journey. Above them the wind tore at the loch, whipping the surface like osprey talons. The salmon, as all the wild spirits of the earth, were wandering among the devastation which had occurred, now hidden by time, lost in memory, softened by the resilience of what remained: wanderers before the storm.

PART THREE

The last salmon

14

The lecture theatre had taken on a pleasant familiarity, as had other corners of the college. The seats were in shadow while only the wide board and lecturer's area was lit. John Howard sat at the end of the second row, looking at the board, listening to the hum of air-conditioning as the professor paused. Eight other students sat in the first few rows. The elevated rows behind them were empty. *Just nine*, thought John, to listen to him, a Nobel prize-winner, Maurice Wilkins. It was a waste. There stood one of the first men to have looked into the structure of life itself, the molecular structure of DNA, and he had won one of the world's most coveted prizes for his part in the outstanding discovery of life's shape, the double helix. And now, on a winter's day deep beneath the Strand in London, he lectured to a class of nine.

He held his listeners spellbound, however, so that in his pauses the air-conditioning devoured the theatre with its hush. No one fidgeted; even Liz and Frank, who usually groped one another in lectures, were transfixed by the tall, gaunt man, the charismatic urgency in his voice.

Codes and chemical symbols were sprawled across the board. Except that it was not a sprawl to those who had watched the professor chalk them up, and heard him explain the significance of each mark. Those who had listened and who, like John, had been through years of Chemistry, could see the order on the board. In its way, thought John, it was as beautiful as a Constable landscape, or Da Vinci's geometric use of line. It was peculiar how science became so like art. He had felt this so many times during his recent years at King's. Science and art were, after all, means by which we defined our surroundings and expressed ourselves. In fact, the divisions between art and science were entirely man-made, created so as to make any particular subject easier to understand. The more subjects John had studied, the more interwoven they had become; inter-related, inter-dependant, each clearer when set in the context of others.

Which, he had concluded, was exactly how life should be seen, interacting, only viable if everything worked within certain limits controlled by living relationships. Wasn't that what Professor Wilkins was really talking about?

It was not like it had been at school when John had understood only those fragments which had excited or intrigued him. Here, at university, he was his own master, not forced to do anything against his will. The doors had been open; he could wander wherever was suggested, not demanded. He was there because he had chosen to be there, despite the fact that he knew he could have been on the trawler or some other fishing boat on the high North Atlantic, or at Loch Maree.

He had been drawn to King's, right from the tentative telephone call he had made, five years ago, to the Chemistry Department secretary who had put him in touch with the Admissions Supervisor. There had been a friendliness, a welcoming atmosphere that was almost tangible, as he had been shown around the college. He had felt that quality ever since in the dark, wood-panelled corridors, the team-like attitude within his year group, the excitement in the huge laboratories where the smell of organic solvents always pervaded. Glassware, multi-coloured chemicals and electronic equipment became familiar and necessary components of John's world.

They had been marvellous years for him. He had worked hard and played hard. The comfort and joy he had had with his friends in Kinlochewe and Mallaig had gradually been replaced by a new life. He had worked on the trawler in summer holidays, or as a ghillie on Loch Maree, but it had ceased to be a lifestyle as it had *almost* once been.

His mother had moved back to Kent, farther east than Stocks Cottage and the River Bewl, away from the worst of the escalating development which yearly spread its cancerous way across the county. She lived again in a cottage, in a village on the edge of Romney Marsh. John had felt enormous pleasure at seeing his mother move back to the sort of environment in which she was happiest. She, like him, had never really settled into life in

London. The city had merely enabled her to educate her children properly and to set them on what she saw as their proper path through life. Charlotte had remained in London, having qualified as a doctor and had married a surgeon who was a consultant at the same hospital.

The shapes danced upon the board, becoming ordered in John's mind. DNA bases paired with one another, cemented by hydrogen bonds, by Maurice Wilkins's words, by an understanding which he passed across to those who listened; the nine students who sat in the shadows while he stood in light.

Having graduated two years earlier, John now was a PhD student, like his friend Chris who sat next to him. The others were all undergraduates sitting the biophysics unit of their courses. They seemed wilder and more outlandish than those students who had been in John's undergraduate year. Nonetheless, they listened to Maurice Wilkins.

The lecture was over and the professor had left the theatre almost before the students had stirred from their thoughts and in their seats. John was unaware of the undergraduates shuffling together their notes until the noise of the chatter broke his concentration.

'You coming for a game of squash, then?' asked Chris. John looked up at his tall friend.

'Why not? You go on and I'll be along in a few minutes. I've just got to sort out these notes.'

'Do it later.'

'Piss off and go and pay for the court.'

'Well, don't be long. The courts are hard to book with all these sodding undergrads using them all the time.' With a haughty shrug of his shoulders, Chris whirled through the swing doors. John smiled as his side-kick disappeared. Chris seemed older these days, his dark hair thinner, his face less child-like than the engagingly ridiculous innocence of their fresher year. He and John had been close friends throughout their undergraduate years and together had remained at King's, with only two others from their year, both to take a PhD, but in different branches of Chemistry. John was researching the biochemistry of migration stimuli and responses in birds and fish. Chris spent his days surrounded by the pungent organic odours of the specialist organic synthesis laboratories.

Alone in the lecture theatre, John caught himself chuckling as he thought of his friend as he had so often seen him, clad in lab coat, his face half covered by a breathing mask because of his perpetual worry about the fumes making his hair fall out or sterilising him.

John's stare fell on to the rough notes and diagrams he had made as Maurice Wilkins had talked. It was incredible how some men could be so brilliant, with so much understanding. There in his A4 notebook was a summary, an image, of decades of work carried out by scientists with imagination and the background of painstaking research. They had caught a glimpse through one of nature's most secret doors, of the very shape and meaning of things. Yet away from those ideas and truths, beyond the safe domain of the university, was a world of harsher, deadly truths, and terrible misunderstanding. John was safe from it all here, in his adopted world with friends and lecturers, or in the peace of his laboratory, within the cloistered security of King's. But he knew it was only a temporary sanctuary. It was like that other place of safety, as it had been then, not so clear in his memory as it used to be, the Weald.

One day he would have to go back out into the world where life itself meant less, or existed on different levels, and no one really cared anything about the structure of DNA. Where life lost its true shape.

At King's he had been looking inward all these years, into the molecular structure of nature. Soon he would have to look outward again, and that disturbed him, for he had fled that once before.

He wondered whether or not university had prepared him any better than the trawler had done, or fishing days in Scotland and Kent. Certainly now he had more of the sort of knowledge that men respected, though that knowledge was useless beyond the personal level unless it was constructively applied.

The symbols on the pages caught his eye again and he thought about his own work, the complicated biochemistry which had seemed, at first, such a jumble and yet, with countless hours of study and research, had gradually taken shape and meaning, like Maurice Wilkins's DNA models. He had enjoyed the long process of making sense of it all, unravelling the secrets of his corner of science.

His career's path felt tidy and clean behind him now, though he remembered that, not so long ago, it had been different. He hadn't known where it was leading him. Then, it had seemed as if there was no purpose to his being on the decks of the *Shadow of Skye*, or lost in the research depths of some biochemical mechanism, or drifting on Maree's cold waters. It was all happenstance, with no reason or order. But there had to be a reason for it, for each and every instant in his life – anybody's life – even if the reason would eventually be of his own making and determination. The experiences of the past converged definitely on a point, or a single direction, in the future. He knew there was more yet to add before he reached that point.

His love of writing had developed in pace with his research. Both had taken him towards distinct limits and had taught him to progress in stages, by constant practice, just as an artist's line becomes more true, as expression commands more purpose. As he pressed on, so the limits withdrew and his world broadened. There was something, after all, beyond those horizons, once marked by trees flanking a silvered ribbon of a Kentish stream, beyond even those delineated by cold granite that rose emphatically from Maree's dark waters. Of course, those animals he studied, and had watched all his life, the fish which were sensitive to migratory signals so astonishingly subtle, they also knew horizons farther away, towards which his own human path led. That route, marked by all he had known, lay carpeted with words.

Each step he took would require of him that he ordered the words, tidying the path behind him.

He had written articles for several country, fishing and nature magazines and as each one had been published he was reminded of his first article in *Trout and Salmon*; the thrill of it and how his mother had shared his pride in what he had done. His peers achieved their own minor victories, strings of high grades at 'O' level, early 'A' levels, music and sports scholarships, places at Oxford and Cambridge ... But none of them had had an article published in a national magazine. He had gone beyond the English students' naive attempts at poetry in the school magazine. He might have failed where they succeeded, but he had won difficult ground where most dared not tread. His mother always insisted that he gave her a copy of every article that was published. He knew that she had a collection more ordered than his own, and one which was shown to more people. It gave him a good feeling. There was someone on his side, down there in Kent, where it had all begun.

With a sudden excitement in his stride, his papers and books crammed in the hiker's bag he always carried around college, he rushed towards the squash courts where Chris would be cursing because he was late.

A great sea with no horizons spilled in light and wave-tossed spray and shuddering explosions of bubbles and blue-grey motion. A great fish with apparently no limitation to the miles across which he could wander speared into the wildness of the dangerous surface. Two others travelled with him; just three big fish on the waste of the high North Atlantic, thudding their way against the vastness. There might have been three thousand, once, on that path, on that tide, a silver cloud in the stormy sea, rushing on forked fins towards Greenland. But they had gone, netted and diseased and poisoned and poached and rid from all the fresh-water systems of the Atlantic coastlines until there were just scattered groups of wanderers. In *their* group, just three, though very large; victors of several migrations and long feeding years at sea.

They were the most prized and yet most elusive of all their kind. Surviving, wild Scottish salmon, they were alert to the myriad dangers of the sea and the fresh-water system which was their home, Maree, far behind their tails. An excitement was in them, perhaps brought about by their knowledge of the proximity of Greenland where the feeding would end the terrible hunger that had dogged them for months. It had been with them ever since the beginning of the long spawning run which had taken them, again, into the shrouding hill country above Loch Maree, beneath a tall, black peak, to lay their future there, in ova and milt on the sacred redds of the Sgurr Dubh. That they had done, with hunger in them, with urgency in them, with the pain of the fresh-water run in them all the time. Now the pain became excitement again as they felt the vibration of the tide which battered a fjord coast and warm water welled up from the deep.

*

John Howard's excitement grew as he watched the girl take off her lab coat. Anna, the tall, fair second-year undergraduate who had bedazzled the younger male lecturers and PhD students alike. No one appeared to know very much about her except that she lived with her parents in Tunbridge Wells and travelled into college every day. She had refused a date with several adventurous postgraduates and had been brandished the 'Untouchable One', or less kind labels. John had spoken to her on a few occasions, usually about the chemistry experiments which he, as a postgraduate, demonstrated to the first and second-year students. He watched her far more than she realised, or he thought she realised; but then all the postgraduates stared hard at Anna.

As he watched her now she stretched her arms back with chest slightly forwards to take off the coat and his feelings for her were accentuated. He knew that other men were looking and wished that he could be less obvious.

It was dark outside the brightly lit laboratory and the windows were gleaming with rain. Everyone was packing away equipment and chemicals after the long Friday afternoon practical session. The fume cupboard motors were all whirring at full speed, yet there was still a slight haze of solvent vapour and smoke in the air. John wound down the window nearest him and felt the refreshing blast of winter-damp air on his cheeks.

'Thank you for helping me today.' It was her, standing by him in her overcoat, her scarf tucked neatly under the collar, her books packed in her leather briefcase. He felt foolish at having been surprised by her approach.

'Oh, that's OK. It's what I'm here for.' He smiled and tried to look less gormless, aware of many pairs of eyes watching them. His hand was still on the window handle. He nodded towards the open space. 'I just needed the air.'

'Yes, it will be nice to get outside tonight after the stuffy lab. Anyway, I love the rain.'

'So do I.' He could think of nothing more to say. She loved rain, for goodness' sake. He had never heard a woman say she even liked rain. She hesitated for just a moment, her long eyelashes completely shielding her blue eyes as she looked down at her gloves.

'Oh well, see you next week.' She turned to leave and he

caught a faint smell of her coat or her perfume, even through the toxic atmosphere. Inspiration suddenly came to him.

'Er, Anna,' he called loudly. She turned to face him and he walked up to her so that he could speak more quietly, terribly aware of those who listened. 'Are you going home now? You live in Kent, don't you?'

'Yes. I'm going from Charing Cross.'

'Ah.' He felt as if he was clearing the bar of the high-jump. 'Well, I'm off to see my mother this weekend. She lives in Kent too, you see. Er, I'll walk with you to the station.'

'All right.' She was looking right at him and he was conscious of a long, embarrassing silence which she broke for them both. 'Will you be long?'

They walked quickly through the rain and the umbrella-armed crowds which seethed down the Strand towards Charing Cross. They shouted at one another to make themselves heard above the noise of the traffic. Out of the college Anna had taken on a different image. She appeared less restrained in her manner.

'Honestly, the rush into Kent and Sussex on a Friday evening gets worse all the time. Where does your mother live?'

'In a little village between the Weald and Romney Marsh. I go to Ashford. I've left my car there.'

'Good, we can catch the same train. I change at Tonbridge.'

'Yes, I know.' She glanced at him.

'There's a train in five minutes, but we won't get a seat. Let's head for the brake-van, if you don't mind the cold. At least there's room to breathe and I won't get some City-type eyeing me up.' He felt surprised that she had asked him if he minded the cold.

'Let's grab a cup of coffee at the stall in the station. That'll keep us warm until Sevenoaks.' Though John had no need to try and keep warm, with the heat in his head and the dampness on his body that was not caused by the rain.

There was no one else in the brake-van and the guard unlocked it especially for them, at Anna's request. They sat on John's coat on the floor, backs against the wooden wall, cradling polystyrene cups of coffee in their hands. The train picked up speed as it neared the fringes of London and it rocked and juddered, reminding John of the galley and sleeping area of the

Shadow of Skye. Far out at sea where the wet wind blew through the night outside and people that he loved were around him, sheltering him from the hostile world beyond. It wasn't so different then with Anna's warmth touching his right side, the glistening rain outside and the train's rolling motion.

'Penny for them?' she said. So he told her, between Orpington and Tonbridge, of some of his time on the deep-sea trawler and his friends in Scotland. She listened and, though he knew that he was pouring out his heart to her, his innermost, private memories, he could not stop himself. She was there, on his own course, as if for a reason, surely for a reason? It was the most natural thing in the world for him to tell the lovely girl at his side about a distant though treasured part of his life.

'You miss it, don't you?' she said as the train began to decelerate on approaching the Medway and Tonbridge.

'Oh yes, but you can never go back, can you?'

'I suppose not. Thank you for telling me about the trawler.' She stood up and picked up her briefcase. He made to apologise for having spoken so much about himself, but she placed a hand on his arm as if she knew what he was about to say. 'No, really, it was great to hear about it. Will you come on the train with me again and tell me more about Scotland? I'd love to go there.'

The lights of Tonbridge station surrounded them and John opened the brake-van's door.

'I'll do better than that. Why don't we go out somewhere tomorrow night? I'll come and pick you up.' He scribbled down her telephone number on the palm of his hand in Biro.

Time. Time to be in love. Time for time to stop. His time, hers, theirs; when the only real moments were when they were together. And to be in love was all that mattered. There was nothing beyond that. John felt that it was why the world was how it was. Without love everything in the world was worthless. He had the time to see that. Through her he saw everything else that he had loved, remembering the stolen moments of youth and adolescence. The delicious rain was her, the struggle for life he had seen in the great salmon on Loch Maree, somehow even that was mirrored in her. And the excitement of the wild, wild sea; that was in her limbs and her eyes.

Even in love he could see that soon it would be his turn; time would start again and he would have to give it all back, all that fathomless love. He knew how he would do it. At last he was realising the means, and the need, which would allow him to give it back. Then, yes, then he could be even with the world, with this time he had been given when he was learning the most precious quality in the universe.

John opened the door of his flat to see Anna sitting on the sofa amid a pile of books and papers.

'I think you should write for a living,' she announced simply.

'Have you been reading my articles?'

'Yes, and some of the stuff you hide away in your desk.' He did not mind. Secretly he had wanted Anna to read his private work ever since they had started going out together.

'There's not much of a living in it.'

'It doesn't matter. You could make enough.' She lifted an untidy pile of A4. 'Why don't you send more for publication?'

'I mostly write essays now, not articles. Or pieces too long for a magazine.'

'Yes. So write a book.' She was emphatic.

'You sound like my mother. She's always badgering me to do more with my writing.'

'Well, why don't you listen to us. Women *always* know best. You can write, but you don't know how to manage yourself. I mean, look at the way you keep it all, in this ... mess. If you organised it and worked to a plan you could get somewhere. I just *know* it.'

Later, while they worked together at the big, second-hand oak table which he had bought from an Oxfam shop in Finchley, she at her course work, he on his research, he said suddenly: 'It's this work. There's no time to concentrate on the writing. This uses up all my time now.'

'You'll have your PhD soon. It'll be over.' Her reasoning startled him. Would it really be over? He had thought of going on in research. He enjoyed it and knew that he might get a post-doctoral research post at King's. But then, deep within him, he knew that to do so would only be ducking the real issue of his future. What stopped him properly pursuing his writing was only fear, not the science which was temporarily in his way, or preparing his mind for order and control.

The writing was the hard path, the unknown, insecure. Research was so much safer, in a place where he had learned to love, where he had found Anna. Yet, of course, he would lose her if he chose the wrong route, the easy way. She loved what was strongest in him; his love of wild nature and his desire to write it all down as he saw it.

15

John Howard's laboratory on the sixth floor of the Strand building was a sprawl of apparatus, papers and books. John sat on one of the high stools, leaning forwards over the bench, burying his face in the dirty sleeves of his lab coat. In front of him was an old Adler electric typewriter and in that was a page, the last page of his PhD thesis. The final sentence was written and in its completion John felt a dreadful anticlimax and an overwhelming fatigue. Chris barged into the laboratory.

'Christ, what a mess!' He walked over to where his friend was slumped over the bench. He saw the page, read the last few sentences and thumped John on the back. 'Hah, you've finished; before me too, you rat!' John heaved himself up. 'Bloody hell, you look awful.'

'Cheers, mate. That's just what I need to hear.'

'Well, what do you expect? You're never seen outside the lab in college nowadays and that rather nice fiancée of yours tells me that you spend all your time in the flat typing and reading. I think I prefer the healthy git you used to be, talking about nothing but fishing and trawlers.'

'It's over now.' John smiled. 'It's odd though Chris, three years of hard work, six if you count our undergrad years, and then, quite suddenly, it's all over. Next thing I know I'll be saying goodbye to King's.'

'Don't you start getting depressed. I can't stand you in that sort of mood.' Chris chuckled.

'No, really, six years and what do we achieve? What's it all for?' He pulled the page out of the Adler and threw it on the pile of papers which made up the thick wad of his thesis. 'This. Has it all been for this?'

'Not exactly, as you know full well. It's what's in your head, what you've learnt, the skills you've picked up along the way, and knowledge ... '

'And knowledge,' echoed John. He looked blankly at the pages of his thesis. Three years of examining the molecular details of migration, the chemical reactions that made an animal turn in a particular direction in the sea or sky. It was nature examined in fine detail. Yet what had he really achieved? Knowledge? But that was only relative to other peoples'. It was true that he had taken the subject a little farther along the road towards understanding. Yes, that was what really mattered, not knowledge, but understanding. It was extraordinary, but the animals he had observed and researched had a far deeper understanding of those migration stimuli than he could ever have.

'Do you know, Chris, that salmon can taste something which is in the water at concentrations of less than one part per billion. They have a sort of chemical amplification system so that miniscule concentrations register in their brains. We still don't know how far offshore they can taste and smell the coast, or even their own river, but it's a very long way.' But why, why did they bother to do it, when running any cold, clean fresh-water system would serve its purpose? Where John, or any scientist, could only analyse, the salmon *knew*. They understood their environment. They were so utterly and completely tuned to the sea, river and loch. The more you looked into the mystery of long-distance migration the more humbling it became.

'I wonder about something else,' said John suddenly. 'I can remember all sorts of odd things from my past, about when I was a little boy fishing in a river near my home and about moving to London and then going back ... ' Something choked the words in his throat as he spoke them, as an image of Stocks Cottage in fair summer weather came into his mind, and the Weald and how property developers had destroyed it all. 'And I remember all sorts of things from my times in Scotland, you know, about the trawler and Loch Maree. I can remember them quite clearly actually, all sorts of things – Christmas, my fishing rod, that first big roach, that first sight of Maree down the glen – and because they're so clear they're so precious. They make *me* what I am, don't they, the way memories make us all what we are?'

'We've all got memories, old fruit.'

'Yes, but how much will we remember about King's, about our research here? All that effort for how much effect, and how much memory?'

'I reckon you're tired, John. You've been burning the old candle a bit too much in recent months. Time to call it a day now and give it a rest. Come on, we'll go and have a beer.'

But it was not only his tiredness talking. It was, again, the fears of a world beyond his own, or the one to which he would now have to return, after the temporary sanctuary of college. Anna was right: he was trained as a scientist though he was not a scientist. He was, or could be, a writer.

He was convinced of one thing, that it was important to write only what needed to be written. It was useless to write for the sake of it, like casting a net in a dead sea. At least he had things to say, in a particular way. All those pictures that he had collected: of the long, island-strewn loch, seen from the hills to the south, beneath an August sky; the savage North Atlantic with a little trawler set against it, like an angry tiger with foam at its mouth; a huge salmon's back awash in the waves at the mouth of the Kinlochewe, a fish alone in billions of gallons of emptiness; or the fairy-land banks of a silver-green stream which once flowed through the quiet Weald, beside a cottage shrouded in wisteria and clematis. All those pictures of how Britain used to be to a boy and a young man who had wandered through it; all those memories which were his, all the places and the wild nature and the love of the people with whom it had been shared. To all those he owed whatever he could give, and he knew that the best he could give was his heart.

Hand in hand on a Friday night John and Anna walked along Camden Road in central Tunbridge Wells. They had seen *Raiders of the Lost Ark* at the Classic and were walking slowly to where they had left John's old Mini. There was no hurry. Anna was spending the weekend at her parents' house and John was going down to see his mother.

'You could look for houses this weekend,' she announced matter-of-factly. Neither of them had thought very much about where they would live when they were married. The flat John rented in Finchley had been so convenient while they were at King's. But now she had her degree and he his doctorate and they no longer needed a place close to the dreaded Northern Line for access to Charing Cross and the Strand. It was curious though; in love John had not felt his usual revulsion for London and the powerful need to escape from it whenever his research allowed. He had, after all, met Anna in London even though she was Kentish, like him. In love they had felt that everywhere was fine, so long as they were together.

'Where? Here, in Kent?'

'Of course, it's our home.' And that, to her, to him, was the most important thing in the world: to have a home, a place where they belonged and that they could cherish.

They stopped at the window of a fishing tackle shop, brightly lit and showing off pristine items of tackle, glossy rods, immaculate reels and all the fascinating paraphernalia of angling. Anna watched her man's eyes, lit like the varnished carbon fibre of the fly-rods. She had seen his eyes like that as they had watched the film. There was so much imagination in him, so much that he needed to express. It gave him an unusual perspective on life. She was glad that she had at least recognised it gradually in the man she was going to marry, for to find it suddenly would have been to detonate a bomb between them.

Like a little boy, like the one he had been almost twenty years ago, John stared at the lovely reels and could almost feel their magnesium-lightness in his palm. The fly-rods had an animal, living quality about them, though they were motionless in the shop window. It did not tax his imagination to feel their flex as they were loaded under the weight of line cast through the air.

'We can look for houses on Sunday,' he said. 'Tomorrow I'm going to show you Bewl Bridge.'

It reached out beneath the summer sun, lancing deep into the border country of Kent and East Sussex. Blue fingers of water parried with dense woodland and lush pasture. Bewl Bridge Reservoir glistened, huge and fascinating in its complexity, in its winding arms, deeply indented bays and broad, jutting promontories. A warm breeze from the south-west ruffled the surface of Copens Reach and Hook Staight, two of the great branches of the reservoir, some of which John and Anna could see from where they stood on the shore.

'Yes, it's lovely. Tell me why you wanted me to see it.'

'The dam was built a few years ago.' He pointed down the lake towards the mile-long structure, splitting the wild shore of Chingley Wood, matted with beech and oak, from the yacht-club area. 'There was nothing much here before that except a few farm cottages and an old millhouse and pastureland, like you can see along the banks now. There was a little river, a stream really, called the Bewl.'

'Where you used to fish as a litle boy.'

'Yes, well, not far away from here, except the stream is abstracted now. This is what's left, what's replaced the little Bewl.' They stared together out over the expanse, she imagining a little boy in wellingtons and short trousers with mud on his knees and hair as dishevelled as summer-blown leaves of oak. He remembered the same little boy, and the adventures he had had by the intimate, winding stream. This was what was left: a man-made reservoir replacing the wet-land of the Wealden plain. At least there was life here, abundant in the cool water, and not sterility in the concrete and brick of the spreading towns and housing estates not very far away. How things changed, so dramatically, so quickly really, so much that when you wanted to show someone your home there were only remnants of it left. Where you had built a young life, other people had razed the substance with which you had built it. So you only had the shell, and the memory was its soul. Anna could only glimpse the precious qualities of his youth in the vista of Bewl and the folds of the countryside around the lake, his country, though he would have to describe most of it now, from the memories deep within him.

'I would have loved to show you how it used to be,' he said.

'You have. I've seen it all.' He did not know whether she meant she had seen it in this view over Bewl, or in what he had told her about his childhood, or perhaps in what she had read in his essays and articles. And he did not ask. He knew she could see it clearly, and that was what mattered.

'This is where I want us to live, somewhere near here.'

'Of course.'

She leaned back against him and he reached his arms around her as they both watched the lake. There was so much he wanted to show her, and share with her. After his years in London, Kent had become something for which he yearned, just like the dream of Loch Maree when he was younger. It was true that the county was becoming increasingly unrecognisable, that building and industrialisation had ruined much of it for ever. But it had a powerful draw for him. He did not know if it was simply nostalgia, or if his roots were indomitably planted in the Weald. Something instinctive and irrational told him that if he was there again, living there, he could somehow prevent any more of it from being destroyed.

It was a simple story, written with passion, about a whale and a long journey through an ocean full of dangers. Every page was crowded either with threats or with scenes of tranquillity. John Howard had painted some of the pictures in his memory with the words he loved to use and had written a book. He had used the pages to vent the emotions which had been pent up within him. In writing about how the whale's world was being poisoned and destroyed he felt a release from the anger of what had happened in the Weald. In his story there were parallels between the existence of a wild creature and his own life. Relationships again, and inter-relationships; the bonding of all life just as he had learnt as a little boy on the river, as a young man on the trawler on the high North Atlantic, and just as Maurice Wilkins had taught at King's. If you wrote about life you wrote about your own or that of a whale or an amoeba. It was all the same, only the perspective could change.

A draught threaded through the old cottage and a door upstairs creaked. Anna sat close to the log fire reading the manuscript while John spread some of the earlier chapters on the dining table they had bought in a junk shop in Tonbridge. He never particularly enjoyed the editing process, especially when a section was full of problems. It was not split infinitives or sentences ending with prepositions which worried him. Those he or Anna could spot and put right. It was the paragraph which did not flow as naturally as it should have done, as if the sentences were carved in hard wood and the edges had not been smoothed, nor the joints carefully worked, so that it was ugly and had no place against the rest of the page, even to the extent that it could ruin a chapter. Yet he felt that each and every paragraph he had written was necessary to the whole, if only it could be smoothed and moulded into the rest ... What was it that Hemingway's editor had said to the great man? That he should just give him the words, the words. But John was not Hemingway and the words were not enough; and nor were the ideas and emotions. They all needed shape and order.

He looked up from his work to see Anna watching him. The manuscript was closed on her lap.

'I thought I could see it before,' she said quietly, 'but I see it better now.'

'What, what can you see?'

She smiled and patted the manuscript.

'Publisher. That's what we need now.'

For a few moments they sat at either end of the dimly lit room, listening to the wind outside and the plink, plink of water dripping through the roof into a bucket they had placed on the bedroom floor upstairs.

'Do you mind this?' he asked, nodding vaguely towards the rest of the cottage, cold and almost derelict down a farm track in a forgotten corner of mid-Kent. With loans, savings and mortgage, it had even so been almost more than they could afford. 'You could have done better.'

'Might have got Harold Fortescue up at Cowsley Manor. He always fancied me.'

'Don't suppose Harry would keep his horses in a place like this.'

'Too small and draughty for horses.'

They stood together, arm in arm, in Bedford Square. A fresh April breeze blew away another shower and the grand Edwardian buildings sparkled in the clear air. Taxis and cars dashed along the one-way road, throwing spray up on to the pavement. It was a peculiar scene for the middle of London, thought John. There were daffodils blooming in the window boxes on some of the buildings and the great horse chestnuts and beech trees in the square stood above lawns and carefully tended flower beds. Except for the endless procession of black taxis, it was a scene more typical of Tunbridge Wells or Canterbury.

A motor-bike courier opened the green door of the publishing house and let it swing closed behind him. Barely had it shut than the courier reappeared. The opening and closing of the door seemed to hypnotise John.

'Maybe we should just post it.'

Anna nudged him. 'We haven't come all this way for you to chicken out now. Come on, a publisher like that probably receives a dozen manuscripts a day through the post. The personal touch must help a bit. It might make them actually read it,' she added as she straightened his school tie, especially ironed for the occasion.

'But why this one?'

'I like the writers they publish. Anyway, they've got a lovely smart door.'

'Oh, that will sound good if they ask me why I chose to come to them. "Well," I will say, "my wife likes your door."'

'So, walk through it now and be my hero.'

In the reception area another courier was standing talking with a security man. The receptionist flicked some switches on the telephone console and looked up at him.

'Can I help you?' John heard the two men stop talking and felt that everyone in the suddenly quiet building would hear him as he choked out the words.

'Er, I would like to leave my b..., my manuscript please.'

'Yes, dear, you leave it there and I'll pass it to an editor.' She answered the telephone again. John stood there, imagining the two men looking at him. The receptionist put down the phone and frowned slightly. John smiled pleasantly at her.

'I wonder, could I possibly leave it with the editor myself, if that's possible?'

She hesitated, then flicked some more switches. 'Hello, Debbie, Angie here. There's a young man in reception with a manuscript. Could you come down and see him? Lovely.'

'Miss Spinks will be down to see you shortly. She's Mrs Kielder's secretary.'

'Thank you. Who's Mrs Kielder?'

The receptionist stared at him for a moment until the ringing telephone saved him further embarrassment. Miss Spinks was much more friendly, though she could not hide the fact that she had seen countless other young hopefuls like John. He felt that he was hearing a well-rehearsed monologue. She took the manuscript, neatly bound and sealed in a large brown envelope and told him that they would be in touch as soon as possible.

'It usually takes a few weeks,' she said. The *usually* said it all.

And what happened *usually* after those awful few weeks of waiting? John did not like to imagine. He watched Miss Spinks turn and walk up the stairs, carrying his precious story with her. Would she even bother to show it to Mrs Kielder, whoever she was?

'Well, how did it go?' implored Anna who had been waiting by the railings.

'Oh, they offered me an advance of half a million quid and asked how soon they could have my next book.'

'Not bad then. Come on, let's go and buy some bitumen so you can mend those leaks in our roof.'

Not that year, that stormy April, not that homebound run – he would miss it. He would not turn his tail to Greenland. He and the hen fish hung on the violent tide, their silver mass, a total of over one hundred pounds between the three of them, poised against the careering tons of water. The migration, the last breeding run, the *last*, would wait until the time was perfect: the year, the tide, the weather system over the North Atlantic would have to be right in every way to a salmon mind.

Alone in the sea they waited. No other salmon gathered with them. Even those fish with home coasts other than Scotland had been so few in number that year, and now even those had ventured on to their breeding runs, spreading again their ever-more fragile silver fan across the ocean.

It was a fan the centre of which the Danes had cut to pieces and now abandoned. The exploitation had ended, for there was nothing left to exploit. The shoaling centre in the wild seas off Greenland, the millions of tons of salmon that returned every year, the certain, ever-rich fishery was fished out. It was gone and the high-seas fishermen had abandoned it as its heart had abandoned them. The salmon were finished.

One day, dreamed the fishermen from all the nations of the North Atlantic, the fishery might recover, like the herring in the North Sea had once done, and the trawlers could work it again, in another happy time, though most knew that the few salmon which may have survived would not be able to replenish their kind to anything like the quantity of those former, halcyon days. It was not like it used to be, when if nature was abused she somehow disabused herself. Too much of her had been torn apart and now she bled like she had never before done.

The trawlermen felt it in the stark cost of their wasted diesel, the scientists knew in the data and charts that had been gathered and prepared too late, or ignored for too long. The politicians had known for long enough, but they had been impotent. They were not strong enough to exercise long-term policies in the face of short-term gains in votes.

And the last salmon knew as he felt the quiet sea, silent despite the roar of tide across his lateral lines. He hungered for that other tingle, buzz and smack of life that might have been teeming around him; there in what was, once, the richest place in the world.

16

Miss Spinks led John up the wide staircase. Ahead was a white-painted panelled door, another barrier, another pause in the long wait he had had. A month earlier, on a fresh April day, he had delivered his manuscript. Now, as he climbed the stairs he was hot in his wool suit, the only suit he owned. He felt desperately uncomfortable and out of place. Sweat bloomed on his forehead.

The summons to return to the publisher had come in the form of a letter from Mrs Kielder suggesting they should meet and discuss John's writing. She had not said much about his manuscript except that she had been greatly impressed. Publication was not mentioned. Nonetheless, Anna had pressed John's suit and they had both spent nearly-sleepless nights as the day of the meeting approached. Instinctively, they both knew that even to be asked to see the publisher seeded great hope that John might become an author.

At the door, as Miss Spinks knocked, John thought momentarily of his wife. She had come with him to the station at Tunbridge Wells before going on to the school where she taught. He saw her face, the love in it that was, he thought, what he most needed to give back by making his writing a success. While she went off to teach every day he was left alone in their little cottage, at peace to indulge in his own thoughts, to paint his word pictures. It was not fair on her unless it paid.

Mrs Kielder was eccentric, John could see that at a glance. He could see the extraordinary Einsteinian abandonment of her hairstyle, the multicoloured socks and the odd shoes, one brown, one red. On a teenager they might not have looked unusual, but Mrs Kielder was about forty. She possessed something of the air of an English colonial lady and her face had fixed on it an infectious smile. She had an aura of fun about her. John could sense, however, a certain sharp professionalism.

'Your whale book has caused quite a stir among our editors, young man.'

'Really?'

'I've never read anything so *green* in my life.' John wondered if everything in Mrs Kielder's world had a colour. 'You must understand,' she continued, 'that we have not yet decided whether or not we can publish it, but, well, there's a chance. I'm recommending it to our chairman.' She narrowed her eyes, giving her face an impishness. 'I want to know a little bit about you. Do you want to be a writer? Or is this whale thing a one-off?'

What John wanted to tell her he found impossible to say: that yes, yes, he desperately wanted to be a published writer and that he had so many stories in his head and so many important things to say. If only he had the freedom to put them all down on paper, for everyone to read; if only those who could pay him had some faith in what he could do, as Mr Wilshaw and Old George at school had done, had believed in his promise for just, *just* long enough for that promise to bloom, to become truth. If only, if only Mrs Kielder and her chairman would give him the chance to give them his promise. Then the whale's tail which brushed across the pages of his manuscript would sweep with such immense power ... But there, in the book-lined office in Bedford Square, he could not say that. Instead, he told her what his inhibitions and convention allowed, while sweat poured coldly down his back and his shirt stuck uncomfortably to him.

After almost an hour of Mrs Kielder asking him questions while she chewed her pencil, she suddenly said: 'Look, I am going to ask you to be very patient. It is all up to our chairman. I will try to hurry him up for you, but he is very busy and will read your book when he has a chance. As soon as he has I will make sure he gets in touch with you.'

As she stood, to end the interview, she said, 'You must never give up, you know. Even if this book doesn't work, though it should, it really should. You must always carry on writing.' She frowned in such a way that John might have laughed if what she

179

had said had not been so important to him. The pencil was fixed rigidly between her teeth, emphasising what she told him.

'Yes, I will carry on writing.' He nodded, calm at last, as he was about to leave. 'So long as I have things to write about.' But time was running out for that. He wrote about what he loved, and much of what he loved was dying. The North Atlantic was losing the life it had contained, the Weald was shrinking before the advance of building developers and high-intensity farming. They were talking about a Channel Tunnel and a high-speed rail link, bisecting the county . . . The madness, the utter, astonishing insanity of it, twisting and mangling the last beauty out of southern England. And north-west Scotland, where the salmon and sea-trout ran; all poached and netted and poisoned. There was not very much time. There was not very much left to love and cherish with his words.

The brothers, Iain and Peter Sutherland, sat in the drawing room of Iain's croft in Kinlochewe. The contrast between them was extreme; Peter the old, stubbled sea-dog, a life-long trawlerman, Iain the refined thinker, the Highlander with a quiet and studious disposition. Yet seeing them together on the wide Edinburgh settee, it occurred to John how obviously they were brothers. Their eyes and mouths, their expressions, could have been juxtaposed. Anna sat stiffly at his side and was the subject of the brothers' stares. Mrs Sutherland entered the room with a tray laden with scones, Scotch pancakes and a huge teapot. John stood to help her with the tray.

'Ach no, Johnny, I can manage. Ye'd best guard that fine lassie from the stares of these two old devils.'

'It's *so good* to see you all,' said John.

'Aye, and it's about time we saw ye again, and your wife,' said Iain. 'It's been much too long, laddie.'

'Well, you were invited to the wedding.'

'In England was it?' croaked Peter, pulling his old pipe from his mouth. He let out a cackling laugh. 'I cannae bear the thought of a day in England, even to see a beauty like our Anna here. Och, but she makes me think I've been too long at sea!'

'How is it now, Peter? At sea, I mean. How's the fishing?' Peter's humour evaporated, as if John had asked him to do some terrible deed. The old man sighed.

'The fishing is all over, Puke my lad. It's barely worth the diesel to put out from Mallaig. The *Shadow*'s not got the range to compete with the big trawlers out nowadays – them vermin boats bristlin' with their damn "lectronics".' There was an uncharacteristic bitterness in him, visible in the tired creases of his weather-worn face. 'The *Shadow* was never built to go even as far as Faroes or Iceland like we used to do,' he continued. 'She was built as a coastal trawler, not for deep sea, not compared wi' those big buggers anyway.' His face lit up with the memory of past trips in the stormy high Atlantic. 'Do ye remember some of them trips, laddie? Christ, we had a time of it, didn't we?'

'I'll never forget them, Peter,' John said. 'What's happened to the others then, Mackerel, Bill and Ben . . .?'

'Mackerel an' me still takes the old boat out for a bit of lobster an' a few sweeps around the Isles, when we can find some boys to work the nets. But ye can't make a living from it now, so it's a good thing we're drawing a wee pension. And Bill got hisself hitched to that Elspeth lass up on Northside. She leads him a terrible song and dance, I can tell ye. He works in the processing plant.' He shook his head, as if to say that working in the fish processing factory was a fate worse than death itself for a trawlerman. 'Ben's gone away down to Glasgow for work, an' goodness knows what he's doing down there.'

'And Hector?' An image of his tall, powerful friend loomed in John's mind's eye, as he always remembered him, striding the decks of the *Shadow of Skye*, dragging ropes and netting inboard, quietly working with his great strength.

'Hector's the only one of us making a real go of it now,' replied Peter. 'He's got hisself a boat of his own. He works it up north somewhere. Seeing his catches I reckon he's nicking the fish out of Faroes.' He laughed. 'And bloody good luck to him.'

So big Hector was the last, somehow making a living out of the North Atlantic where so many had failed.

'It's about time ye told us your own news,' suggested Iain. 'Ye come back to us a married man and goodness knows what else ye've been up to.'

'He's become an author,' put in Anna. 'His book is going to be published in the spring.' Proudly she squeezed John's arm.

'Well, well, ye're full of the surprises,' bellowed Peter. 'But then I always said ye had a way with the words. Used to talk too much and work too little, so I s'pose ye've found the right vocation!'

'Ach, a writer, is it?' said Iain. 'That was always one of your dreams, Johnny. Have they all come true for ye?'

'Some of them, yes.' And some had gone for ever.

'There've been no salmon for three seasons now. A few grilse in the summer, but none of the big greybacks in spring or autumn.' Iain sat with John in front of the dying embers of the peat fire, as they had often done between John's trawling trips. The others had retired to bed. 'Not even many sea-trout left now. And to think how it used to be on Maree. Ye remember?'

How could he ever forget? It had been unbelievably rich, the tumbling waves alive with migrant *salmonidae*. To think that they had all but disappeared.

'Too late for recriminations now,' continued Iain. 'And they can't bring back those fish.'

'They could restock, plant new ova or alevin up on the redds,' suggested John, almost absent-mindedly. Iain Sutherland took his pipe from his mouth and opened his eyes wide, glaring at the young man.

'*Maree fish*, Johnny, they can't plant those. You should know better. They're not like other salmon.'

He was right, of course. John's research at King's had proved that, shown graphically and scientifically what the Gaelic people had known all the while, that salmon are very specific to their location, that they have a home and a definite migration path and pattern, stronger than a race of aboriginal people. The salmon were wanderers, nomads, until the call of fresh-water from the high hills, *their hills*, called them home.

'Those damn poaching gangs up from Glasgow. Ach ...' Iain spat the words towards the fire, but the peat embers had not the strength to spit back at him. As he had said, what use was recrimination now? People had known what was happening all those years ago. They had known about the poaching gangs, the inshore netting, the high-seas fishery, the poisons and the sheer bloody-mindedness which had set a species on the rack.

But there were a few, great, wild Atlantic salmon, though not in Loch Maree. Bladed fins knifed the Greenland tide on the extreme range of the species, high, high up towards the Kane Basin north of Baffin Bay. Two thousand miles from home, they had followed the krill, and escaped Japanese and Canadian fishing fleets, pushing northward even as the season tried to drive them south with hard fingers of ice and failing light. There seemed no hope in this far, cold place, but then there was no hope elsewhere. There was only a sea which spoke with an ever-weakening voice, a parody of past ocean sounds.

Those three fish were lost in a world of faint blue and violet, a sea which sizzled as it froze. Waves jostled the sheet ice and the very breath of the tide was suddenly grasped in the awesome polar night. Deeper they swam, completely out of the light, where the oxygen concentration was uncomfortably low and they had to work their muscles slowly so as to avoid excessive lactic acid build-up. The void spoke nothing to them, neither bidding them to turn for home nor demanding they remain in the frigid basin cemetery. No nearby shoals tickled their lateral lines to influence them and no distant tastes enticed them. They had to guide them only what a salmon-mind remembers.

They gyred on the abyss, unseen, unheard; but imagined by a young man in a croft in a land which bore their home waters.

John stared at the notice:

Woddle and Banbridge
Building the Future of Kent

It stood by the road proudly displaying what the building firm intended to do on the adjacent fields. 'Woddle and Banbridge have acquired this land for an exclusive development of 400 two-, three- and four-bedroomed homes.' Far across the fields John could see an old church, a few old Kentish cottages and a farmhouse, a lovely community nestling in the Weald by fields where cattle now grazed. In the early spring sunshine it was an idyllic scene, the cottage gardens a haze of daffodil yellow and the luscious green of April.

What had made John stop was the way the notice seemed to press out into the road as if its owners wished to vindicate their own existence with the fact that they were going to build upon that land. Also, beyond its ply-board expanse, lay the vista of a

Wealden valley where a stream flowed, a tributary of the Great Stour. The hills reached and rolled up towards the village. What a lovely view for those people who lived there, thought John; yet soon their curtains would remain drawn upon the grotesque mangling of those pastures. *Four hundred houses*, in a space where you could not imagine a hundred could fit. But there had been another reason that the notice had caused John to push heavily upon the brake pedal and get out of the car to look at the fields. It was the name, the second on the notice: Banbridge. Mr William Banbridge had been the man who had bought Stocks Cottage and Mr Billings's fields.

Banbridge was not a common name in Kent, and where Stocks Cottage had been was only ten miles away. Were there two property developers with the same name working in the same area? It had to be him, now with a partner in the same environmental crime.

'Mr Banbridge will see you now, sir.' The pretty secretary gave John a sexy smile and showed him through to a plush, freshly decorated office. David Banbridge, son of the late William Banbridge rose from the black ash desk and strode over to shake John's hand.

'Mr Howard, the journalist, sir,' announced the secretary.

'Thank you, Jennifer. That will be all.'

Banbridge was only a little older than John, dressed in a beautiful three-piece tailored suit, silk shirt and Italian leather shoes which seemed to float upon the pile of the carpet. His voice was firm and faintly high-class, though there was a trace of East London in it. The clothes, surroundings and a good public school education, thought John, had smoothed out the manner and accent which would have given away the man's background. He indicated a chair at the desk for John.

'It's about the Charter development?'

'Yes, beneath Great Charter village. I saw your notice.'

'Are you going to write about it, or do you want to buy a property there, perhaps?' The question was deliberately provocative.

'Oh, I'm writing an article about it. You might have seen some of my pieces in the local papers about other communities in the Weald ...'

'I've seen your name in some of them. I'm afraid the subject doesn't interest me very much, unless, of course, it's a community that affects our development plans.' Banbridge sat rather precisely with his elbows on the desk and his fingers joined and steepled. On that desk was a copy of the *Financial Times*, not a local newspaper in sight. He appeared to be careful about what he said, somehow wary of John Howard whose expression was cold, pent-up and dangerous.

'So what do you do, exactly, when a community is affected, like Great Charter, for example?'

Banbridge hesitated before answering. 'We are bound by the Planning Authority. It is the duty of the planners to make sure that any existing community is not adversely affected. We are very careful, as you know, to build homes only of the very highest quality.'

'I don't know, actually. Quality in what sense?'

'Have you seen any of our developments, Mr Howard?'

'Oh yes.'

'Well, then you have seen the sort of houses we build.'

'I have seen them, but I have not seen very much quality.'

'What do you mean?'

'Mr Banbridge, the developments you are cramming on to the Weald are hideous. Granted, they are no worse than any of the others, but they do not suggest high quality to me, in any sense. They consist simply of as many houses as you can fit into the space available with no deference to the natural surroundings and only what concessions are forced upon you with respect to any existing community by the Planning Authorities.' John took out a notebook as if in preparation for any comments Banbridge would make. He felt a sense of purging, being able to say what he thought about the man, actually to his face instead of indirectly through an article. It could only have been better if it had been William Banbridge.

'That's not exactly fair. Our homes win awards. If the planners didn't allow it we would not put houses close together ...'

'So you get away with what you can and pass responsibility to the next man?'

'Mr Howard, people have to live somewhere. We build very pleasant homes and do not have any trouble selling them to a willing public.' He smiled as if he had delivered the *coup de grâce* in the argument.

'They buy because they are deceived. By you, by the estate agents who artificially inflate the property values, and because there is nowhere of better quality for them to buy at prices they can afford. Also, I would suggest, you probably have the planners in your pocket. What do you say to that?'

'I say that is almost libellous, Mr Howard.'

'I'm only asking you questions, as a journalist.'

'Well, *I suggest* you don't write any such thing in your little country paper, and stick to the facts. Which rag is it you work for, anyway?'

'Oh, I'm a freelance. I work for whoever buys the articles, local or national. Didn't I tell you where I'm going to put this piece? It's going in there.' He nodded towards the pink paper on the table. Something in Banbridge's eyes told John that the man was taken aback. An article in the *Financial Times* about a property developer in a beautiful area of the countryside could be very bad for business.

'Look, I don't know why you have chosen my company. There are much larger developers working in this area.' John put down his notepad. When he spoke it was calmly.

'Do you remember a development of your father's between Paddock Wood and Horsmonden, not far from where Bewl Water is now. It was about fifteen years age. A housing estate.'

Banbridge frowned. 'My father did a lot of work over by Paddock Wood.'

'Yes, he did, just as you're doing over here. This particular estate was put on some farm land, not unlike that on the hillside below Great Charter. There was a stream and lots of oak and beech, and in summer the fields ... Anyway, your father bought up all the land there and ... and destroyed it.'

'I'm sorry, I'm not entirely with you. What my father did, what we're doing at Charter ...?'

'It's history repeating itself, I suppose. Except this time there's a bit more opposition than your father had. Just a bit. Me, and the villagers at Great Charter.'

'Oh, you live at Great Charter. You're a NIMBY!' Banbridge raised his eyes towards the ceiling as if having explained the real reason for John Howard's interest in the development at

Charter.

'No. I don't live there, and it's not in my back yard. But I lived where your father stuck that other development.' John shivered. He had the man cornered, at last, and he could vent his anger on him, smother him with the hate he felt. 'I've interviewed the villagers too.' He tapped his briefcase with his foot, indicating the reams of notes he had made. 'And I've closely examined the plans, and I'm going to interview members of the Planning Committee which granted you permission for the development. 'I'm going to write a bloody great article, Mr Banbridge, about Charter, with nice big photos, and tell what the villagers have told me, and about how you don't give a damn about the people in this area or about their countryside. *I* don't care a damn about your committees and official plans, and the laws which say you can go ahead and take your bulldozers across those fields. I don't care about your Freemasons or your architectural institution or any other organisation you hide behind. You can mention libel all you like, but what is going in this article is the truth. I'm going to give them the story before and after. I can show them the fields and the river now and I can show them what it will be like, thanks to your father.'

Spinning on cold, deadly emptiness, the three salmon turned southward, their world totally hostile, indifferent to their passing. There was no quarter in the immense tide at their heads, no ceasing of the endless bombardment of fisted currents and jagged ice tearing at their flanks. An Arctic storm battered them and drove them down beneath giant icebergs which groaned in the enormity of the wind and wave motion. The polar night taunted the Atlantic salmon with its weird Aurora lights and lightning to the south. And the wind screeched in the waves and through ice mountains.

Alone they swept, never more than a few feet from one another, some final quest at their fins; the last of their kind, the last from Scotland, the last, big, autumn salmon, ready now to ride the rains from the hills on their last migration.

17

Iain had telephoned from Kinlochewe with the news. There had been the best run of sea-trout into Loch Maree for years. Even better, some fly-fishermen had seen one or two grilse, summer salmon, among the sea-trout shoals. None had been caught, but Iain knew the fishermen to be experienced and unlikely to make the mistake of confusing grilse with large sea-trout.

Were they vagrants, some fish from another system which had run Maree accidentally? It had happened before; indeed it was a natural phenomenon of the species that a very small percentage of maiden fish returned to a system neighbouring their own, or even one farther afield. It was very unlikely, however, now that salmon had disappeared everywhere. The systems north and south of Maree had also been devoid of salmon for several seasons. Unless they were escapees from fish farms, the grilse seen by the fishermen just had to native Maree stock.

And if the grilse were returning, thought John, was it possible, just barely possible, that there might be some autumn salmon that year, survivors of previous migrations? Yet it seemed too much to hope for, after so many seasons when not a single big salmon had been seen or caught for hundreds of miles around Loch Maree, that any could come back now. John had had dreams before, ones that had magically become real for short periods of time. Maree had lived for him, come to him from a black and white photograph in a book to surround him with colour and mountains and motion and waves where silver fish swarmed; and Kentish streams had bubbled and slid across the backs of red-finned roach and marble-camouflaged trout. All gone now, the life in those dreams.

It had been a hot summer in the Weald and the landscape was

parched. The little streams had dried to stagnant pools and the merest trickles, though their foliage-rich banks were ribbons of green in fields which were brown, buff and dusty. The grain harvest was almost over and giant combine harvesters crawled and toiled like dinosaurs through swathes of wheat and barley, followed, so soon, by flames as the farmers burnt off the stubble. Some days it was as if all southern England was on fire. Columns of blue smoke towered like thunder clouds and the air was thick with black smuts and the smell of burnt straw. It was not a natural landscape anymore, the rural south, but a battleground where farmers forced out of the land more than it was capable of producing without being damaged, and men like Banbridge devoured most of the rest. It had happened so quickly, within John's lifetime, and the momentum that the destruction had gathered was surely too great for it to be stopped.

Despite the weather, John was pale. He had spent most of the summer indoors, writing and typing, preparing articles and a manuscript for another book. His writing barely brought them sufficient income and in order to pay the mortgage and bills he had to spend most of his time at work. Anna had given up her teaching job in Tunbridge Wells and had borne their first daughter. While taking delight in his family, John knew a despair in what was happening all around him.

Articles in national newspapers did not stop men like Banbridge, they merely caused a little embarrassment, and, anyway, had to be edited to death to remove the possibility of libel. That removed their sting. You could write about any of them; property developers, farmers, poaching gangs, high-seas netting, and you only made enemies. It was not as if any individual was particularly to blame, beyond his own weakness of spirit. They were only existing within social and legal frameworks which happened to be in opposition to the best interests of the environment. It was policies which needed to be attacked, and the policy makers in Westminster and Brussels. It was they who made the decisions as to how Britain would be carved up, how Kentish villages would become sprawling conurbations, the towns massive and without soul, the Weald sliced apart with a high-speed rail link, communities severed, woodland and flood plains desecrated. The individuals like Banbridge who actually did the deeds were merely instruments of a greater and devastating force. While the framework existed so would Banbridge and all his counterparts in the various disciplines of destruction.

If only, he thought, cabinet politicians could be forced to live in homes blighted by the close proximity of the new link or motorway, or deep within the claustrophobic hell of the town developments. If only the Environment Secretary had been born in the Weald and had known a childhood like John's in a cottage in a tranquil valley. If only people had memory of things beautiful, and vision to act today for the sake of tomorrow, then it all might have been different.

Those salmon, though, against all the odds, against all the political committees and destructive influence, could they possibly be returning?

It was night, warm and humid in that still August, and John could not sleep. He half-expected to hear his daughter crying out for a feed or a nappy change, but all was quiet in the old cottage. Anna was asleep and he watched her for a while in the dim light before going downstairs. He had learnt which creaking steps to avoid so that he could descend with barely a sound and not disturb his daughter.

Late night was his favourite time nowadays, when the cottage and its little garden lay as quiet as a secret, and the sounds of the Weald punctuated the night. Owls and bats, rustlings in the bushes, a squeal out in the fields, all part of the mysterious peace. He could think in the relative cool of the late night more clearly than during the day with its heat and disturbances. He could not get Iain's telephone call out of his head, and thoughts of the grilse in Loch Maree. He was excited at the thought of the cooler, wetter air in Scotland, and especially at the prospect of seeing wild salmon again. He would have to go, to see for himself, if there really were *salmonidae* returning from the sea after all this time.

John's old laboratory on the sixth floor of the Strand building was empty. It looked much tidier, though dustier, than when he had occupied it. It was peculiar to think that he had spent three years at work essentially in this large room with its view out over the Aldwych and Bush House. Behind him was the glass panel in the door through which he had often watched the Thames running beneath Waterloo Bridge.

The door opened behind him. He half turned to see the head of Chemistry enter the lab.

'Dr Howard is it?' The professor's soft voice brought back memories of lectures and seminars, of struggling through examinations and the exploration of the frontiers of science.

'Hello, Prof. I just wanted to see it again.' He nodded towards the stacks and rows of glassware and chemicals.

'Of course, of course. I often go back to Cambridge to see my old haunts. It helps one to think more clearly, somehow.' He looked up at his ex-student. 'You're a writer now I hear, Howard.'

'Battling through with freelancing. It's not easy.'

'Still, not many scientists become writers. You wrote a book, didn't you?'

'I've just finished another. A novel, actually. But they don't pay so well as articles.'

'You're going to stick at it, are you? Or do you want to give science another crack?'

'I don't know. I have a family now, Prof. Maybe I'll go into journalism full time. I miss the science though. It was safe, somehow. It was a nice way of life.'

'Not anymore. Not safe, I mean. This lab isn't used much nowadays. What research is done is mostly funded by industry – we can't do what we want to do anymore. It's not the way science was meant to be done. You should stick to the writing and be thankful you're out of it.'

'I want to write another book,' said John suddenly, realising the fact fully himself only in the instant that he spoke. 'I suppose that's why I came back here.' He smiled at the professor as if that would better explain himself. 'If you can re-attach yourself to the past in some way, to a time when you felt utterly secure, it helps you take the next step ... This book I want to write ... is a big step for me. It will be difficult.'

It was a migration. Urges had drawn him, powers which he did not yet fully understand, but which inexorably drew him. It was his past speaking to him and his future calling. It was his book, the one he wanted to write, the crystallisation of fact and remote history, of the wild, wild sea and the wandering, questing spirit. And love – that was in it, coursing in it, in him. That was what he could weave most strongly through it, love for what he had known, the last precious quality the world possessed.

Close together the three fish neared the coast of Scotland. Perfectly poised on the tides of high summer they threaded through the Hebrides passage and on into the quiet Minch. Now it was just a dash away, the Ewe–Maree system, a blast of fins for the three huge autumn salmon. Even though they had not returned on a breeding migration for four years, the fish were accurately navigating their course, none leading, just a shoal sense holding each of them on line. Messages came to them, from sea-floor, sky and distant coast, from converging electromagnetic flux lines. Each fish analysed the voice and taste of the sea and none of the three were confused. Their past spoke to them and their future called, directing them on what they might have known was their last migration.

In three fish, one hundred pounds of salmon flesh; all that remained of the billions of tons that had been a species; and all the wisdom of long-distance migration and mastery of their dynamic environment.

They heard nets out in the Minch, but these were not salmon nets. They were seines, searching out the surface for mackerel. In those waters salmon nets had not been drawn for years. Even so, the sound reminded them of southern Greenland's greatest danger, they sloped down into the sea and veered from their course until the vibration of mesh against tide was far beyond their tails. Now the indented sea wall of western Scotland spread out ahead of them. They tasted the sea, knowing its signals, feeling for its familiar currents and the passage which would lead into Loch Ewe.

He had crossed the Medway, gone under the Thames, traversed the Ivel and the Ouse in darkness. Now John Howard's old car strained its way through the dawn and the East Midlands. Familiarity made the long journey seem comfortable, especially this early in the morning when there was relatively little traffic. The landmarks were guiding him and measuring his distance from Kent, or the distance yet to cover to Wester Ross. Grafham and Rutland Waters, multi-thousand acre lakes, the largest reservoirs ever built in Europe, lay off to the west in Cambridgeshire and Leicestershire. He would usually have stopped off at these two lakes, to take in their wide skyscape and the miles of water where trout rose and fishing boats drifted.

It had often occurred to him that the construction of a reservoir in lowland England was the one and only massive engineering function which did more good than harm. The flooding of a valley changed the environment. The reservoir replaced overworked farmland, yielding a lake to replace all the acres of marsh and wetland, and miles of river and stream, which had been polluted throughout the lowlands. With the draining of Romney Marsh in Kent for agricultural use, so Bewl Water had become the most important site for wildfowl in southern England. The artificial had given back, in some way, what had been taken from the wild. Bewl, Rutland and Grafham were civilised man's concession to the need for open, fresh water. John knew, though, that what had been taken from that wild place in the north, where he was headed, could never be replaced by the artificial.

As he had first done fifteen years before, John stared down the glen towards Loch Maree, her crimson waters gleaming beneath the dusk. To the eye it had not changed a bit in all that time. The island-strewn loch still spread between what had become to him, by long acquaintance, a friendly mountain-scape. Beinn Eighe and Slioch were in silhouette against the warm glow of the sky, but the loch's surface cast the brightest light in the scene. If more men could see that light and the fairy-tale islands, the awesome slopes of mountain; if more could know of what once swam in those waters, that light ...

It was unthinkable that what was so alive to the eye was dead at its core. *Salmonidae* were the life-substance of that loch and now they were all but gone. Iain's words were dancing in his head, as they had been since the telephone conversation back in August: 'The grilse are back. They've been seen.' So the heart of the system was pulsing yet. Now, in September, would autumn salmon run? Would the ultimate glory of the *salmonidae*, quest Maree's waters just one more time?

John instinctively knew that his own migration to this place must have been for a reason, one just as powerful as the salmon's. In the end it was all instinct, for salmon, for people;

everything worthwhile, all truth, was instinct. Lies and destruction and committees and politics could not exist in harmony with instinct. It was too pure a thing, it spoke from the deepest parts of living creatures. By men it was only glimpsed and then it brought truth to the forefront and they could see clearly. Maurice Wilkins at King's had seen this truth and instinctively recognised it, in his crystal pictures of DNA; Gavin Maxwell had seen it in an otter's form twisting in the silver tumble of a waterfall at Camusfearna. And John had seen it in a rolling salmon's back, huge and poised on the waves by the river mouth, and a fin, a signal, forked and merging with the millions of gallons of peat-stained water from the hills.

Instinct was bringing them together again, man and wild beast. There was no doubt in him, not any question that it would not be so: there were native, wild salmon now in that loch. They had come home one last time. Soon he would be with them.

18

'Aye, its a fact. There are a few grilse. I've seen them myself.'
John was bombarding Iain with questions about the salmon.
'There's no big ones, just grilse, four or five, maybe. They're a
wee bit stale now, for they've been in the loch since July. They
came in with one of the sea-trout runs.' Iain looked at his young
friend's expression. No, lad, there's no salmon, no big autumn-
run brutes, I mean. Not yet. Still, now's the time they run, in
later September. Ye never know; if we have a bit of rain in the
hills . . . Ye never knew what might come up from the sea.'

'I just *know* they're there, Iain. I can feel it. You know – that
Gaelic sixth sense you go on about.'

'So what if they are, Johnny? What will ye do about it?'

'See that they get a chance to reach the redds up at Bharranch,
I suppose. Just that.'

'Ye'll have to stay sharp then, lad. I saw those Glasgow boys
about again. They're after the sea-trout, but, well, a grilse would
pay their petrol. And an autumn salmon, och, they'd all stay
drunk for a year.'

'Poachers! Do they know about the grilse?'

'Bound to, ye couldn't keep grilse quiet in these parts. Their
spies will have told them the day the fish ran into the Ewe.'

That night it rained. Up in the attic room he always used in the
Sutherlands's house, John listened to the comforting sound.
Weather, real weather coming off the Atlantic, relief after the
drought back in southern England. The shoals would move now,
riding the rain from the hills, up into the high, moorland country
where there was gravel to make their redds, or deep pools and
lochans in which to hide until the November spawning run.

But an organised gang of poachers would also be glad of the

weather, so that the sea-trout and grilse would push up out of Loch Maree and into more confined waters where they were easier targets for nets and illegal 'stroke hauling' equipment.

If Iain was right and the poachers did know that there were some grilse in the system, their campaign would be vicious. The money to be made from wild Scottish sea-trout was big enough for them to organise themselves with military precision, with the same ruthless single-mindedness towards their goal. But for salmon, the whole operation would escalate. They would be armed, they would have spies and scouts, even among the ghillies and gamekeepers, the very people best disposed both to protect the fish and to give information to destroy them. They would be in contact with one another by radio and they would have several vehicles which could move around the difficult terrain with ease, probably four-wheel drive cars as highly tuned to their task as police and mountain-rescue units.

The weapons they could use against the salmon ranged from simple nylon monofilament gill nets, lethal, cheap and haphazard, to gaff hooks and the stroke haul, weighted treble hooks which could be driven into a salmon's flesh. Fastest of all would be cyanide compounds, or Cymag, poured in upstream of where the salmon lay. Waiting accomplices downstream could scoop out the dead fish with hand nets. The whole river, from eel and brown trout to the salmon, even the aquatic insects, would be destroyed, though only the largest trout and salmon taken.

John felt himself becoming increasingly tense as he listened to the rain. Had he come all this way just to see the fish, the last salmon, ripped from the water on their most urgent migration? Had those huge fish, if even they still existed, endured so much and returned for that? Would it be like Maxwell, seeing his otters killed one by one, and Camusfearna burnt to ruins?

The police could not help unless there was a crime actually being committed. There was no law which said that men could not sit in Land-Rovers surveying the river bank with binoculars. Even if those vehicles were searched nothing would be discovered. The cyanide, ropes, nets and all other incriminating equipment would be safely stashed and buried. The poaching gang would do its deed under cover of night, in a wild place, far from prying eyes. By dawn they would be long gone and only fish scales on rocks, flattened heather or salmon carcases which had been missed would suggest that they had ever been at work; that and an empty river.

Even if they were caught, actually in the act of netting or poisoning a pool, and then brought through the long process of prosecution, the fines were ridiculously lenient, paid off in less than a single night's work. Why was it that magistrates seemed to view all poaching as it had once been, poor men sneaking fish away for their under-nourished families, stolen from fat land-owners who would, anyway, never miss the odd salmon? And why did the law impose such a pathetic maximum penalty for an act which had been responsible for the extermination of salmon and sea-trout from countless river and loch systems throughout Britain? There it was again, policy-makers, law-makers, and men who would exploit the loopholes, the leniency, the weakness of it all. It undermined the human spirit.

You could not even blame most of them, reasoned John as the rain drummed heavily against the roof-slates. Theirs were the jobs which had been lost as ship-building closed down on the Clyde; theirs was a Scotland which could not support the jobs the men needed. They had turned, instead, back to the land and the water, and sought whatever those could give them.

It was the big men who were to blame in the poaching racket, the organisers who ruthlessly arranged distribution of the salmon and trout, those who gave shotguns, pistols and knives to their henchmen, and who sent their gangs to pillage a river, by what-ever means, just so long as there were salmon to sell at a fat profit. And for wild salmon the profit was enormous, worth the death of a gamekeeper or a policeman who was foolish enough to get in the way, worth the destruction of a river.

It was two in the morning and the rain was falling less heavily. Unable to sleep, John rose and decided to drive out along Glen Torridon, where a single-track road followed the A'Ghairbhe branch of the Kinlochewe river towards Lochs Clair and Bhar-ranch. This was the time, after all, when the poachers would be at work.

Quietly he left the house, but not so quietly that Iain Suther-land did not hear his young English friend creep down the stairs and out of the front door. The old man shook his head. There would be trouble soon, up the glen, and Johnny was bound to be at the centre of it. The lad had always felt things so deeply, his fishing, his work, the Highlands. He had a passion about him. Now he had this obsession about the salmon. He could not think or talk of anything else; just the salmon, all the time. Iain wished that he had never made that telephone call back in August. Johnny should be safe and warm now with his family, back in his home, Kent – that other obsession of his. Still, there was never any going back, every Highlander knew that in their hearts: you had to press on with courage. As Iain Sutherland saw it, you had to face the devil to know the love of God. Though Johnny would not see it quite like that. It came to the same in the end. On his knees in the quiet house on the edge of the village, Iain Sutherland prayed for his friend.

Rain and wind whipped the Renault as it toiled along the lonely single-track road. John caught glimpses of the flood-whitened river as it bounced and roared its way along the boulder-strewn valley. Eighe, black and immense, was off to his right, though most of it was invisible, shrouded in thick cloud. Ahead, also unseen in the storm and the night, was Sgurr Dubh, beneath which was Bharranch. He drew up the car into a passing place and switched off the engine and lights.

From where he had parked he could see the surface of Loch Bharranch, lashed by rain and wind, and also a part of Loch Clair. White streaks showed up against the black rock over towards the west. That was Sgurr Dubh. No one was out there, he was certain of that. Whatever sea-trout and salmon had ventured this far up the system would be safe for the moment. This, though, was where they were most vulnerable to the nets or gaffs, up in enclosed waters on the Sgurr Dubh burn itself or the reed-fringed river joining Bharranch to Clair. Here two men could work through the night and remove whatever fish were in the streams.

Loch Clair itself lay on the Coulin estate and in the loch was a salmon farm, cages containing artificially reared grilse, grown on for the insatiable table market. Any wild fish that took this route up towards Loch Coulin, via Clair, and the Coulin pass, would be relatively safe from poachers, because of the proximity of the estate owners and salmon farmers. The huge autumn fish were most exposed on their journey up into Clair itself and beyond to Bharranch. Also, ideally for the poachers, the system here was in no place more than a mile from the road.

On some night soon, when the autumn runners came up from Maree, John knew that this was where the gang from Glasgow would strike, raking out the last of a species.

When he woke, the storm had passed and it was dawn with the sun beginning to nudge its light through the dips between the mountains. To stretch his legs and to shake off the stiffness and aches produced by sleeping in the confines of the car, John walked across the wet moor to Bharranch. He followed one of the burns down to where it streamed out into the loch over gravel and small boulders. From there he could see almost the entire surface, except where points jutted out and hid the loch beyond. Away from the burn-mouths the water was calm. As he watched, a small sea-trout jumped by the peaty flow from the burn. Already, then, the migrants had pushed this far up the system. The autumn salmon, if there were to be any, would not be far behind, especially now that there had been heavy rain to draw them up into the high hills. Soon. As Iain said, 'Ye never know what might come up from the sea.'

Oxygen-rich water sizzled across his gills, and a taste he knew washed over his tongue. The taste of the past, his nurturing ground, the spawning burns – it was all there – life and death up in the high system. Here on Loch Maree, as the wind from the storm in the night abated at dawn, he felt safe in this sea within the hills. It was not so big as the ocean he had just crossed, he was comfortable here and knew the places to lie where seal, cormorant or otter would not find him, though he was far too large to be in danger from any predator in fresh water. Only men could kill him now.

It would be time soon to gird his muscle to the steep flow of the Kinlochewe, he and the two big hen fish. The sea-trout were already running, collecting by the river mouth and spilling up into the turbulent, peaty flow. There were not many of them, but there had not been many on his last two runs. He could smell grilse, too, and knew that they had already made a dash for the upper lochs. He would let them all go before making his own bid for the burns with the females.

Later that day a fishing boat rode through the swell, near where the three salmon lay on gravel close to shore. They heard the buzz of the outboard motor and the rhythmic thump of its bows hitting the wave. For some time after it had passed there was nothing unusual to be heard, but gradually the cock fish heard another sound, a slurping of something awash in the waves, coming in from behind. He stayed very still, poised to burst from the gravel at a hint of danger.

It was the boat, carrying two fly-fishermen. Drifting broadside to the waves the fishermen cast in front of the boat, each with a team of three flies. Up ahead of them was the bay known locally as Whisky Bay, marked at its southernmost end by the Whisky Stone, a noted lie for big sea-trout. The fishermen adjusted the direction of their drift so that they would slide down on to the Stone. It was at this spot, almost two decades earlier, when sea-trout and salmon were prolific in the loch, that one of the fishermen had hooked a giant sea-trout of record-breaking proportions. That fish had towed the boat half-way across the loch before it broke the line which had restrained it. Now, there were no sea-trout in the bay, though there was a prize fantastically more valuable.

The cock fish saw the flies, dancing smoothly in the waves near the Stone. In a flash they were gone. There was something tantalising about them, though slight vibrations and sounds kept him motionless on the loch-floor. The smallest female, however, a twenty pounder, lay up ahead. She had felt and seen nothing until just one of the flies hit the wave directly above her. It hovered there a moment, its claret colour rich in the peaty water, like the blood of a small fish, its hackles vibrant and oozing with life. As it began to move she turned on it, rising from the gravel, excited at the power in her own fins, wanting to hit and destroy the fleeing shape which was so reminiscent of a darting capelin, then the flushing red of krill. Still it sped away and she accelerated, suddenly oblivious of everything else, even the cock fish at her tail. In the moment before he reached her she had wolfed down the fly and had lost interest in it, ready to spit it from her jaws now that she had killed it. Her alimentary system had ceased to function as soon as she had entered fresh water. It was enough to have attacked and caught the beguiling object, as she would have done a skittering sedge or bedraggled crane fly. She knew joy in using her graceful body in pursuit.

But she could not rid herself of the fly. It had gripped into the cartilage at the scissors of her jaws.

The fisherman had seen the giant turn in the deep and fling itself towards his fly. He had held it poised in the wave, waiting until the fish had taken it and turned back down. Then he drove the hook home and felt the incredible weight of the gleaming, ferocious animal out there. Without looking at his companion, he called out a cry not heard for five years on Loch Maree: 'It's a salmon, man. I've a salmon on!'

The surface exploded as she leapt, her head shaking as she tried to tear herself free of the annoying sting in her mouth. In the air she flattened out and the fisherman's rod bucked in his hands. She tore away, just below the surface, throwing a bow-wave before her, thrusting out towards deep water. Driving relentlessly into the black loch, her lithe body ran arrow-straight from the shore; but a tremendous weight was building at her head, forcing her at last into a slight curve. Still she kicked while the great muscle-banks of her flanks poured out their energy to her tail, forked and open, blasting her towards what she imagined was sanctuary.

Her first run took her a hundred yards from the boat. In frustration at the weight of line she dragged behind her she leapt. To the fishermen, even so far away, the salmon looked huge; a glorious, silver leaper.

The line was twisted around her, cutting into her, and again she jumped in the great spectacle of the *salmonidae*, and still the weight dragged at her, forcing her, slowly, painfully, in the direction towards which she did not wish to go. She pulled her head savagely against the invisible force, and it jabbed back at her, relentlessly. So, instead of running from it she turned towards it, thudding her tail at it, shooting towards the boat which had now drifted well out of the bay.

They saw her swim beneath the boat, and the line streaming out behind, until the fisherman had reeled in the slack and again felt the fish, now in towards the shore, running among the boulders. He lifted the rod high and applied as much pressure as he thought the tackle could bear. The fish panicked, flaying at the surface, her tail whipping up the gravel beneath her.

This far she had come, to be stopped now by something she did not understand but which frightened her. There was little pain, but she sensed the danger was extreme. And it would not leave her. She could not even attack it, manoeuvre against its cunning. She knew now that close to the shore, where there was the noise of waves, and sand and gravel to throw with her tail, weeds and rocks where she could hide, was the place to do battle. She would twist and force her body through the shallows, against the pull at her head, until the lactic acid stilled her muscle, or her great heart burst. Seeing a weedbed up ahead she ploughed her way through it, then between boulders, scratching her head across sharp stones in an attempt to rid herself of the infuriating device that was set there. She, who was the mistress of seven migrations and years on the wild tides off Greenland, would not stop until she was free or dead.

The bend in the rod was fixed against the fish's weight. Both fishermen knew that they would have to lead the salmon out into deeper water, for if it stayed in the shallows there were too many obstructions for the line to snare. To break on a salmon was unthinkable. They needed the proof of its flesh; a *salmon*, not even a grilse but a full-blown, autumn-run wild salmon.

But the fish would not stop her careering dash, shaking her head and twisting her body as she ran, no matter what lay in her path. She rode hard over gravel which scratched her belly down to the flesh, she rammed her head into unyielding boulders and hurtled through weedbeds which clawed at her and the line trailing behind. And escape came to end her panic and begin her final struggle. Even as the man was beginning to turn her, trying to prevent her from reaching the next weedbed, the line broke and he led out a cry of anguish and his friend sat dazed at the spectacle and the loss.

The waves had subsided, as if in awe of the energy just expended by the big hen-salmon. Foam, strands of weed and particles of sand marked her passage along the loch shore. The fish had disappeared, as abruptly as she had arrived in her silver swirl of bristling fins over the fly.

The public bar of the village hotel was crowded. The activity concentrated around the large table between the window area and the bar. Here, side by side, sat the two sea-trout fishermen, and they were surrounded by locals, tourists and other visiting fishermen, several of whom John had never seen before. The McEwans Export and the whisky both flowed liberally and the sea-trout men spoke ever more commandingly of their adventure on the loch that afternoon.

'I tell ye it was a salmon. No doubt about it,' insisted Hugh Macdonald, the one who had hooked the fish.

'Rubbish, man,' argued Rory MacPherson, the local head ghillie. 'There's nothing bigger than a few maiden grilse in the loch, nothing at all. I would have seen them.'

'Och, MacPherson, ye'd disbelieve yer own mother, even if she had the evidence of the big fish to slap in yer face. I'm telling ye, if ye disbelieve me then yer calling us both liars. We saw the fish as clear as daylight, man. Right under the boat she was.'

'Aye, 'tis a fact,' put in Jim Murdoch, his friend, 'and the best bit we havenae told ye yet.' He looked meaningfully into his empty whisky glass. It was swept out of his hand by one of the visitors and replaced by a full one. With a brief nod of thanks he continued. 'There was a bigger fish with her. He was right behind her the moment she came at the fly, as if . . . Well, he was a dirty great monster of a salmon.' He lifted his arms to intimate either the fish's size or the truth of what he was saying, while he still grasped his glass. 'May the Lord strike me dead as I sit here if anything but the truth passes my lips.' And everyone knew it was true: a pair of very large autumn-run salmon, at least, had entered the Maree system.

'So, how big was the one ye hooked?' The voice belonged to one of the strangers, a short, mean-looking man who had merged with the crowd, but John Howard had noticed him earlier and had noted the attention he was paying to the fishermen's story. He would be one of the poaching gang up from Glasgow. Why could they not have kept quiet, the fishermen? Why blurt it all over Kinlochewe and the Highlands that there were autumn-run salmon in Maree? Did they not know that the wrong ears would hear, sooner or later, probably listening at that very moment and even asking for details?

'Twenty pounds and she wasnae half the size of the big fellow,' answered Hugh. The little man's eyes narrowed. His ruthlessness was almost a visible presence among the crowd. Danger was etched in his face, like some hard-bitten mercenary. John wondered if anyone else had sensed this about the stranger in their midst; yet they kept on talking about the fish.

'Tell us exactly where ye hooked it, Hugh,' called another voice.

'I'll no' listen to any more o' this nonsense,' growled Rory MacPherson. 'There's not a fish in that loch, or anywhere here-abouts, bigger than ten pounds. And that's a fact.' He pushed his way through the crowd and out of the hotel. That's it, Rory, thought John, give them a good act. You know as well as I do that it's true. There *are* dirty great autumn fish in the system and you probably knew it the day they ran up from the Ewe; but you're too canny to let the poachers know about it.

So she had got away, the first salmon to be hooked by a fisherman. That was not surprising considering that they were after sea-trout and the thought that they might hook a giant Atlantic salmon would not have occurred to them. Their tackle would have been designed for much smaller fish, not twenty pounds of tide-nurtured wild beast. She had been on the hook for almost ten minutes, they had said. That would be around the limit of her endurance. The lactic acid in her, and the oxygen deprivation, might well kill her, even if she managed to shake herself free of the hook and the line, or stones had not cut her too badly during the fight. Some survived after such a battle, if they were enormously strong, for nature had designed their bodies to withstand the tremendous shocks and stresses they would have to endure on their tortuous migrations.

It was good, anyway, to know that there were at last some salmon in the system, though John wished that fewer people knew about the miracle. And yet such a thing as this should be known by the whole world, shouted from the mountain tops . . . If it wasn't for those like the narrow-eyed man from Glasgow.

That night John spoke to Anna by telephone. She told him that there was still a drought in Kent and that no one was allowed to wash their cars or use garden sprinklers. Bewl Water, she said, was at its lowest level since the valley was first flooded. If the rain did not come within the next week or so, the water auth-ority was going to switch off the supply and there would be standpipes in the streets. As she spoke he watched rain trickling down the windows of the hotel. His daughter was asleep, but had been asking after him for days: 'When Da home?' Knowing that made it all the harder for John to tell Anna that he would not be able to come home for a while.

'There are salmon here. One was hooked today, and lost, thank God. But there's a gang of poachers who would love to get their hands on fish like that ... No, no, I won't get into any trouble, I just want to ... well, you know.'

She knew, and she did not argue with him. It would be utterly impossible for him to leave Wester Ross if there really were salmon there, after so long, before they had set some redds and given their kind a further, tenous hold on the system, on survival. Her husband loved Kent, though she knew that her news of the drought was almost nothing to him: his passion for the wild north-west and the spectacle of *salmonidae* on a home run had more significance to him by far than the draining of Romney Marsh's last wetland or the urbanisation of the Weald. There was still something wild and glorious in the heart of Britain. The heart still pulsed, almost unheard, and John was there where it was strongest.

October came in as wet as September had left and John's days were filled with walking along the river and loch shores and on the hills from where he had a good view of the river valley. The Kinlochewe was in full spate and the lochs brimmed with peaty water which burst into them from white burns and from them in roaring torrents, building enormously as they gathered and swept down towards the sea.

The holiday season was over and John saw few tourists. At the end of the second week in October the fishing season closed and the lochs seemed particularly empty in the absence of sea-trout fishermen. He became part of a lonely landscape in grey, watching areas where he knew the fish would be most vulnerable to poachers.

Just below Loch Clair, very close to the track, was a lochan. The water from this spilled over a sill and down into the A'Ghairbe. Here the water was restricted and the movements of any migratory fish, even small sea-trout, could be seen as they forced their way through the shallow torrent over the sill. John remembered stories about this place, about how gamekeepers and ghillies would stand and count the grilse and sea-trout rushing up to the Coulin chain of lochs from Maree. At times of flood several hundred a day could spill up into the lochan from the river. The most ever counted, on an August day in 1933, was 620, at least half of which were grilse and salmon. On one good day as John watched, as rain drove hard at his back, he counted seven fish bow-waving their way across the sill, all sea-trout. They were the last brave runners of the system.

John Howard was not the only river watcher, and he knew it. Malevolent stares came from the windows of vans and Land-Rovers, or via the gleam of binocular glasses from the hills. The poachers carried out their clandestine operation so that only those who knew the valleys well would have known of their presence. They knew too, John discovered, exactly where best to watch. Frequently, as he approached the lochan below Clair, or the narrow river joining Bharranch to Clair, he would see a Land-Rover driving quietly off. He would see the tyre marks of their vehicles in strategic passing places where the road ran near to the river, and he saw their boot prints in the peat by numerous river pools. By their activity, he knew they were ready and primed for their task. Only the lack of salmon kept them from striking. If they netted out or poisoned the system now for the sea-trout, they would lose the chance of valuable autumn-run salmon.

19

At last they moved. Two shadows, side by side, stealing across the shallows off the point of Whisky Bay. Twinned fin-beats launched the salmon together out into the abyss of the loch where they turned almost due south towards the smell and sound of the Kinlochewe in flood. Their passage to the high system was open for them, already run by the sea-trout and few grilse which had been in Loch Maree. They were the last, and the heaviest pair of fish ever to run those waters, enormous even by the standards of their species. Yet the darkness of their age was hidden beneath the gold and glisten of their immensely powerful flanks. Their backs were steely-grey, topped by the black sweep of erect dorsal fins, like blades, like the terrible forks of their spread tails. The awesome apparitions eased their way beneath Slioch's cliffs and into peaty Dead Nook Bay where the taste of the high system was intense. Already the river row hissed across their lateral lines and water gushed through their gills, pulling at them, tempting them up towards the ultimate goal and glory of the *salmonidae*.

They rode the river through backwash and glide, smothered in the white water of rapids and held motionless at the surface by insane water torrents. Across the fiercest turbulence they leapt, the only time they revealed their passing to creatures of land and air.

Human eyes saw; eyes narrowed with menace, eyes wide with astonishment.

As they came at him, first a bow-wave, then their bodies lancing the smooth water of the sill, they seemed to still the river's flow with their power, firing out into the air and crashing back into the waiting waters. This was why John was in that remote glen, to see such a sight, even to feel the cold splash of river which they threw up in spray. It put a conclusion to his thoughts, made him know certain things with a clarity which had not been there before he had seen the great salmon thrash their way into the high system. It was the last picture he needed to shape with words; the salmon's last, graceful, ariel curve, remembered for ever. Nothing in nature, nothing in the living universe could be as dramatic as that. There they were, muscle dressed in chestnut and lilac, glowing with reflected light, mirroring the colours of the river valley, now made golden by the peaty water. They were so big it took a man's breath away, yet their shapes were perfectly married to the ferocious current, so that at no time did it seem possible that the millions of tons of water which swept over them could ever drive them back down to Maree or the sea. Of course, the Gaelic people had known all the time. The salmon were the ultimate gift from the sea-god, carried with his own power, with the power of the wild, wild sea itself at their fins.

The narrowed eyes of another man also watched, but they saw different things, or the mind of the man interpreted differently. For what he saw was wealth, not, this time, money to be made by selling salmon for the table market, but a far more lucrative source. Such a pair of huge Scottish salmon were destined for the taxidermist. Others, even individual fish, that had been set up and taken to auctioneers in London had fetched remarkable prices in recent years. But a pair, so big, set up together in an enormous glass case ... He would probably be able to retire.

When later he tried to piece together the events which followed the arrival of the salmon in Loch Clair, John found that they were difficult to order properly. It had all been very fast. He could not even remember how the day passed, except that he had gone as usual up to Bharranch where he knew the salmon would run. Perhaps his action had even directed the poachers, for they might easily have assumed the salmon would run up into larger Loch Coulin towards the spawning burns up there.

It was early evening when John noticed a Land-Rover and van parked together in one of the passing places on the road, half a mile from where he stood on the shores of Bharranch. In the next passing place along was parked his own Renault and it was this that abruptly held his attention. Inside, in his car, sat two men. At that range he could see only the shapes of their faces, looking out towards him, sinister in the Scottish dusk. For a moment he froze, at once trying to disbelieve his eyes and frightened by the menace of the situation. Anger rose in him and he lurched off towards the road. Then, at the one place where he could see along the river which ran from Bharranch down to Loch Clair, he glimpsed another figure. *Of course*, that was where the poachers would have to take the salmon, hidden, except from where John now stood, at a part of the river which was so narrow that two men with a net or gaffs could catch anything that was passing up the constricted flow.

Then John saw that there were three men by the stream, two of them crouched among the reeds and the third standing on the bank in a place where he could watch the road and a wide area of moor. He had also seen John Howard who was running again, not towards the road, but towards him, shouting as he came.

The two men in the water knew nothing of the young Englishman rushing at them across the moor. Their concentration was fixed on the water gushing between them. Already a big sea-trout lay on the rocks, gaffed out as it was forced on to the shallow water in its attempt to run into Loch Bharranch. In the pool below the men had seen the two salmon, poised to run the rapid. In a moment they would come.

She was up, the water a constant detonation across her lines, a fizz and buzz and crack at her nerves, careering through her mouth, across her gills, and her power was enormous; forty silver pounds thrusting at the current. She knew the cock fish was at her tail and soon, together, they would be in Bharranch with only the breeding burn from the Sgurr Dubh ahead of them. Another migration, another fantastic two thousand miles from the sheet ice in Kane Basin behind her. Now she was home, her last run, her last chance to set her eggs beneath Sgurr Dubh.

The water raced at her and slowed her passage almost to nothing. Her tail bent to the current's force, driving her upwards. Gravel scraped at her belly, as it would soon when she spilled her eggs into it on the redds, with the cock fish again at her tail . . .

She had not seen the silver hook resting on that gravel, or the stooped shape by the bank, crouching and hidden against a backdrop of rock. As it moved, in the instant she sensed danger, she had already swept her power at the river, and the gaff rammed into her flesh, stabbing pain and thick metal deep into her quivering muscle, down into what she bore for the river, her eggs.

The man stood, letting out an involuntary cry of joy as he swept the gaff handle up and felt the weight of the fish. Then the whole world exploded in his face, the river erupting at his feet. The gaffed fish arched her body even as the cock-salmon leapt across her, coming down hard on the gaff handle. In that instant, also, John Howard was across the water and had thrown himself in blind rage at the man.

John was not even aware of the shock of cold water. Instinctively he focussed his attack on the poacher, hitting out and screaming insanely, kicking at him as they tumbled in the stream. Then there was hard rock at his back and still he hit out, punching into whatever part of the man was within his reach. For a while he felt the punches returned and something scratch across his face, but soon the man fell infuriatingly limp in the shallows where John was kneeling. Even then he continued to batter him, sobbing and shouting things which later he would not remember.

The hen fish was oblivious to the fighting men which had tumbled across her back and then downstream. The broken gaff hook was lodged in her flank, though the force with which it had been driven into her had disappeared. She felt she was free and now her companion was pressing heavily into her from behind, holding her against the river current. Again she swept her tail, painfully regaining the ground she had lost, and together the two fish lurched their way against the current, their backs exposed now in the shallow torrent.

He was using his fists, elbows and knees, in an attack which had been festering now for weeks, for years, even decades. All the hate in him exorcised itself on the unconcious poacher. A warning came through the fog: the other men were almost at him, running, one armed with a knife, the other with some sort of cosh. He turned his ferocity on them, leaping from the water, leaping, leaping, thrilling at the pain, the energy coursing in him, the glorious ascent, the madness, the final, last understanding, the joy in his extreme violence, the wet, cold explosion in him, a salmon shattering the water barrier from the high hills, the wild, wild sea . . .

'Johnny, can ye hear me, man?' The voice came through quiet and soft. Was it memory? Why was it sounding now in his ears? Hector's voice, warm on the wind, as he had heard it all those years ago on the deck of the *Shadow of Skye*. Why was he so cold? He opened his eyes: a fog across his vision, a face, Hector's face. Yes, it was Hector, his old friend, and he was beginning to remember. He was cold because he was wet and lying half in the river. He felt the man lift him from the water and lay him down in the heather. 'Ye just lie still, Johnny, ye're all right now, yer friends are here.' John saw Iain's face then, next to Hector's, framed by the Sgurr Dubh mountain behind them.

Then the sound of running water was in his ears and he felt himself relax. It was the Bewl flowing through a quiet Kentish valley with dace and trout rising at autumn sedge flies. This time there would not be a Banbridge to still those magical waters, for he had battered the life from all the Banbridges in the world. Iain's face came back into focus. Iain. They were at Loch Maree then, ready to push the boat out and drift beneath Beinn Eighe for sea-trout. No, that was long ago, when the fish were plentiful. They had been, hadn't they? He knew they had been, because Hector was there and Hector had been with him on the trawler and what fish they had caught up on the Faroes' banks . . .

'Iain, what's happening . . .?'

'Ye've been in a fight, Johnny. Poachers, ye remember?'

His vision cleared and he felt the ache across his temple and a stab of pain in his ribs. He remembered, scenes of his berserk anger coming back to him.

'Where are they?' He tried to pull himself up but fell back with a gasp of pain.

'Ach, just stay still,' insisted Hector. 'The police have them all. We got them all. Ye were not the only one watching the river, lad. Iain here's been watching it, and them poachers, for weeks now. Soon as the big salmon got into the high lochs he called the police.' From where John lay he could turn his head and see the road. There he saw a flashing blue light and a group of men bustling around all the parked vehicles. As they spoke a police helicopter thud-thud-thudded its way through the mountain passages, its searchlight lancing through the dusk towards the sprawled rabble of men.

'Ye thought the law wasn't enough to stop them, Johnny,' said Iain. 'And maybe it wasn't by itself; but with a little bit of help from us, eh? We timed it just about right, I reckon.'

'Did we, Iain? Where are the salmon? Did they get away?'

'That I don't know, lad. Ye must have seen?'

'I saw them gaff the female. God, she was *huge*. But I don't know ... '

'No, you don't know. No one ever will with salmon. Given time, given just a bit of a chance like ye might have given them – well, when next it rains ye never know what might come up from the sea, as I told ye.'

'See that, Johnny,' said Hector, his big hands turning John's head gently towards the river. 'It's tears from the hills for those fish ye love so much. It's tears for the salmon.' The river, the waters from high Loch Bharranch, fell away to Maree and secretly on to the sea.

It was all quite clear now. Life and death, and the struggle in between, generating their own clarity. Some birch leaves lay on the ground nearby. Wonderfully curved and crisp in their autumnal death, they rustled in the cold breeze that came across the heather moor. Everything was in continuity, the curve of those leaves, the curl of waves over Bharranch, the rise of rock to the peak of the Sgurr Dubh where the broad sky opened, wrapping the landscape in colour and translucency – the curve of a leaping salmon.

Of course there was cruelty, and always would be, just as there would be the opposite. It was all part of the continuity, the spectrum of nature, or the natural pattern of life. Had he not seen it in its great and tiny form in DNA, and in the most majestic leap of the *salmonidae*? And there was senselessness in some of that life, in some men, as there was also great sense. It was only difficult to determine what was right and wrong or even if these qualities could be defined in nature. Men would always be a part of that conflict with their surroundings and the other living creatures of the earth. Some men simply lived nearer the limit which might be called cruelty by others. Who could really, honestly, judge it all? No one had enough knowledge, though perhaps there were those with enough understanding.

What was certain was that some life and some death was dramatic. And there would be many tears shed by the hills for the Atlantic salmon.

In the cottage deep within the Weald, John Howard listened to the wind. It was the first cold wind of winter, hard from the north-east. The whole story was there for him to tell, complete now, all its parts connected through the years. In his hand was the pen his mother had given him all those years before, in another Wealden cottage. It hardly seemed possible that so much had happened within what seemed a very short span of time. The destruction of a species, yes, but it was more than that. It was the destruction of lifestyle, of a quality of life which would never, ever, be recaptured. There was not the time left.

John knew that his battle with the poachers was only part of what he had needed to do, to vent what had been compressed within him for so long. The main part had still to be worked, though at last he had the means to fulfil the promise he had made to himself all those years ago on a hillside above Loch Maree. He had said then that he would paint what he saw, in his own way, for others to see, beauty as it was then. He unscrewed the cap and held the glistening nib to a sheet of paper. It shone with that fugitive light he had seen elsewhere. He began to write, calm inside: 'The Last Salmon'.

He swam west, away from Scotland, and again he leapt and shattered the crinkled surface. A thousand million deaths lay behind him and he was the last, the very last, falling down into the infinite dilution of his kind. But far to the east, above Loch Ewe, above Loch Maree and a river snaking down from Bharranch, in a twelve-inch-deep burn gushing in a winter torrent from the mountains, a batch of eggs stirred beneath the gravel.

Far from the mainland the last salmon eased himself between the reaching teeth of the Hebrides and into the ocean's waiting throat. He paused just once, spiralling down into deeper, colder water. He was part of the void then, a last representative of a species; and no human eyes would ever again see him. The gleaming leaper undulated, drifted, and was lost for eternity.